MILL CREEK MYSTIQUE SERIES

A collection of stand alone, small town, romantic suspense novels.
Each book can be read independently but features characters from the
Mill Creek town.

Suggested Reading Order
Trent's Redemption
Hidden Identities
Breaking Point
Kane's Reckoning - Coming Soon
Legally Bound - Coming Soon

BAILEY THOMAS

Hidden Identities

MILL CREEK MYSTIQUE
BOOK 2

BTA PUBLISHING

Published by BTA Publishing

Cover Design: Melody Pond

melodyypond.weebly.com

Interior Design: A Fabulous Production

(@afabulousproduction on Instagram)

PAPERBACK ISBN: 978-1-967156-04-7

Second Edition: March 2025

Contents

To my wonderful husband: You are my inspiration, support system, and happily ever after.

In loving memory of Marsha.
Your big heart and unwavering support will be deeply missed.

One

THE PULSE FROM THE beat of the music vibrated down Aimee Lang's spine as endorphins flooded her body. Memories of dancing with her father filled her head while lyrics from a popular western song echoed through her ears. She shimmied against the vinyl seat of the booth, longing to join her friends who were on the dance floor.

Friday Fresh was her favorite event at Two Stepping Bar and Grill because they showcased local bands the second Friday of every month. Listening to up-and-coming performers of all types ranked high on her list of favorites, a cathartic experience allowing her to support artists who took risks to share their love of music.

She loved music almost as much as she enjoyed making up stupid little moves and dances. Her father had shared his eclectic love of music with her, and together they'd danced their way through life. To most, their moves had been pathetic, perhaps even silly, but to them, choreographed masterpieces.

A giggle escaped her lips until the warmth encircled Aimee's heart from those memories began fading. When would she stop torturing herself by remembering the past? That life had ended; now she had to focus on the present.

A prickle of awareness washed over her body. Aimee inhaled, moving her neck from side to side. Her gaze scanned the crowd until she saw the hulking man with all his muscles who appeared to be casually leaning against the wall, listening to the band. Clarke Dragoon was anything but casual and pushed all her buttons, from his overbearing personality to his rugged good looks. He'd won over the residents of Mill Creek when he'd helped her friend, Margaret "Maggie" King, out of a perilous situation not long ago, but Aimee had to keep her distance, even if it grew harder every day. Since she couldn't trust her decision-making skills toward men, it was easier to avoid romantic entanglements altogether. She would not make the same mistake twice.

What she wanted more than anything else was to break a damn sweat on the dance floor. To stop observing from the sidelines while everyone else got to enjoy their life—but that was the point. Now, her job was to embrace a new existence and not fall into any norms of the past.

Warm air circled around her body from all the activity surrounding her. Maybe she could allow herself an hour, an amalgam of her old and new self. How much trouble could that cause? That thought rolled around in her head while her heart beat against her chest in excitement. Who would even know?

"You okay, Aimee?" Maggie asked, a frown marring her face, but concern radiated from the depths of her big green eyes.

Aimee hated all the secrets, but that burden would squarely sit on her shoulders until she died. "I'm fine, just tired from a long week."

"I don't know about you ladies, but I'm parched from shaking my derrière," Irene quipped as she approached the table.

Laughter erupted around Aimee at Irene's comment. That woman had a heart of gold, but that didn't mean this petite woman in her late fifties with those beautiful blue eyes and long white hair was a pushover. Neither was Maggie. She fought for the people she loved, but her charm came from her subtlety. There was no doubt Aimee had been lucky in the friendship department since moving to Mill Creek. Both women were fun, loyal, and loving. The burden of not being able to tell them the whole truth weighed on her, but she'd made an agreement that which couldn't be altered. Her lungs constricted with that knowledge.

Maggie headed toward the dance floor. "Oh, I love this song."

Her declaration interrupted Aimee's maudlin thoughts.

"It's time to throw caution to the wind. Dance on wood instead of the vinyl on your seat. You're not fooling anyone," Irene added, extending her hand to Aimee.

Holy smokes. There were times like this when she really thought Irene possessed the ability to read minds. Yes, Aimee wanted to dance, and again, what harm would come from it? It's not like she had a signature move that would give away her identity. She made a snap decision after scanning the surrounding area. Her body vibrated with excitement.

Aimee slapped her hand into Irene's and smiled. "You're right, but only one dance."

Irene's grip closed around her hand, pulling her closer to Maggie. "And at least two encores."

Maggie's pleasure lit up her face when she saw Aimee. "Crap, now I owe Irene twenty dollars."

"What?" Aimee stopped moving, her gaze going back and forth between her friends. "You bet on this?"

"Of course we did. You practically forced our hands with your stubbornness," Irene said, shaking her shoulders to the beat.

"You're both incorrigible," Aimee replied with a laugh. She threw her hands in the air and twirled to the beat.

Before long, her cheeks strained from the size of her smile. She felt alive. The three laughed and danced through another song before the band slowed it down to a familiar love ballad. A slight twinge of longing pinched Aimee's heart as she watched Trent Jacobs, the town's sheriff and her boss, navigate his way through the couples gathered on the dance floor toward his fiancée, Maggie. Those two were a perfect pairing, and Aimee didn't begrudge their merriment. They made each other insanely happy. It was the fact that her dream of love, family, and a picket fence would never happen.

Trent slid Maggie against his body and gave his assistant his best puppy-dog face. "I know it's ladies' night, Aimee, but I need this dance, then she's all yours."

"If it keeps you smiling at work, dance twice," Aimee replied.

He winked at her before twirling Maggie farther into the mass of dancers.

A hand snagged Aimee's arm, halting her exit from the dance floor. "Don't leave now, hot stuff. I need a close-up after watching your sweet performance," a man she hadn't seen before said while he tugged her closer. His breath smelled like stale beer, and his brown eyes were dilated. His fingers dug into the tender flesh of her upper arm, making her wince. "Curvy and plump."

She jerked her arm back to try to break free of his grasp. "Take your hand off me right now. I'm not interested."

"Don't play hard to get." He tugged her against his body.

Aimee's ire erupted at this man's barbaric behavior. She'd never been a pushover, but a sense of *déjà vu* assaulted her. There was no way she'd allow herself to be trapped or powerless again. Straightening her spine, she placed her hands on his stomach and shoved herself backward and out of his embrace. "I said—"

"You nitwitted Neanderthal, no means no!" Irene barked from behind her.

Aimee turned away from the man and looped her arm through Irene's. "Thanks for having my back. What a jerk."

"Anytime, dear," Irene said before she turned to give that man one last glare. "He needs a serious attitude adjustment and lessons on how to be a gentleman."

Once they reached the booth, Irene ordered three water bottles from their waitress. Aimee took a seat and fanned herself with her hand. She'd forgotten how much energy she burned when dancing.

A familiar deep voice caused her to look up. "Do you want me to remove the trash you bagged?" Clarke motioned toward the jerk who watched her from across the room.

"No, it's handled. Besides, I think Irene scared the crap out of him." She appreciated that he'd asked her instead of making a scene.

Clarke nodded and headed back toward the group of men he'd just left.

When the band finished the ballad, they announced a fifteen-minute break.

"I love slow songs," Maggie purred as she approached the table, her cheeks rosy and her eyes bright.

"That's because you and lover boy engaged in dancing foreplay," Irene announced like a host of a wildlife show on television.

Aimee burst out laughing at Irene's reply, especially when Maggie's mouth popped open and her eyes went huge.

She slid into the booth next to Irene. "Oh my God, at least Trent didn't hear you. You'd embarrass the poor man."

"What? I'm old, not dead," Irene said, before twisting off the cap to her water the waitress had delivered.

"Ladies, I'd like to introduce my friend, Noah. Noah, this is Irene, and you should remember Aimee," Trent said as the two stood in front of their table.

Noah extended his hand to each woman. "Irene, Aimee."

"Noah, it's so good to see you again. When did you get into town?" Maggie asked before hopping out of the booth to give him a hug.

"A little while ago. I sent Trent a text to let him know I'd arrived, and he told me to meet him here."

"Let me get you a beer, buddy," Trent said, getting the server's attention.

"Well, at least you're willing to come to the table, unlike our friend who prefers the shadows." Irene pointed to Clarke—who lingered in the background chatting with Lance Charles, Trent's deputy sheriff—and waved them both over.

"Irene, he's a good man. Maybe he's just overwhelmed by your constant critique of him," Maggie admonished.

Irene raised an eyebrow. "Oh hush, it builds character."

"Sorry, we only allow her out every so often," Aimee said as her cheeks tightened into a slight smile.

Irene turned her attention toward Noah. "You, honey, are easy on the eyes. Are you single? Visiting for a little R and R?" she asked, waggling her eyebrows.

Noah's cheeks reddened, but he recovered, rolling with the punches as he said, "Wow, that's quite a welcome. It seems I made the right choice in moving to Mill Creek. All this lovely female attention will be good for my soul."

Everyone laughed except Trent, who grumbled at Irene. "Be nice, or you're going to chase away all the eligible bachelors."

Maggie's eyes widened briefly before her eyebrows drew together, concern written all over her face. "Don't get me wrong, having you here permanently is awesome, but are you okay? Did you retire from the FBI?"

Lance and Clarke joined the group in time to hear Maggie's question. Everyone turned their heads back to Noah, as the group waited on his answer.

Noah shook his head. "Nope, too young for retirement, but my boss, Special Agent in Charge Tim Guzman, offered me a new assignment. I start in a few weeks. The best part is I can live wherever I want, provided there's an FBI office close, which means Boise fits that requirement."

Trent slapped his friend on the back. "Hot damn, that's great news. Welcome to Mill Creek, man. I'll give you the official tour of the area tomorrow."

"Perfect, and a real estate agent," Noah added.

"I guess it's up to me to get the conversation back on track before we all smack backs and celebrate. Right or left? And do you even know how to throw a ball?" Clarke asked.

The waitress delivered a new round of beer and drinks to the table. Trent handed one to Noah and snagged one for himself. "To friends and new beginnings," he declared, raising his beer and clanking each glass and bottle. "Don't worry, Clarke, Noah will pick up your shortcomings."

The guitarist started to play a riff, signaling they were back and interrupting the banter between the men.

"That's our cue to leave. Enjoy the dancing, ladies," Trent said to the group. He pressed a kiss to Maggie's lips before guiding Noah, Lance, and Clarke toward the bar.

"Let's dance," Maggie sang out, grabbing Irene's hand and holding one out to Aimee.

Aimee declined with a wave. "I'm going to head home early. I've got a terrible headache starting, and I'm exhausted."

Maggie grasped Aimee's hand. "Do you need anything? I can have Trent take you home."

"No, I'm good, and I'm not leaving this second. Go dance," Aimee replied, shooing her friends to the dance floor. "Besides, it's Mill Creek, not some big city," she tacked on, not wanting to have an escort as her friends headed toward the crowd.

Aimee sat and listened to a few more songs before making her exit. When she reached the big front doors, she turned to say goodnight to the bouncer and exited. The cool, damp air from fall wrapped around her heated body, carrying with it a subtle scent of pine and rain. Mountain living appealed to her, especially the gorgeous views of the stars at night. Tonight was darker than normal since the stars were hidden behind a thick blanket of clouds.

Droplets of water dotted the sidewalk, which caused Aimee to alter her route by taking the shortcut through the alleyway between the bar and Knotty Pine Tree. She paused briefly at the opening of the narrow passage to look and listen because being drenched, cold, and taking the long route held zero appeal. Bright lights illuminated each end but left the middle section darker. No noises or movement caught her eye, so she squelched her concerns and strode down the pathway.

Around the halfway mark, she heard male voices and laughter in front of her, but the big metal trash bin blocked her view. She slowed as she approached the square object. Beyond the metal structure were three men, and the one in the center was the jerk from the bar. The beat of her heart quickened and caused a rush of blood to pound in her ears. Like a slot machine landing all sevens, her brain registered the mistake she'd made. Now, being cold and wet a little longer didn't seem like the worst choice. Decision made, she propelled her feet to move with purpose and would ignore anything they said.

"My luck has improved tonight," Jerk-o announced to his friends. He stepped directly in front of her, blocking her path.

Refusing to show this idiot any fear, she forced steel into her words and gave him a piece of her mind. "Get out of my way. I already told you no, and nothing has changed—" The words abruptly stopped as her breath whooshed out of her mouth when he yanked her against his chest and into his arms.

"She's that girl I told you guys about earlier. All I want from you is to finish our dance."

Aimee struggled against his grasp. "You're upsetting me. Just let me go. I don't want to dance."

He pressed his face next to her ear and whispered, "Come on, don't embarrass me in front of my friends. Besides, who wants to go home alone?"

Aimee's eyes widened at this creep's gall. She jerked her knee up, disheartened when she narrowly missed his groin. He'd sidestepped her attack and shoved her backward. In a flash, she twisted her body to miss the wooden pallets stacked off to the side but landed hard on her hands and knees. Her skin burned from the asphalt and rocks that tore her flesh.

"Stupid bitch," Jerk Face spat out as he moved toward her. "I told you, I only want a fucking dance. What's your problem?"

To her surprise, instead of being attacked, all she heard were the pounding of footsteps as the three men retreated. Aimee grimaced as she lifted her body from the ground, her knees raw and bleeding. Her white tropical knit skirt and long-sleeved T-shirt did little to protect her skin from the ground or the elements. Her legs trembled, threatening to give out, so instead of ending up back on the ground, she sat down on the stacked skids. When she looked up, a hulking form headed in her direction. *Clarke.* Taking a moment to catch her breath, she flashed back to the night she loathed.

She'd escaped. Had pushed her body as hard as she could toward the big gate that separated the house from the road. The sound of a single gunshot echoed through the air. Aimee's breath caught in her throat while fear crawled up her neck. Her footsteps lumbered as she struggled to stay upright. Seconds later, her face slammed into the newly laid turf; a mixture of grass and dirt infused her senses while her knees dug into the soft ground. In the distance, a flicker of red, blue, and white lights caught her attention, a beacon of hope encouraging her to keep fighting—to keep moving forward.

A deep voice bellowed out her name a second before strong arms hefted her body off the ground. Her memory faded as warmth infused her body. Clarke cradled her to his chest. Tears streamed down Aimee's face and bit into her cheeks from the cold air that funneled through the corridor. The adrenaline that had coursed through her body moments ago retreated, leaving her limbs heavy and her eyes drooping from exhaustion.

"I've got you, you're safe now," he crooned, sitting on the same spot she'd just occupied.

He supported her in his arms as if she were precious to him. This strong, virile man with his bald head, numerous tattoos, and blunt attitude could be so soft and caring. So many people misunderstood him. They lumped him into different categories due to his appearance or his motorcycle. Human nature seemed to gravitate toward making judgments without seeking facts or details in many situations. Something she, too, was guilty of doing when she'd first met him.

"I know," she replied, content to stay in his arms for a little longer while she soaked up his body heat and tightened her resolve.

"Can I see the damage?" he asked, his dark brown eyes angled down to assess her.

When she nodded her consent, he kept her anchored against his body with one hand while he used the other to lift each leg and inspect her knees. After he finished, he tilted her head up with his index finger so he could see her face. His movements were gentle. His brows were drawn together while he studied her. The clenching of his jaw was his only sign of anger. A deep, sudden intake of breath shifted her in his arms.

"I'm sorry, I should've insisted on taking out that trash earlier. That man, he was the one from the bar earlier, right? I'm guessing the other two were his friends?" He exhaled a deep breath and the sincerity of his gesture caught her off guard. The warmth of his breath feathered across her skin.

She nodded. "He wanted to finish his dance, and when I tried to knee him where it counts, he shoved me to dodge my attempt."

Clarke's smile transformed his face. "I like a fighter. I'm just sorry he avoided your knee. He deserved that and much more."

"I don't want to excuse his behavior because it sucked, but I don't think he meant for me to get hurt. I think he's just an obstinate pig."

"So, I guess that leaves me with the 'what the hell were you thinking?' when you broke what I'd call rule number three."

"What are you babbling about? What's rule three?"

"You know, rule one: stranger danger. Rule two: don't jump in front of moving vehicles, and rule three: avoid dark alleyways when alone. No, scratch that, every damn time."

Aimee pushed out of his arms and stood. "Your timing was perfect. Now I need to get home. I appreciate your concern, but I don't need a lecture."

"I'd beg to argue; however, I'll give you a pass tonight if you promise I can walk you home to clean and bandage those knees. That'll satisfy the protective side of me. I'll call Trent on the way so you can file an assault and battery report on that dickwad."

Aimee panicked. A police report would be the exact opposite of what she was supposed to be doing—lying low. That certainly did not live up to blending into her newly crafted identity. She could practically hear the US Marshal in charge of her protective detail reinforcing, ad nauseam, the importance of staying in the background and embracing her new identity. She hadn't seen that loser before, so he had to be a tourist, which meant the odds of seeing him again would be slim. The thought of letting him go stung, but she had other concerns.

She thrust her hand against the impenetrable wall of Clarke's body and stopped him from standing. "You can walk me home and help me with my knees. I'm not filing a report because of a stupid decision."

Clarke's brow lifted. "Run that past me again? What he did was wrong on so many levels."

"Yes, he overstepped. I'm not going to ruin his life because he made an ass out of himself. I know you don't understand, but it's my decision." She turned and took one step down the alley and winced. Her knees hurt from the movement.

"You're right, and for the record, I don't agree with your decision. Let me give you a boost to your place."

Did this man miss anything? She winced shaking out her hand. Her world went sideways for a second time tonight. In a flash, his strong arms slid around her body, hoisting up against his chest. Damn him, she liked how she felt in his arms.

She directed him toward her place on Main Street above one of the stores. It wasn't much, but it was all she needed now. After he ascended the stairs in the back of the hardware and feed store, she removed her keys from her pocket and laid them in his outstretched palm. She expected him to put her down, instead he easily held her and unlocked the door in one fluid motion.

Once inside, she flipped the light switch on the wall by the door and pointed to the sofa. He hesitated momentarily before depositing her on the center cushion.

"Where's your first aid kit?" he asked. His gaze roamed the small living area.

"Bathroom under the sink, and the washcloth on the towel rack is clean."

She took the opportunity to study his powerful, muscular frame as he moved to get her supplies. He had to be at least six feet five inches tall and weigh over two hundred pounds.

Even at his size, his motions were efficient and graceful. He was comfortable in his own skin. His presence took up most of the free space in this tiny studio.

When he returned, he squatted in front of her and examined her wounded knees. Carefully, he wiped away the dried blood, added antibiotic ointment, and applied several bandages.

When he finished, he looked up and watched her for a few seconds. "Do you have any frozen vegetables in the freezer? That'll help with the bruising."

"Uh, no, I have a tray of ice, though."

He nodded and made his way toward the kitchen. When he returned with ice wrapped in a towel, he instructed her to alternate icing each knee. "I know a thing or two about icing injuries. This'll help keep the swelling and bruising down."

She wondered what type of injuries he'd sustained, but the words stuck on her tongue. "Thanks, Clarke."

He took a seat on sofa and ran his gaze over her body. Her skin tingled under his intense scrutiny. "I've got be honest, I'm pissed at myself for not taking care of that douche earlier. I also wish your knee would've had him singing soprano. Are you okay?"

"I'm fine, really," Aimee replied, then shifted the bag of ice to her other knee.

"How long have you lived here? Are you still unpacking?"

That question threw her off balance and wasn't what she'd expected him to say next. "No, I decided to purge a lot of things from my life when I moved here. When this space became available, I jumped at the opportunity. The location is prefect. It's easy to clean, and Daniel and Lana have placed me in charge of security for their Hardware and Feed Store."

His eyebrows scrunched together. "What does that mean?"

"I'm kidding, it's our joke," Aimee replied on a stifled yawn. "I'm sorry, it's not the company. I'm exhausted."

"Understood. I'll head out so you can rest." He pulled out his cellphone. "Give me your number so I can call you. Then, you'll have mine. If you need anything, don't hesitate to use it."

She hedged for a moment, then relented. Having friends helped her blend in and build her new life, but she still controlled what she shared and how close she allowed anyone to get. She called out her numbers while he diligently typed the information into his phone. Seconds later, her phone vibrated, so she answered his call before adding his data to her contact list.

"Good night, Aimee." Clarke said. "Lock the door after me," he added after he crossed the threshold and closed the door behind him.

His concern and thoughtfulness about her safety caused a spot deep inside her chest to expand. Knowing she had support mattered to her.

It was nice to have a few people you could count on from time to time. Loneliness sucked and could overwhelm a person.

That thought made her stomach flutter with hope, until her mind caught up and stomped on that bubble until it burst. She didn't deserve a do-over with her life. She was alone for a reason.

Two

CLARKE DRAGOON HOVERED HIS mouse over the camera icon on his monitor's display before clicking it. A ritual that was ingrained in him, not that he'd expected to find anything amiss on his footage. When you had more enemies than friends, you learned to put in safeguards. His thoughts turned to the day his mother's sister, Elizabeth Pickle, had informed him she was giving him her house. That had been right before she'd been diagnosed with Alzheimer's, well before she'd moved into a long-term care facility.

His aunt enjoyed life to its fullest, and being a flight attendant had allowed her to travel the world. His mother had always teased her sister since she had these wild thoughts zipping through her head that typically ended with a streak of paranoia. Now, Elizabeth lived in Boise at a memory care facility. This past June, he'd decided it was time to move into her home, but he'd kept her name on the deed. He liked the mountain setting and the small town of Mill Creek.

Getting used to nosy residents took patience, but the bomb shelter his aunt had built into the basement during the original construction trumped any negative. Those layers of protection provided a buffer between his personal and work life.

Over the last four months, he'd been occupied with renovating his new home. He was proud of his accomplishments, from the updated kitchen, bathrooms, new roof and windows, to the fresh coats of paint inside and out. The bomb shelter, which he now called his command center, had been perfectly constructed from the beginning. It had its own ventilation system, air filtration, reinforced walls, and an emergency exit, which saved him a good deal of cash. *God, I love my aunt.*

All he had to do was transform the shelter's interior into a wonderland. He'd worked with an electrician to rig the space for all his high-tech gadgets, which included a secured area with a biometric lock that housed his weapons locker, medical supplies, bug-out gear, food, and other gadgets he'd acquired.

Frustration still pulsed through his system, even after his two-mile run earlier. He could blame it on a sleepless night, but his culprit had bright hazel eyes with curves and a killer smile. Aimee's adamance about not pressing charges and reporting last night's incident bothered him. That asshole deserved to be prosecuted to the fullest extent of the law. It made him itch to run into the bastard so he could educate him on the proper way to treat women.

He finished reviewing his surveillance footage and started to cycle through each individual camera feed. He rubbed his eyes with the heels of his hands and let out a deep breath. Why hadn't he taken care of that bastard when he'd seen him being handsy with Aimee on the dance floor? The world didn't need men who acted like that, and Clarke had a real problem with anyone who victimized women, children, and animals. Had that douchebag threatened Aimee, making her afraid to defy him? No, she wouldn't allow that, she had too much pride.

There was also the disturbing fact that her home had zero personal items--no mementos, photographs, or magazines. Hell, she didn't even have food in the freezer. Not that it was wrong either way, but most people at least had a frozen meal or something. If he hadn't known better, it looked like a hotel instead of her home. The place she'd lived for the last ten months was barren.

He clicked on the next camera and did a double take at the screen. *What the hell is my neighbor doing?* He shot out of his chair, ascended the stairs, and exited his house, rushing toward Irene, who clung to the top rung of a ladder. "What the hell, Irene? Are you trying to kill yourself?" Clarke asked in a stern tone, shielding his eyes from the sun as he looked up at her.

"Good grief! Didn't your father teach you that you shouldn't startle a person while they're on a ladder? What does it look like I'm doing, my hair?" she shot right back at him as he looked up at her.

He had to give it to her, she was determined. She redefined "busybody," but her mind worked like a race car. He'd never admit to this out loud, but she had a heart of gold. Her cantankerous spirit was another matter altogether. A Mill Creek lifer, she protected everyone and everything she cared about, right down to the books at the library where she worked.

He grabbed a hold of the ladder to steady it. "Get down, right this minute. I don't want you to kill yourself. I'd be the number-one suspect."

"If the brooding shoe fits, Mr. Dragoon. Besides, you'd be lonely without all my attention. Oh, and who would complain to the sheriff regarding your insane need to walk and inspect your property? What's the rock count this week?" she asked, while she worked her way down each rung.

Clarke smiled and rubbed his head. He stepped back to make room for her when she got to the bottom step. Once she was clear, he climbed up to inspect the section of gutter that had held her attention. After several minutes, he identified the problem. "These gutters need to be cleaned out," he said, then moved closer to the sagging section.

She folded her arms over her breasts and huffed. "Thanks, Captain Obvious, I had that much figured out."

"Stubborn woman," he muttered under his breath. "Okay, this section separated from the weight of all these wet leaves and debris. One clamp from the hardware store should solve the problem. This fix and a clean out should take about three hours, more or less."

Irene held Clarke's gaze. "You're offering to help? That could ruin your bad boy reputation."

He cocked his head at the small woman. "That's a risk I'm willing to take. Stay away from that ladder. I'll be back in a bit."

Irene called out to his retreating form, "Keep the receipt. I'll pay you back."

C LARKE GUIDED HIS MOTORCYCLE into a parking space outside the diner to catch an early lunch. He planned to call Aimee after he ate to see if he could bring her food.

Mill Creek might be a quaint, small town, but it had some amazing restaurants. The town's architecture appealed to him with the mix of wood, brick, and siding. He loved the long wood-planked sidewalks on Main Street, complete with horse hitching posts. Pretty much each building had its own look and style, which made it unique but showed personality. The residents were good-hearted and loyal, even if the gossip mill worked overtime.

He glanced at his phone when he received the text message alert and grimaced. The psychologist he'd been dodging for the last two weeks had now resorted to messaging him. He knew it was procedure, but it irked him to have a shrink digging into his personal space. Clarke was confident he could discern if he were having a mental breakdown or losing his shit. He didn't need a therapist to sugarcoat it and ask repeatedly, "Tell me how that makes you feel." His psychological fitness evaluation would have to wait.

He'd return the call after he finished his mandatory leave. That last assignment had been a clusterfuck and would haunt him forever. By his calculation, he had just over a week left to figure out what the hell had him all twisted up. He enjoyed his time off. Now, he poured his energy into home improvement projects. It'd been a nice change of pace to let his guard down some and not sleep with one eye open. His aunt's home had now been converted into his primary residence, and he liked the idea that he'd lain down roots. Not sure why that appealed to him, but it did.

Mentally, he complied his to-do list for after lunch. Since the forecast had called for more rain on Sunday, the gutters became a top priority. Hoping to see Aimee put a smile on his face. He wanted to verify that she was doing all right from last night. Also, he wanted to see if she'd change her mind and press charges.

The chimes above Knotty Pine Tree's door jingled as he moved over the threshold. He'd looked forward to Saturday's special all week long. The owners, Peter and Sally, were masters in the kitchen, but Sally's fried chicken and fixings were legendary. Clarke planned to order two servings—one for now, and the second for dinner later.

When his vision adjusted to the interior lighting, he scanned the restaurant for an open booth. He'd taken no more than three steps before his feet stopped dead in their tracks. *What the hell?* Disbelief slammed into him while his hands curled into fists at his side. His body coiled tight, ready to strike. Clarke was torn momentarily over confronting that very same dickwad from last night who'd just finished speaking to Aimee sitting in a booth in the diner. Or follow him outside and let his fists do the talking. Although he'd love to hunt that man down and make him pay, he chose Aimee over revenge.

AIMEE DIDN'T HAVE TO turn her head to confirm what her body already knew. She'd sensed Clarke's presence the moment he entered the diner. She turned to greet him as he approached the table. His eyes were drawn together, and a scowl stretched across his face.

"What the ever-loving hell is going on? Is that thug harassing you?" Clarke asked in a deep, low voice she hoped didn't carry to other tables.

She motioned for him to sit and waited for him to fold his large frame into the booth. His dark brown orbs scanned and cataloged every minute detail. The man missed nothing and had her at the center of his attention. There was no point in holding anything back. He'd dig until he found out what he wanted to know. The sooner she could put this behind her, the better.

Aimee pinned him with a look. "I'm not entirely sure. He approached my table and uttered an apology then left. I didn't say one word to him. I'm not sure if he saw you and left or if that was all he wanted to do."

"I think you need to tell Trent. I don't buy it."

"As I said last night, it's over. Hopefully, that's the last time I'll see him. I'm pretty sure he's a visitor, since I haven't seen him around before last night."

Clarke put his elbows on the table and exhaled. "I don't agree, but I'll respect your decision. Something is off with that man. Promise me, if he *just appears* again, you'll let me know immediately. If that happens, then you should report all of it to Trent."

Her insides churned with indecision because a part of her agreed with him. That man should be held accountable for his actions. People can't force others to do things against their will. He'd scared her half to death last night. The problem was, she'd made a promise when she'd entered the Witness Security Program to embrace her new identity—to live in the shadows and blend in. A police report and potential court hearing were the opposite of that pledge. A simple fact that she couldn't divulge to Clarke or anyone in her life, which meant keeping secrets. *God, why did I take that damn alley last night?*

"I'll promise to let you know," she said, turning her attention toward the menu on the table.

Those words she meant, but she knew he didn't miss her sidestep about reporting the incident. The glimpse of disappointment that flickered in his gaze bothered her. Hopefully, she'd never see that man again, and this would be a moot point. This whole WITSEC thing sucked, but she couldn't go back and undo the past. A lesson she'd mastered in her life.

A waitress stopped by their table with a pad of paper and pencil at the ready. "You two ready to order?"

Aimee closed the menu. "The special and a slice of apple pie. To go, please."

The waitress jotted down her notes and turned her attention to Clarke.

"I'll have the same, but with two specials."

The waitress smiled and winked at Clarke, who seemed oblivious to her flirting. His entire attention was directed at Aimee. "How are you feeling today?"

Pursing her lips, she took a quick survey of her body. "I'm good."

"Whoa, slow down, all those details are overwhelming me, sweetheart."

"My knees are a little sore, but nothing I can't handle," she said, ignoring his arrogance.

She glanced past him to look out the window then snapped her head further to the right. Dark plumes of smoke stained the air surrounding the hardware store and her studio. The deep wail of sirens and horns from the firetrucks reached her ears moments before she saw the streaks of red metal pass the diner. People walking down Main Street either stopped to stare or hurriedly moved toward the frenzy. She grabbed her purse and zipped out of the booth. Determination and anxiety fueled her steps as she ran toward her home. *Please don't let the fire destroy that box.*

"Aimee, wait!" Clarke hollered at her retreating form, but she kept running full speed toward the disaster.

Her heart pounded against her chest. The acrid scent of smoke filled the air. Ashes and heat slapped her flesh as chaos surrounded her. The orange-and-yellow flames provided the backdrop while firemen jumped into action. Hoses were scattered all over the ground while another man worked on securing the end of the hose to the hydrant. A deputy arrived seconds later, jumping from his vehicle helping to secure the scene.

"Ma'am, you must get back," a fireman shouted at her. His outstretched arms ushered her away.

"This is my place, above the store," she pleaded.

Once again, she tried to dart around his arms toward the stairway in the back. Her throat burned from exertion and the thick smoke permeating the air. Visibility was low, but she thought she'd make it until a large hand wrapped around her forearm, snapping her back against a solid wall of muscle.

Clarke's deep voice addressed the fireman. "I've got her."

She didn't know what irritated her more, the finality in Clarke's voice or how she melted into his strong arms when he anchored her to him. His hold never loosened as he walked them backward away from the danger and toward a safer area. Basically, removing her from the equation so the focus could return to fighting the unruly blaze.

Aimee lifted her head and in a rough voice said, "I wasn't trying to interfere. I just wanted to save..."

Clarke's hand moved to stroke the back of her head as tears stained her cheeks. She lost track of time as they silently stood together, watching the scene unfold. His support mattered to her and reminded her that she wasn't alone at this moment. The seriousness of the situation and his actions overwhelmed her.

After working its way through a spectrum of colors, the black smoke had transformed to a grayish white. The flames had receded, which had to be a good sign, even though the smoke still blanketed the building. Hopefully, her treasured items were spared and would be recovered unscathed. If she lost those few precious mementos of her former life, she might as well have died herself.

"Aimee?"

She stiffened and wiped her eyes dry before pulling free of Clarke's embrace to see who approached from behind them. "Oh, Mr. Davis, this is so horrible," she said, then turned toward Clarke. "Clarke, this is Daniel Davis. He and his wife Lana own the Hardware and Feed Store."

Clarke extended his hand. "We've met. Daniel and Lana, I'm sorry this happened. It sucks. Have you heard anything or know where the fire originated?"

Daniel's lips went flat. "Lana and I know it didn't start from within the store, so we're guessing the attic. Since the fire's almost out and the crew is tackling hot spots, it shouldn't be too long."

"Hey, guys." Trent greeted them as he approached the group with a fireman flanking his side. "This is Mason Gerald, Fire Chief of the Mill Creek Fire Department."

The fire chief nodded. "I'll make this quick so I can get back to the task at hand. We have a fluid situation, but we're gaining ground. I should know more after we investigate origin and cause. Trent will gather contact and pertinent information, and I'll coordinate with his office tomorrow."

A crackling sound burst over the chief's radio, followed by a man's voice. "Chief, you're needed back at the command center. You're going to want to see this."

"On my way, Lieutenant," Mason said, then released the button attached to his left shoulder from the walkie-talkie. He inclined his head to the group and retreated toward the big red truck.

"Aimee, how are you holding up?" Trent asked, his gaze darting between her and Clarke.

"Okay, I guess. All of it's so shocking. It looks like I'll need a place to stay for the night."

Daniel and Trent answered her simultaneously, "It might be longer than a night."

"You can stay at our house. Maggie would love to have you with us," Trent supplied.

Clarke choked back his laughter. "Please, she'd be a third wheel at the house of love. You could always stay at mine. I wouldn't mind the company, and I have a spare bedroom too."

Maybe she was crazy to consider staying with Clarke, but the thought of staying in another hotel room while she waited for the verdict on her life to be delivered made her uncomfortable. It paralleled a time she never wanted to repeat. Besides, this wasn't forever, and it would give her a chance to get to know him better.

"If you weren't always an ass, Dragoon, you'd actually find the woman of your dreams," Trent said.

"Return to your corners, men," Aimee chided. "Clarke does have a point, so maybe I'll stay with him for a night to two? If it's going to be longer, I'll just get a room at the hotel. Maybe the damage won't be that bad."

"Absolutely your choice, but you get to tell Maggie," Trent said to Aimee, then turned his attention to Clarke with a finger pointed in his direction. "You're on notice. Mind your manners, and take good care of her—like your life depended on it."

Aimee smacked her forehead. "Good grief, you two should be locked in a room together until you can say nice things about each other."

Clarke chuckled at Trent. "She's probably right, but don't tell her that." Then, he turned toward Aimee. "Let's settle our bill at the diner. We'll eat our fried chicken for dinner."

She cocked her head toward the smoldering building. "I should probably grab my truck. It's parked behind the hardware sto—"

"Leave it. It's safer to stay out of the way. If it's damaged or if we need to bring it to my house, we'll deal with it tomorrow. Besides, you can't just drive over all those hoses," Clarke rebuked.

Aimee cocked her head and raised a brow. "Tone, Mr. Dragoon."

Clarke stared at her for several seconds. "It's Clarke, and I thought we were past that issue."

"It depends on if you irritate me by getting too bossy," Aimee shot back. She picked up her pace toward the diner, purposely leaving him in the wind.

When they cleared the threshold of the diner, Sally practically tackled them. "Is everyone safe? What happened?" she asked, then folded Aimee into a hug.

"Yes, but we won't know he details until Mason finishes his investigation," Clark supplied, pulling his wallet out of his back pocket.

"Where are you going to stay tonight, Aimee?" Peter asked through the window that separated the counter and kitchen.

"Clarke offered his spare bedroom. Tomorrow we should get a better picture of the damage," Aimee replied. "We wanted to stop by to pick up our food and settle our check."

"What check? Someone doesn't have that shitty of a day in our town and expect to pay for dinner. It's on the house," Peter said, his head practically shoved through the opening now.

"I love that man," Sally crooned. "Give me a minute to assemble your meals."

Clarke nodded at Peter and cupped Sally's arm. "Thank you, it's much appreciated."

"Yes, you both are so kind. Thank you for dinner, Sally and Peter."

In no time, Sally handed Clarke two bags stuffed to the brim with containers. Aimee had a feeling they'd ended up with more food than they'd originally ordered. Her cellphone chirped from her purse.

"Thanks Sally," she replied with a smile, then answered her phone. "Hi, Maggie."

"Oh my God, I just spoke to Trent. Are you okay?"

"Yes, I was at the diner when the fire started."

"Oh, I should've known. It's Saturday—Sally's special. Are you sure you don't want to stay with us? We could have wine and talk."

"No, I'm good and wouldn't be that great of company. I'm tired. Clarke will barely know I'm there."

"Uh, I'm pretty sure he will. If you change your mind, call me, and we'll pick you up."

"Will do. Talk to you tomorrow." Aimee ended the call and put her phone back inside her purse. She followed Clarke to the parking lot. The next day or two should be interesting, to say the least. The thought of not being entirely alone appealed her. If she had any luck, maybe her box survived the fire and tomorrow she'd be able to retrieve it. When she'd woken up this morning, this was not where she'd seen her day headed, but at least no one was injured.

Three

T HE NEXT MORNING, CLARKE sat at his kitchen table with his service weapon disassembled. A steaming cup of coffee was placed on his left, and all his solvents, oils, and cleaning materials were lined up on the right. He applied solvent in the barrel using a small brush and put it off to the side. He grabbed a cotton cloth to wipe down the remaining components. A meticulous process he rather enjoyed. When the oven timer dinged, he moved toward the oven to pull the biscuits out. He returned to his task, using a toothbrush to clean the recoil spring, and then brushed down the barrel again.

He flicked his wrist to check the time. Unsure of when Aimee would rise, he debated whether to start cooking the rest. He'd wait until he saw or heard sounds of life before he finished the bacon and started the eggs.

He snagged a cotton swab and applied a tiny amount of gun oil on the tip. He worked the rounded end on all the shiny surfaces, recoil, and slide. When he finished, he reassembled the gun and tested it to ensure all components fired properly. *"You always take care of your firearms so they'll take care of you."* A motto he'd adopted from one of his instructors.

His disappointment had shocked him when last night had ended earlier than he'd wanted. He'd enjoyed the small amount of conversation they'd shared and now wanted to get to know Aimee even more. She'd been exhausted from dealing with all that shit in a mere twenty-four hours. Also, her absurd determination to be allowed into her studio worried him.

What she'd been hellbent on saving, he couldn't fathom since he hadn't seen much of anything. The part that had almost brought him to his knees was the sheer look of defeat and acute loss of hope that had filled her eyes when she'd been denied access. That suffering had gutted him.

In that moment, he would have done anything to erase her pain. Then, when she'd melted into his arms, his body had vibrated with a different type of hunger he'd struggled to quell. This beautiful, sassy, and voluptuous woman called to him. Hell, her smaller frame nestled perfectly against his body. And her hair normally spilled out of some messy bun with tendrils falling alongside her face, but yesterday, she'd worn it down.

He wouldn't deny that achieving horizontal time with her would be amazing, but his confidence in the fact that she'd never agree grounded him. What he needed was to put a lid on his attraction. This wasn't the time. He'd devoted his professional life to protecting others, which didn't leave any room for emotional entanglements. Those were complications that weakened him by making him vulnerable, not something he wanted to experience again. In his line of work, the enemies he made with each assignment weren't always locked away in prison at the end.

Perhaps his self-imposed celibacy for over a year had his mind going haywire. His last assignment had been more grueling than others, and he didn't want any distractions during his downtime. He shook his head rapidly and exhaled—how had he gotten on this subject? He didn't want to think about work or his reluctance to find another assignment. Control was what he needed in his life. He had that stripped away as a teenager and had vowed to do whatever it took to maintain control over his life and outcomes.

The shuffling of feet interrupted his reverie and had him lifting his head to greet his sexy houseguest. When he'd given her a T-shirt of his to wear last night, he hadn't thought that one through. Now, he might never wash it again so it retained her intoxicating smell of coconut and vanilla. His shirt engulfed her smaller frame like a dress but clung perfectly to her round, full breasts, even as she wore a bra, and showcased her curvy, muscular legs. His body tightened from a zap of arousal that image stirred deep down inside him. Nope, he would not go there.

"Morning. How'd you sleep?" he asked, needing to shift his focus.

A little yawn escaped her mouth before her eyes went wide with alarm as she zeroed in on the table. "Is that a gun? I-I don't like them. Can you put it away?"

Okay, that wasn't how he'd expected her to answer his question or that the sight of his weapon would cause such distress. "Sure, I'll put it back inside my gun safe," Clarke said.

He moved toward the door and opened a cabinet. When his thumb was placed on the biometric reader, the door lock disengaged so he could stow his weapon. When he turned around, Aimee stared at him with her mouth agape.

"You store a gun in your kitchen in that futuristic contraption? What do you do for a living?" she finally asked.

"It's a special safe that only opens for me. I work for the government. All my firearms are safely locked up. When you live in a rural area, it's not a bad idea to have them close." Clarke decided to keep the other reason to himself. She didn't need to know that his chosen profession had inherent risks tied to it.

Her feet were firmly rooted in place while he could only assume her brain processed whatever had caused her strong reaction. The scene before him vaguely resembled a flight-or-fight scenario, which both intrigued and bothered him. The tension radiating off her body had morphed into tiny trembles.

Unsure if he should dig deeper or change the subject, he opted for the later. He'd revisit that conversation later. "So, I've made biscuits and gravy for us. Give me a few, and I'll finish frying the bacon then cook our eggs. How do you take yours?"

Her shoulders dipped at his change of subject. "All ways. I like eggs, but I love bacon! I could be called a bacon-atarian."

Clarke smiled at her enthusiasm. "That's a woman I admire. There's coffee in the pot or juice in the refrigerator. Help yourself. I'll have the rest finished in a few."

Fifteen minutes later, he loaded the plates with steamy piles of scrambled eggs, crisp bacon, and two biscuits smothered with gravy. Once the plates hit the table, he grabbed the pot with the remaining gravy and the pan of biscuits, placing them on hot pads on the table.

"Oh, this looks amazing," she replied, then took a bite. "Mmm, delicious, and these biscuits melt in your mouth. What's your secret?"

His heart soared with her compliment. "I can't take any of the credit. It's my mother's recipe."

An abrupt tightening in his throat had him closing his eyes for a moment to control that pain. He couldn't believe he'd just casually shared that memory. He never went down that rabbit hole. Avoiding any and all recollections made his life easier since it kept his guilt and anguish buried deep where it belonged.

Clarke cleared his throat and threw out a lifeline in hopes of a topic change. "Where did you grow up?"

She forked another bite of eggs into her mouth and chewed before providing an answer. "Akron, Ohio."

His spine straightened while he cocked his head. "So, you're a bona fide Midwestern girl? I never would've guessed. You don't use the typical slang."

Her gaze snapped up to meet his stare, and her posture went rigid. "Well, it's true. And you?"

"Midwestern also. That's why I asked. Anyway, I grew up in Michigan and never really left. Even went to the Big House."

She took a sip of coffee and put it down. "What's the Big House?"

His eyes went wide as he pushed himself back from the table. "Seriously? Michigan University. Where did you go to school? Mars?"

She put her fork down and stared at the plate in front of her. She showed no signs that she'd reciprocate, and the air had thickened between them. The minute he'd directed the conversation toward her, the easy exchange had evaporated. Had he embarrassed her? Maybe she hadn't attended a university, which didn't matter to him.

"The Ohio State. Graduated in four years with a degree in accounting."

Although she spoke the words mechanically, her answer couldn't have stunned him more. She had to know more than she was letting on. They were university rivals, for God's sake. How did you go to OSU and not know about MU? He knew for a fact that each respective bookstore sold disparaging shirts regarding the other university.

At a loss for how to continue, he forged a different path. "Would you like more food?" he asked. When she raised her hand, he served himself another round. "Being Trent's assistant is far from number-crunching. What made you take that job?"

"I hated accounting. Trent's job sounded fun, and I needed a change. Here's a newsflash, not everyone has a career in the same field as their deg—"

She snagged her ringing phone off the table, answered it, and moved out of the room. Obviously, she wanted privacy for that call. He understood that need, but something about their conversation just wasn't adding up. His mind analyzed every word until he'd produced several theories.

Deciding to tackle the dishes, he cleared the table and had just washed the last dish when his cellphone vibrated in his pocket. Caller ID told him it was Trent, so he swiped his finger across the screen. "What's up?"

"I've spoken to the fire chief," said Trent.

"And?"

"He's cleared Aimee to *briefly* enter her home and retrieve whatever belongings she can recover. Then, she needs to meet with Mason and me at the station in about an hour."

"Okay, I'll relay the message," Clarke said and ended his call.

When he turned around, Aimee had just cleared the kitchen threshold, her facial features drawn tight. "What message?"

She listened, and when he finished, she wrapped her arms around her middle. Her easy demeanor had evaporated. Whoever had called must've given her news she didn't like.

She walked to the kitchen sink and paused to look out the window. "We need to get moving. I want to go to my place before this meeting."

Interesting, his first thought had been that being summoned to the sheriff's office wasn't a good sign, but not for her. Her complete focus was on getting to her apartment. Maybe her call had been about the meeting so she already knew what was coming. She'd gone back to keeping him at an arm's length.

Clarke put his phone into his pocket. "Was your call related to the fire? Do you know what's going on?"

"Nope," she replied in a tight voice, her eyes downcast. "I'll get changed so we can go. I'm sorry you have to chauffeur me around this morning. Hopefully my truck wasn't damaged so I can do this myself and not burden you any further."

Her attempt to brush off that phone call irritated him. Something had her panties in a wad, and he wanted to know what or who had caused that reaction. He wasn't entirely sure he deserved that view into her life, but he couldn't help himself because he cared about her.

He detested secrets, especially when they were being kept from him. She had his curiosity meter at full throttle. He knew he had this insane need to fix all of life's injustices, but sometimes one failed.

When she scooted past him to head to her room, he captured her elbow to halt her progress. She wouldn't look him in the eye. "Hey, I don't do a damn thing unless I want to. You don't have to shoulder all of this alone unless you choose to."

He released his grip. When she hesitated for a second, he thought she might open. Instead, she continued moving forward and out of his sight. What the hell did she have stashed at that barren apartment that was so important? Most men he knew had more stuff than she did.

Yet, there was something about this very woman who commanded his attention and made him want to find out each undisclosed truth and reason behind it. To say his curiosity had been piqued put it mildly, but that wasn't a solid reason.

AIMEE SUCKED DOWN A deep breath, desperate to purge the negative thoughts twisting her insides. There was no way this fire had been intended for her. She sucked another deep breath. If that didn't work, she was pretty darn sure she'd puke down Clarke's back while he drove his motorcycle toward her apartment. Hell, the first time she'd ridden on a two-wheel motorized vehicle was yesterday.

She hadn't wanted to make a fuss so she'd kept her mouth shut and followed his directions. The ride hadn't been horrible, which had surprised her. It had actually made her feel courageous, like she was taking a walk on the wild side.

Today, the vibrations of the engine, mixed with the proximity of the passing vehicles and her stress, caused her stomach to clench even harder. Clarke had been so sweet to her, silently reinforcing again that she wasn't alone. He had a strong moral code. This was something she'd learned not too long ago when he helped Maggie and Trent.

At times, that man contradicted every perception made of him. Yet, she'd lied to his face and stomped on his concern. She had no other choice because her life was scripted, and he didn't have a role in it. A lesson she knew all too well but fought to master when he valiantly supported her.

When she woke up this morning, she'd never imagined she'd get a call from Jake Lyndon, US Marshal, in charge of her WITSEC detail and handler. That man had missed his calling—he would've been an excellent army drill sergeant.

Wasting no time on pleasantries, he'd jumped right into the purpose of his call, wanting to know why there was an arson investigation at the hardware store where she lived. Then, he'd peppered her with questions to assess her risk and if she thought her location and identity might have been compromised. When he asked if there had been any other incidents, she'd known keeping the alley incident quiet was best.

Exhausted from the verbal marathon she'd been forced to endure, there was no way she'd tell Jake about what had happened in the alley the other night. He'd explode and probably move her out of Mill Creek, forcing her to start over again.

She loved the small town of Mill Creek and her friends. Plus, a new place wouldn't have Mr. Dragoon. He was firmly off limits, but she enjoyed their banter. After she'd calmed Jake's concerns and had recited his WITSEC code of conduct—be your new identity, stick to the script, master your backstory, and forget who you were—he'd ended the call.

How had her life escalated from low key to out of control in two damn days? Holy hell, there had to be an invisible magnet attached to her forehead that sought out all manner of evil. Could this day get any worse?

Shit, I shouldn't have said that. If course, it can always get worse. The lack of vibrations and rumbles underneath her body pulled her back to the moment. Clarke had parked in the rear of the building right next to her truck.

Aimee vaulted from the back of the bike and shoved her helmet into his hands. "Thanks for everything. I'll see you around."

A deep voice stopped her hasty exit. "I'm not leaving you to face this alone." When she spun around to argue, he cocked his head with a brow raised then continued, "You can fight me or you can accept it. Either way, the outcome will be the same. This is called support."

Great, now she could add "noble" to his growing list of accolades. She wanted to push his buttons but shitting on a person who cared was pretty low. "Thank you, but you stay here. I'll be back in a few minutes, then we'll head to the sheriff's office."

"You're welcome. Give me your keys. I'll check out your truck while you're upstairs."

Reaching into her oversized purse, she dug out the keys then tossed them to him. Afterward, she turned to ascend the staircase toward her front door. The smell of charred wood mixed with something else she couldn't identify overwhelmed her. The siding and wood that covered the walls were blackened and bubbled from the heat of the fire. The window next to her door had blown out.

She ducked under the crisp yellow do-not-enter tape and walked inside the shell of where she lived. Her vision narrowed with purpose as she strode toward the small closet area on the far side of the room. Prickles of hope stabbed at her scalp when she noticed the floor wasn't damaged. Maybe her treasured items had survived. There wasn't one damn thing in this studio that mattered other than the box under the floorboard.

The bag she carried hit the ground at her side as she kneeled. She rooted around until her palm gripped the handle of the flathead screwdriver. Carefully, she pried and wiggled the loose board while she held her breath. When the plank popped free, she dropped the tool and covered her mouth. A wave of dizziness swamped her system, forcing her to close her eyes.

When she opened her eyes, a tsunami of emotions battered her insides. Tears leaked over the edges, trailing a stream of wetness down her cheek. The box remained intact and appeared undamaged with the exception of a fine layer of soot that covered the surface. She opened the box and immediately removed the pistol, placing it off to the side. She smiled, and her heart soared when she grabbed her treasured cards, photos, and rings.

The tension in her shoulders dissolved while she shuffled through each item until she found her absolute favorite. A family picture of her mother and father from when she'd been ten years old. They'd just returned from dinner celebrating her mother's birthday. She lightly rubbed her thumb over their faces, willing them to hear her apologies.

The flickering of red and blue lights stained the blackness. She was back on that grass. All she had to do was stand, then run toward salvation. It wasn't that far, maybe fifty feet, but she had to stand up so she could make her feet move. A burst of hope blossomed in her heart. She planted her feet firmly on the green surface and sprinted as fast as she could, flailing her arms and calling for help. She worried about her father, but her only chance at saving him was in front of her. Only a few more steps, then she could put this nightmare behind her. Why weren't the police coming toward her? Why were their guns drawn and aimed at her? Oh God, had one of those goons followed her? Was he behind her?

The creaking of wooden boards snapped her back into the present, her head whipping to the left. A man's silhouette appeared before an open door with light, dust, and soot particles filling the air around him. Her pulse quickened as she shoved the gun into her purse. She carefully tucked the other items back inside the container. How much had he seen? She straightened her legs and added the box to her handbag, studying Clarke to see if she could read his expression. *That damn man has no tells.*

"I told you to wait downstairs," she snapped.

Clarke shrugged, giving away nothing. "And I told you to be quick. It seems we both didn't listen. Your truck wasn't damaged. We need to leave so we can meet Trent and Mason."

Aimee forced herself to walk past Clarke like she hadn't a care in the world. The reality was that her knees wobbled, threating to send her down the stairs on her ass. Not sure what he'd seen, but it seemed better than to give him a chance to question her. Deep down, she knew she had no right to be mad at him. She was the one who'd lied and was keeping all these secrets. Then, she chuckled at herself for being so stupid and at the irony of the situation. *Normal people didn't hide a box of stuff in their floorboards. Shit. Shit. Shit.*

Aimee turned onto Main Street to head toward the station. Her stomach, after performing a series of somersaults, chose that moment to remind her that barfing remained a real possibility. She forced herself to repeat the mantra she'd adopted after her first introduction with the FBI. *Don't spend time or energy worrying about everything—focus on the shitty problem facing you now.*

She parked her truck and waited for Clarke.

"Hey, Trent, Mason," Aimee said, as Clarke walked up behind her.

"Did you get everything you needed from your apartment? Hopefully, it wasn't too damaged?" Mason asked. "Unfortunately, all your clothes will have to be washed to remove the smoke smell."

Shit, Aimee hadn't even thought of taking any clothing or toiletries. "Yes, thanks, I appreciate the opportunity."

She stepped sideways to gaze at Clarke, who remained ramrod straight with a face devoid of emotion. What the hell? Her gaze jerked back to Mason, whose face reflected his concern with this situation. She hadn't noticed his scar that traveled from his left ear down to his throat when he'd worn all his fire gear the other day. A shiver worked down her spine with what could have caused such a gruesome injury. The wound did nothing to diminish his rugged good looks, but it had to have hurt.

Trent pointed toward the large room. "Let's meet in the conference room."

He strode toward the room and flicked on the light. Aimee followed behind him, taking her normal seat on the side, while Trent and

Mason sat at each end. Clarke chose to stand by the closed door and leaned against the wall. He was still lending his support, but all the warmth behind it had cooled.

"Aimee, the fire has been ruled arson. There was no V burn pattern present. That, combined with the lack of accidental causes, multiple points of origin, and broken glass scattered over the burn area paints an ominous picture."

"Like Molotov cocktails?" she asked. Her pulse quickened, beating against her chest. She shot a glance at Clarke. His face had hardened to the point she thought it might shatter. *Shit.*

Mason nodded. "Yes, and we're currently running each piece of glass for fingerprints."

"Do you know of anyone who'd want to hurt you or is capable of perpetrating this attack? When we met with Daniel and Lana this morning, we asked them the same question," Trent asked, his eyes filled with concern.

Aimee sat quiet for a moment trying to process that question. Clarke had clarified that he wanted her to report that guy, but she couldn't. A sudden urge to please Clarke had almost changed her mind to report that incident, but Jake's threat of moving her away from Mill Creek stopped her cold. She liked her friends and the new life she'd built.

She turned back to Trent and shook her head. "No, no one comes to mind."

Clarke stepped toward the conference table and took a seat next to her. "Maybe it was that man from the bar the other night who didn't like that you'd refused him."

"No, I'm sure it wasn't him," she blurted out before giving Clarke a warning glance. "Wanting to dance is not in the same category as tossing a Molotov."

"What are you two talking about?" Trent interjected. "What happened, Aimee?"

"Pull the surveillance footage from the diner and see for yourself," Clarke said without removing his gaze from her.

She squirmed in her seat. "Nothing that hasn't happened a zillion times at a bar. A man wanted to dance, and I said no. He didn't like my answer and got pushy."

Clarke leaned forward, tapping his fingers on the glossy surface. "What happened later is what I'd label as behavior outside of normal."

She raked her fingers through her hair. "On my way home, I ran into him in the alleyway. He got in my face, demanding I give him that dance. He got handsy, so I tried to knee him and missed because he pushed me backward to avoid my attempt. That man was drunk and acting stupid. In the end, nothing really happened, which is why I chose not to report it."

Clark sat back in his seat and folded his hand over his flat stomach. "He caused her to scrape her hand and knees. The next day, he approached her inside the Knotty Pine Tree, right before the fire started. He should be a suspect."

"He apologized and left. His timing doesn't mean he started that fire. God, you two—people make mistakes or may even act like idiots, but that doesn't mean you ruin their lives. Don't get me wrong, what he did was wrong and stupid, but sometimes we should give people the benefit of the doubt. He did express regret." Aimee thought she'd nearly snarled those words. Being tied to a crime was a serious deal and could ruin a person's life.

"I must agree with Clarke. That could be motive, and the timing fits. I'll pull the surveillance in the alleyway and see if there's anything around the hardware store."

The tension in the room seemed to radiate off the walls. She saw their points, but she had to protect herself and what mattered to her. She didn't want to take another call from Jake, especially when he'd threatened to move her out of Mill Creek if he felt she was compromised.

Trent rested his elbows on the table. "Aimee, mark yourself off for administrative leave for the rest of this week off to recharge and sort everything out. All of this can take a toll on a person."

"I don't need time off—"

"It wasn't a request," Trent said. He slid his notepad across the desk toward Clarke. "Take a look at my notes, add anything missing, and include physical descriptions. I'll see what I can get from Knotty Pine's cameras. If I'm successful, you'll need to come down to confirm his identity. Then, I'll announce him as a person of interest regarding the arson investigation. If you change your mind, I'll add battery and assault to the list."

Mason slid a file folder toward Aimee. "Inside are copies of my investigation and subsequent report for your records and insurance. Coordinate with Daniel and Lana on insurance claims and repairs. They have the same information."

"Thank you," Aimee replied, flipping through the contents of the folder.

Clarke scribbled notes and capped his pen, resting it on top the pad. The scrape of his chair across the floor as he stood drew her attention to him. "Thanks Mason, Trent. We'll talk soon, and if you need Aimee, she's staying at my house for the time being. If that changes, we'll let you know."

After she stood, Clarke placed his hand on her lower back, ushering her toward the exit.

When she cleared the opening, she turned to him. "I need to stop by a few stores. It shouldn't take me more than an hour."

She couldn't imagine that he'd want her to stay now, but that conversation needed to happen in private when she returned to his home. His generosity and willingness to provide solace confused her. Her misfortune wasn't *his* problem, and she didn't want to be *his* burden. The right thing for her to do was to set him free him of that notion. Not being able to be truthful to this man gutted her.

Four

C LARKE'S ANGER AND DISILLUSIONMENT pulsed in rhythm with his heart rate. His mind reviewed everything as he drove home on his motorcycle. Now he sat in his kitchen waiting for her. He'd formulated this plan, and the time had come when he required answers and the damn truth. If Aimee refused to talk to him, he'd have no choice but to ask her to leave. He could tolerate a person who had reasons for sharing limited information, but this nagging feeling she might be lying to him bothered the hell out of him.

The swing of the back door, followed by the strike of her boots against the wooden floor, filled the quiet space. The sound grew louder as she moved through the laundry room toward the kitchen, where he waited.

When her profile came into view, he announced his presence by saying, "We need to talk."

"Shit," Aimee shouted and dropped her bags to clutch her shirt. "What the hell, Clarke? You scared the crap out of me."

A few seconds passed before her shoulders lowered. She picked up the bags and placed them on the counter then stepped into the kitchen, taking a seat across from him at the same table they'd shared only hours before at breakfast. Time slowed while they stared at each other before he interrupted the silence with his simple demand.

"I'm here to listen. You choose where we start." His voice was deep and unwavering. He wanted her to come clean and provide something without this turning into an interrogation or, worse, causing her to shut down even more.

"Listen to what, my erratic breathing? Geez, my heart is flopping around somewhere on this floor," she said, then stood, already retreating from the room.

Desperation and frustration tore at his chest. He wanted her to trust him and not keep shutting him out. "Stop," he said, his hand slapping the table. "You knew about the arson investigation, didn't you?"

Damnit, he blew it while managing to do the one thing he didn't want to do. This woman had him tied in knots, and he needed to dig deep to control his reactions.

He gave her a few moments to respond. When it became clear that she still planned to leave, he tried a different tactic. "Where is the woman I've gotten to know over the last several months? That question, sweetheart, was the easy one. All I needed was for you to tell me the truth, to let me know you're capable of being honest with me."

Her form stiffened even more while her back expanded with her deep breath.

At this point, he could only press forward. "You showed zero signs of shock or fear during that meeting. That would be a normal reaction to a person learning that arson was to blame for the fire. That tells me you knew prior to the meeting and had time to process that news. That also means when I asked you about your call, you omitted that tidbit. So, either you have zero ability to feel or you knew before the meeting."

When she turned around, her facial features were schooled, but her tone was sharp and direct. "You don't know anything about me, except your misguided infatuation."

He sat back in his seat, ready for the promise of a challenge. "Interesting how you deflected my question. I'll take that as a yes. Let's see if I can go two for two. Were you just acting when you demonstrated a strong dislike of guns?"

He caught a flash of something he couldn't quite identify in her eyes before she quashed the reaction. Then, she turned her gaze away from him again. The fight that had burned hot inside of her body mere seconds ago had cooled. The sudden, ragged breath she involuntarily inhaled tugged on his resolve. Her hands curled into fists at her side while she battled whatever had her tied in knots.

"I don't like them," she pleaded with a slight wobble in her voice.

Moments passed in silence with what he could only assume was her indecision on how to proceed. Finally, she removed her purse from her shoulder and rooted around inside until she produced the firearm.

He watched in horror as she held the gun by the barrel with the muzzle aimed at her. When she placed the gun on the table, her hand trembled. Her eyes were vacant. If she were acting, she should win an award.

He inhaled a slow, deep breath to regain his composure, because she'd surprised him with her actions and her faith in him. To lose his cool now would only shut her down. Her vulnerability dripped from every pore, and it did strange things to him. A protective streak surged from deep inside his gut. He forced himself to remember that he only had room for lust in his life. He didn't do feelings or emotions—those only served to expose a man's weaknesses, like love and family.

Either of those would complicate his life, making his job even harder. "Never hold a gun that way. It's dangerous. Is it loaded?"

She shrugged. "I don't think they sell them with bullets in it."

His brown eyes went wide then narrowed. "Gun safety is paramount. If you don't know how to use one, you shouldn't carry it. I'm not trying to be an ass—" He motioned to the end of the gun. "The muzzle should always be pointed in a safe direction. Not at yourself or anyone else unless you intend to use it."

"Okay, that makes sense."

He picked up her gun and performed a press check before releasing the magazine. "It's not loaded. If you dislike guns, why do you have this?"

"General protection."

Reminding himself to keep the irritation out of his tone, he said, "It's hard to protect yourself without bullets or knowing how to use one. Where did you get it?" The real question he wanted answered was, who did she need protection from?

"A gun show. It was a private sale."

Her answer couldn't have surprised him more. A girl who didn't like guns went to a show to buy one? He'd heard some far-fetched scenarios in his lifetime, and this one was right up there. Nothing in her mannerisms hinted that she was being dishonest. Even her novice handling of a gun seemed genuine.

His enforcement training kicked into overdrive producing numerous questions he wanted to ask. He tempered his reaction, because interrogation wasn't the objective, but he did feel confident in his assessment that survival was her goal.

"Let me guess, a cash sale? What's going on, Aimee? You have friends who care about you. You're not alone. Assault and criminal arson are serious, especially when the common denominator that links the two together is you."

"The arson could've been aimed at the hardware store or the Davis family," she countered.

The legs of the chair scraped across the floor as she slid it backward, but instead of taking a seat, she remained standing. She slid her gun off the table and stuffed it back into her bag. She'd squared her shoulders and had rebuilt her walls to shut everyone out.

Fuck that, Aimee—he'd wedged his foot in that gap and would keep prying it open little by little. "Unicorns might exist too," he said, winking in her direction.

She shot him an exasperated look. "Listen, I'm not a side project that you need to tackle."

He laughed at her comment. "No, you're a hot mess—isn't that what you ladies call it? A project has a blueprint, a start and finish, and progresses logically. You, sweetheart, are the exact opposite. I happen to love your style. It keeps me on my toes."

A smile spread across her face. "Thanks. I do appreciate your hospitality and willingness to help with the streak of bad luck that's shadowing me. As for my actions and reasons, I've made some bad decisions in life that cost me dearly. One was a bad relationship, and it seemed wise to take precautions to protect myself."

"Life is simple but complicated; that's the best and worst parts of it," Clarke replied.

He walked around the table, driven by an overwhelming need to hold her since he couldn't erase all the hurt and pain she'd experienced. Grasping her arm, he moved her close enough to rest a palm against the soft skin of her cheek. "Talk to me, Aimee. Give me a chance to show you I'm different. I can sense there's more to your story. Don't you know by now that I'd do anything to support you? All you have to do is let me in."

She stepped back out of his reach. "Oh, I know you're different. That's why I showed you the gun. One day at a time, Mr. Dragoon."

Clarke could live with that as long as they had open communication between them. It took time to pick off a scab and divulge thoughts and feelings on topics that were painful. There were demons he preferred to keep buried. He'd heard the unspoken words that she wasn't ready to divulge more, which didn't bother him. He planned to earn that trust and couldn't wait until the day he'd know everything about her. Chasing women wasn't something he did, but with Aimee, he couldn't make himself walk away from her. His mother's wisdom popped into his head: *"Anything worthwhile in life takes time and patience."*

"If it's okay with you, I'll stay here tonight then check into the hotel tomorrow. It doesn't sound like my place will be ready for a few days. If you'd rather I leave now I totally understand." Her comment interrupted his thoughts.

He shook his head. "Yes, because I'd have no one to flirt with if you left, and proving you wrong will make me happy. Besides, I happen to like your company. It beats a quiet house."

Her eyebrows scrunched together. "Prove me wrong about what exactly?"

"My misguided infatuation is dead on, and you have a spectacular ass," he replied, waggling his eyebrows.

Her face crinkled up with a smile. "You're going to be the death of me, aren't you?"

"Not death, but panting my name could be a distinct possibility."

She put an arm on her hip. "You're incorrigible, but you do know how to make a woman feel desirable, I'll give you that much."

"Not any woman, Aimee. You," he clarified in a tight voice.

She walked down the hallway. Never in his life had he wanted to kiss a woman as badly as he did her. To confirm her lips would feel as soft as they looked. His brain short-circuited in her presence. He needed a fucking beer and fresh air.

Decision made, he'd use the afternoon to clean out Irene's gutters since he hadn't gotten to them yesterday. The clamp he had to order online because of the fire was scheduled for delivery in the morning. This way, he could get the bulk of the work done today and finish the job tomorrow.

On his way out, he knocked on Aimee's door and announced, "I'll be next door at Irene's working on a project. Shouldn't take more than a few hours if you need me."

"Okay, thanks," she hollered back.

This would give him a chance to clear his head while he figured out to how to earn her trust so she'd confide in him. Whatever had happened in her past still haunted her, which only increased his concern. Nothing about this woman made sense in a logical way. He'd bet his last dollar that she had a good heart and intentions, but danger and stress made people act irrationally.

RICHARD PARKER'S WEEKEND HAD been perfect—not the camping part or the adult version of hide-and-seek—because he'd found the person he sought. Inside the bathroom of the apartment he'd rented in Boise, Idaho, he stared at his reflection. Finally, his months of cultivating a relationship with Alice had paid off. He'd almost unknowingly blown this chance by refusing her invitation to spend the night on Friday. If he had, he would've missed the call she'd placed on Saturday.

The paper bag he'd brought with him crinkled as he opened it, placing it on the floor. He unbuttoned his blood spattered long-sleeved shirt and deposited it into the container. This process continued until he was naked. The reflection he stared at in the mirror showed a lean, muscled body with fair, freckled skin and wavy, reddish-brown hair. He'd come a long way from the thin, scraggly kid he'd been.

Pulling a few tissues from the box, he pressed them under the tap to wet them. The white cloth bloomed red from the specks of blood he swiped from his skin before throwing the used wad in with the clothes.

He padded out to the family room and squatted in front of the fireplace. Newspaper and kindling built the base. He struck the match against the box, inhaling the strong smell of sulfur as orange flames engulfed the paper. Once the kindling burned hot, he tossed a small log into the mix and headed toward the shower.

When steam billowed from the shower, he tugged the curtain aside and stepped into the tub. A sigh escaped his lips as the hot liquid slid down his body. He placed his hand on the wall, lowered his head to let the water beat down on his neck. His plan had finally produced actionable results. Rotating his neck, he stretched the tight muscles in his shoulders. He detested the messy work, but he'd do anything to help his brother.

The bar of soap he palmed yielded a big, white lather as he worked it between his hands. Meticulously, he washed his body from head to toe, scrubbing every inch. Then, he repeated the process to ensure he'd washed every morsel of death off his body.

When the water stopped flowing, he toweled off and dressed in a pair of boxers. He padded toward the fireplace with one last thing to accomplish before he made the call. Sparks traveled up the flue after he stoked the fire. When it settled, he nestled the brown bag in the center of the red-hot embers. The bag slowly ignited. Red and golden flames danced in celebration, engulfing the container to burn away his sins.

Over the years, he'd grown up and had evolved under his brother's protection. A sense of belonging and a little love could change a person forever. Incandescent light spilled from the open refrigerator, illuminating the small, sterile kitchen. The ice-cold beer hissed when he lifted the tab. Every day since his brother had been wrongfully convicted, he'd waited patiently for this moment.

After taking a long swig, he swiped his phone from the counter where he'd left it earlier. He couldn't wait any longer to update Dean Walter, his lawyer and longtime friend whom he'd met through his brother. "Dean, it's Richard. Grab a seat—I've got news. I finally have the location of our missing person."

The faint squeaking and movement of a desk chair filtered through the quiet that filled the line. Finally, Dean responded with a measured " Are you sure?"

"Confirmed it myself," Richard answered, then took a drink of his beer.

"Finally, some good news to share when I visit my client. His depression worsens with each passing day of his sentence. It worries me."

Richard knew Dean wouldn't say much over a phone line, his discretion and caution always at the forefront. He crumpled the empty can of beer and flipped it into the trash. "You tell him to stay strong and that our plan is in full motion. His days behind bars are numbered."

"Did you acquire the real estate?" Dean asked.

"Yes, I'm ready to contact our suppliers and get the product moving. I've even added some extra surprises into the mix. The more chaos, the better, but none of this will work without a court date for the appeal."

The sound of Dean's pen scribbling down notes as they spoke had stopped. "The paperwork has been filed, and any more evidence that comes to light will help. I should have an answer any day now. Thanks, Richard. This is excellent work. Keep me posted, and I'll do the same."

When the fire died down, he grabbed the poker, stabbing at the pile of ash and embers to ensure no evidence remained. Tomorrow, he'd clear out the ashes and throw them into the dumpster. Now, he needed to pore over his plans to make sure every i was dotted and t was crossed. His family deserved nothing less. It was a good thing he was a planner.

AIMEE HAD HATED THE tension between her and Clarke when they entered the station. The only person to blame was herself. A part of her wanted to tell him the whole truth, and that knowledge scared her. Something had shifted between them. She couldn't put a finger on why, but his touch ignited a fire within her body. A tingle of awareness grew in her belly, which was a complication that she didn't need in her life.

This man who exuded a strong mix of confidence and virility was dangerous. The rational part of her brain slammed the brakes on her emotions until they burned a bright cherry red. Nope, this had to stop. A line in the sand had to be drawn, one she didn't dare cross. There was too much at stake, and she had too much to lose. Instead, she decided to demonstrate how thankful she was for his support. She'd prepare him a home-cooked dinner. This would show him that he mattered to her.

She surveyed the items in his pantry and refrigerator, deciding a savory chicken pot pie would be perfect. She loved to cook and wanted to put his gorgeous kitchen with all the finest appliances to use. First, she measured and mixed the dry ingredients for the crust, but before she cut the butter into the mixture, she needed some tunes. Attaching her cellphone to an electrical outlet, she found her favorite playlist and let it play through its external speakers. The rhythm of the music had her dancing and chopping vegetables. Soon, the pot simmered with heavenly scents, signaling it was time to pour the contents into the baked pie shell.

As she waited for the timer to ding on her homemade delight, she allowed her mind to drift. How different would her life have been if she'd met Clarke before her husband? Her heart seized for a minute because she knew her father would still be alive.

The second pang came when she contemplated how stupid she'd been to judge Clarke only by his cover when she'd first met him. Sure, his confidence and arrogance got on everyone's nerves, but behind all of it was a protective and caring man. Standing in front of the kitchen window, she used the sink as her dance partner and did a little two-foot shuffle, followed by a hip undulation to the sultry beat of this song.

"Delicious," a deep, male voice projected into the room over the music.

A scream ripped from her throat as she spun around, armed with rolling pin. "Geez, can't you make noise when you move like a normal person?"

Clarke leaned against the door frame, slowing raising his hands into the air with a lazy smile crossing his face. *God, how long had he been there watching me?* A shiver of awareness zipped up her spine and warmed her cheeks.

Desperate for a distraction, she sniffed the air and wrinkled her nose. "If you've finished your chores, it's time to hit the shower, 'cause you stink. Dinner will be ready in about fifteen minutes."

The wink and smile he flashed about melted her insides. "Yes, ma'am."

She moved to her phone, her fingers flying across the screen until she pulled up a list she hasn't listened to in over a year. It had been too hard, yet tonight she couldn't think of a better set to play. Each song had been performed by her mother. Her heart surged with happiness at the thought of sharing this medley with Clarke, even if he didn't fully understand what it meant to her.

Soon enough, the scent of his soap, woods, and clean man wrapped around her senses right before his front brushed against her back as he pulled a bottle of wine out of the wall rack.

"Your meal deserves a bottle of wine. You like white?" The breath of his voice tickled her ear. He held the bottle for her inspection and approval.

"Wine makes me happy, and chardonnay is perfect," she said. She liked the goofy grin that spread across his face. He looked good smiling. "Let me pull the chicken pot pie from the oven then we can eat."

A few minutes later, all she heard were moans and a fork scraping across his plate. "You know, the way to a man's heart is through his stomach. This is really good, thank you."

His delight made her giddy. She enjoyed the sheer pleasure that each bite brought him as he chewed. "Thanks, it was one of my mother's favorite dishes to make."

"Past tense...how did she die?" he asked in a soft voice. The intensity of his gaze radiated his empathy.

Tears were not part of her dinner plans, so she grabbed her wine to gulp down a big drink. Hopeful those few precious seconds would help to quell the hurricane of emotions raging inside her. "My mom died of an aneurysm when she was thirty-eight. Sudden and devastating is what I remember the most."

"I'm sorry, losing people you love before their time is one of the cruelest experiences life can dish out. I'd love to hear about her."

Those six words meant so much to Aimee. She couldn't remember the last time she'd spoken about her mom. Certainly not since she'd entered WITSEC, but tonight she wanted to break another rule. She forked a bite into her mouth and savored the flavors.

Her mind pored through so many wonderful memories until she picked where she'd start. "She had this zest for life, and her music reflected it. She could play anything, but guitar and piano were her favorites. It's really why I love all types of music. This playlist is a compilation of her greatest hits."

She wasn't sure why she'd exposed so much, but in a strange way the timing had been perfect for this cathartic release. Remembering her mother erased some of the darkness that had enveloped Aimee. She loved her family and missed all those special times, like game night, movie night, Christmas morning, or barbecuing on the weekends. Her father's last words echoed in her thoughts. *"Don't let this define you. Make something out of your life. No matter what, don't look back."* Dammit, her tears morphed into tidal waves that crashed over the edges.

Clarke's big hand shot across the table and grabbed hers. His warmth infused her cold fingers. Then, he rubbed tiny circles on her skin with his thumb. She loved how his deep voice wrapped around her, lending his comfort. "Thank you for sharing something so important to you. I wish I had the power to go back in time to erase what had happened for you."

Such a simple sentence packed with so much promise and intent, she couldn't help but smile. If he only knew how much he'd have to erase.

After dinner, they worked in perfect tandem, clearing the table and loading the dishwasher like they'd done these tasks numerous times. Turning around, he leaned against the counter and gazed down at her.

"I think it's only fair to share a story with you about my life." The intensity of his stare mesmerized her. "My senior year of high school, my mom had learned that our neighbor's daughter hadn't been asked to prom and was devastated. She was a cute girl, but a total geek—we're talking straight As, mathematics, and science. That said, I adored her because she made me laugh and loved to play video games. So, after talking with my mom, I concluded that I'd ask her to be my date. Every girl should get that experience—"

"You mean dating you?" she sassed.

He thumped her nose with this finger. "No, smart ass, we were friends. What I meant was the whole prom experience. I was the one who was nervous because I didn't know how to dance. I had two left feet. So, my mom launched 'Operation Dance-off' and every night for two weeks she showed me different dances, and we practiced. It was undoubtedly the worst and best memories of my life."

"Why worst?"

"Uh, 'cause I danced with my mom every night for two weeks. If my friends had found out, the amount of ribbing would've been legendary. But, in the end, prom was a success, and I owed it all to my mom," he said, then pointed between them. "Just remember, this information is classified."

Aimee patted his cheek. "Ah, poor baby, but you survived. I like that story, but those terms were not agreed upon, so no promises."

"I do too. My mom's heart was bigger than her body. I think we should dance to honor our moms. You in, twinkle toes?"

Aimee's cheeks strained under the huge smile that covered her face. *My dad would so like this guy.* She deserved one night of fun, but afterward she had to go back to the life of Aimee Lang. "You leading, or should I?"

He didn't answer her question with words. Instead, he grabbed her hand and tucked her against his rock-hard body. Butterflies took flight in her belly as her happiness soared throughout her body. Their dance moves changed, song after song, matching the beat. She hadn't laughed this hard in a long time.

Tonight was beyond special, and Clarke had just given her a memory she'd treasure for years to come because he'd managed to blend her past with the present without even knowing it.

"Thank you, this night was perfect and I needed it," she said as she stepped back.

She couldn't help herself as she twirled for good measure, then winked at him before heading toward her room. *God, I'm an idiot, but there's no denying I'm on cloud nine.* She ignored the punch of attraction, because her focus had to remain on blending into her surroundings. This man wouldn't know how to do that even if he were wrapped in camouflage from head to toe with his mouth taped shut.

Five

T HE NEXT MORNING, AIMEE glanced at the clock and smiled. She couldn't remember the last time she'd slept this late. Tossing back the covers, she padded stealthily across the hallway toward the bathroom. She needed a shower and caffeine. Then she'd figure out what she had to accomplish today. Trent's decision to have her take the week off had bothered her at first, but now she saw his point. It gave her time and space to handle everything.

Thirty minutes later, she exited the bedroom, fresh, dressed, and ready to tackle the day ahead. She walked the entire house, looking for Clarke, which was empty. A twinge of disappointment hit her belly. Darn it, she'd missed him this morning. It'd been fun getting to know this man's routine and what made him tick. It was the small things that he did every day that fascinated her.

Then, she remembered he planned to finish fixing Irene's gutter after delivering some package. Wait until she told Maggie and Trent that one. It wasn't that long ago that Clarke and Irene had exchanged insults daily.

Aimee changed course and walked toward his den in search of pen and paper. The room had bookshelves on three sides full of various travel and destination books. In the center of the space sat a desk with a leather surface, adorned with gold painting along the edges. A wingback chair and table were on the left, and a wooden file cabinet with a flat-screen television were on the right. The room didn't fit his personality, but she wasn't about to judge him again.

At his desk, she opened one of the drawers and sucked in a sharp breath. She sat in the leather chair and pulled out a framed picture of a family. No, scratch that, it was Clarke's family—mother, father, and sister. Why would he keep a family picture in a drawer? What was he hiding?

She pressed mouth into a flat line while her mind nosedived to the worst conclusions. Underneath the frame, she found a pen and pad of paper to scribble out her note. Why hadn't he mentioned the other members of his family?

Heading to town to grab a few things from the store then the station. Be back soon. A

She placed the note under the framed picture she'd put on top of his desk and walked toward her truck. Interesting that he expected truth and openness, yet here she found a family picture tucked away. It seemed his transparency was only one-sided.

Well, she'd learned long ago that trusting someone only caused hurt. Everyone had secrets, and it was just a matter of time before those cryptic words destroyed someone. That was not a mistake she'd make again. A good reminder—Clarke was strictly a friend.

"YOU'RE MISSING THE BOX with my Halloween dishes," Irene hollered to be heard over the stomping and thumping noises Clarke made as he moved around in her attic.

"Good God, Irene, you have too much crap," he mumbled in a super-loud voice. "Oh, wait, found it. Hey, it's with two boxes labeled Library—Halloween. Do you want those too?"

"No, I used to decorate for the children and to be festive, but it's too difficult to get all the holiday boxes back and forth. I should just donate it to the school or something..."

The sadness in her tone echoed clearly, causing a pang of regret in his chest. Irene could be a huge pain in his ass, but she loved making people happy. Plus, any woman who had these many decorations loved the holidays.

Irene was no exception, but a prideful woman, so his next comment needed to be strategic. "I remember helping my mother and sister decorate. Well, I hauled the boxes with my dad, and they made it look festive and pretty on the inside. Dad and I were in charge of the outdoor decorations."

She pointed to the kitchen as he descended the stairs with a box in hand. "You mean your mother and sister told you their vision while trusting you to execute in the yard," she deadpanned.

He huffed. "I'd like to say no, but I guess you're correct."

He put the box he carried on the kitchen table. He hadn't thought about those memories in a long time. He chuckled at all the costume wars he'd had with his sister over who had dibs on what characters or theme. All she'd ever wanted to be was Wonder Woman. What he wouldn't give to fight with her one more time or to be able to help his mom and dad.

Irene slapped him on the back. "You deaf now from all this manual labor?"

Clarke spun around, accepted her proffered glass of lemonade, and shrugged. Damn if he'd admit to having an emotional moment as he strolled down memory lane. "Sorry, and you were saying?"

"Doesn't your family decorate anymore?"

"No, unfortunately, they're gone. I miss those days. Hey, I'll make a deal with you. When I'm home, I'll transport your boxes of holiday crap so you can decorate. How does that sound?" Clarke's phone vibrated in his pocket. He snatched it and glanced at the screen then answered, "Hey, Trent. Twice in less than a week. I must be your new favorite resident," he said loudly to goad Irene.

"Nope, not really. Yet I tolerate you now. I need to talk to Aimee. Her phone keeps going to voicemail. Is she with you?"

"Um, your mandatory vacation stipulation might be why she's ignoring you," Clarke said. He took a big swig of lemonade and tipped his head in appreciation toward Irene, then mouthed, *really good, thanks.*

"Ha ha, but seriously, this is an emergency. I have a triple homicide that's been reported just outside of town at a campground. Mondays are typically slow, except I still need a person at the station while we process that scene, which will require extra hands and time. See, I can't go one day without her."

Clarke's mind snapped to Aimee. Was she okay, and why wasn't she answering her phone? "A triple is not good. I'll head home to see what's up, and then I'll have her call you."

"Thanks, man," Trent replied and disconnected the line.

Clarke turned to say goodbye to Irene, who waved with one hand and gave him a bag of homemade cookies with the other. "That obvious?"

She smiled and winked. "Yes, now, share those with Aimee, and don't think I won't check. I'll take you up on your offer. Thanks, Clarke."

He hustled across her yard and through his until he'd unlocked the door to his house. He called out, "Aimee, hey, we need to talk. Trent needs your help."

Not a sound came from the house. Her room was empty, and she wasn't in the bathroom. He was about to see if her truck was in the garage when he saw the light on in his den. The frame caught his eye, as did the note underneath it. He was relieved that she'd left a note, yet dread hit his gut when he dialed her again, only to get her voicemail. *Where the hell are you, Aimee? I hope you're okay.*

He tried her phone once more before hanging up at her voicemail prompt. Well, he couldn't leave Trent hanging, so he dialed Trent to let him know he would stand in while they waited for Aimee to call.

He snatched up the note and shoved it into his pocket. The engine on his motorcycle fired up moments before he zoomed off toward town. When he arrived, her truck wasn't in the parking lot. That caused his stomach to clench with worry. He barked his greeting into his ringing cellphone without even looking at the screen first.

"About fucking time, where have you been?" he snapped, his gut tightening even further.

"Uh, Clarke, it's Tamara Gunderson. Is everything all right? You seem on edge."

Fuck me. No, everything is a fucking mess, thank you very much. And no, I don't want to talk to my psychologist. "Expecting someone else, which is obvious. I'm fine," he responded with as much sincerity as he could manage, considering the situation.

A momentary pause followed before he heard her flipping pages. "You've been hard to nail down for your mandatory psychological fitness eval. How about this Thursday?"

He walked toward the back lot to see if Aimee had parked there by chance. "Can't, but I'll let you when I'm available."

"I understand from your debriefing report that your last assignment went sideways. Those situations and the line of work you perform are the reasons we have these types of evaluations. To return to active duty, these meetings have to be completed. Do you want to try for the following Wednesday?" she pushed. A pen tapped lightly in the background.

Shit, no truck, either. His irritation meter ramped up a little higher. He didn't have time for this shit. "Hey, I'm in the middle of something, so I'll have to call you back." Clarke terminated the connection. That might get him a demerit point in his psychological file, but he didn't give a damn.

He burst through the front doors of the sheriff's station to find it empty. At Aimee's desk, nothing indicated that she'd been there. A stack of folders and messages were scattered on the surface, waiting for her return. Where the hell could she be?

While he waited, he texted his boss Aaron Sanchez, US Marshal Chief Deputy, that he wanted to use two weeks of his accrued paid time off. Immediately, his phone chirped with a reply text. *WTF, I thought you were storing PTO days to see if HR had a cap on the amount a person could rack up? You okay? I just hung up with Tamara.*

Clarke rolled his head from shoulder to shoulder, listening to his neck crack and pop. His fingers hovered above the keyboard as he let out a deep breath. *I'm fine, and for the record, no one likes meeting with her. I've got a few things in motion that I need to wrap up before we discuss my next assignment. Two weeks.*

Two weeks, but set up a meeting with Tamara for the first week of November.

"Asshole," Clarke muttered.

He glanced at the clock on the wall for the umpteenth time in the last three hours. He'd eaten all of Irene's cookies, and still no sign of

Aimee. He had her number displayed on his screen, and ready to hit the dial button when the station doors flung open. Activity flooded the area as Trent and his deputies returned from the crime scene.

"Where's Aimee?" he demanded, his face revealing his confusion that she wasn't at her desk.

"I don't know. I've left her several messages to meet me here. What happened out there?"

"Hey, Lance, roll the bulletin board into the conference room. You can set up the crazy wall in there. Close the blinds too."

Deputy Lance Charles nodded and disappeared into the conference room with a box of what Clarke assumed was evidence.

Trent approached Clarke, so there was zero space between them. His voice low, but direct, he asked, "Did you two have a fight?"

Not where he'd thought this conversation was headed, but at least he could answer honestly. "No."

"Good, keep it that way."

"Tell me what you found, because I don't like how Mill Creek's crime rate has increased over the last few days." Clarke put his hands into his front pockets.

Trent stared at him for several long seconds. "Agreed, but if you want information, then you owe me some. Tell me who you work for, no bullshit."

Clarke rolled his eyes and huffed. "Oh, you're still pissed that FBI Special Agent in Charge Guzman wouldn't tell you. I'm not a spook, if that's what has your tighty-whities twisted."

"Don't make me ask again, because we both know the squeaky-clean background and bat cave are a little extreme. Maybe you're paranoid and doing a lot of therapy for those issues?"

"I'm a US Deputy Marshal, paranoia is a job requirement, but you could say that my job has similarities to that of a spy. I do deep undercover assignments with people who should really be wiped from the earth or at least locked up forever. My employment is certainly high risk with average rewards because many of my enemies walk free afterward, which means if I were located by one of them, it would be bad."

Trent's lips pressed into a tight line for several seconds. "You're demented but a tough motherfucker—not everyone is cut out for those roles. If it makes you feel any better, now I owe Noah money. I told him you were too much of a pussy for that type of gig," Trent whined before slapping him on the shoulder.

Clarke flashed him the middle finger. "The respect is appreciated, but your assessment of my abilities hurts me."

Lance popped his head out of the conference room. "I'm ready when you are, Trent."

Trent motioned toward the conference room. "Let's go over the evidence. It's not good, that's for sure."

Once inside, Trent closed the door behind them. "Lance, Clarke is a US Deputy Marshal and is going to lend his expertise on this investigation." At Lance's acceptance, Trent continued, "We have three unidentified victims who died from multiple GSWs from a 9mm handgun. They were found at the campsite just off the US Forest Service road that goes to Tale Peak Observation and Radio Tower. At this point, we have no clear motive. One victim was shot in the face, neck, and groin. The other two died of wounds to the chest, neck, and head. Similar, but could the shot to the face be personal or just bad aim? No witnesses have come forward at this point, and there was minimal evidence at the scene. No casings were recovered from the ten rounds fired. The man shot in the groin did have fibers in his hand, which appear to be hair. We'll know more after forensics and the medical examiner perform their jobs."

"Hair? Do you think they had a fight that led to murder? A fight that got out of control?" Clarke asked.

Trent shook his head. "It's long hair, so it wasn't from those three bodies."

"Where are the pictures of the vics?" Clarke asked.

Lance headed toward the door. "I'll go get them. They should be finished printing."

Trent flipped through his notebook. "We have the estimated TOD in the range of twenty-four to thirty-six hours."

Lance returned with a stack of prints he handed to Trent. "Here are the photos from the scene."

He flipped through the stack, handing them off to Clarke. "The prints are being sent to AFIS."

Clarke's heart practically jerked to a halt. The picture that grabbed his attention also confirmed his suspicion. He planted two photos on the table and stabbed the face with his finger. "This asshole is the one from the bar. Did you pull up that footage from the alleyway the other night?"

Trent sat up straighter and reached for the laptop in the middle of the table. "Yes, I had planned to review the footage today, but this call took priority." After a few keystrokes, he accessed a file on the laptop before turning it around so they both could see the video.

Clarke rubbed his thumb and forefinger over his eyes. "Yup, that's our dead man from the bar and alley."

Trent turned the laptop around and studied the video and photos in more detail. "That's makes this investigation more interesting."

Clarke was about to add more to that statement when he heard Aimee's voice outside the conference room door. She knocked and opened the door. A whoosh of air race out of his mouth, taking a pound of stress with it. She was okay and unharmed. Now, he had to decide if he should throttle her or hug her for causing him all this worry.

"You okay?" Trent asked, turning his chair so he could face her. "We've been trying to reach you most of the day."

"I'm fine. Sorry I missed your call. I turned my phone off for a bit. Do you still need my help?"

"Not now. Clarke filled in since everyone was needed to process the scene."

Her eyes widened. "What happened?"

Lance provided a recap of the investigation for Aimee. "Homicide, three males at a campground by Tale Peak."

Aimee's mouth gaped, but she looked at Trent when he spoke.

"I'm sorry to make you do this, Aimee, but I'm going to need you to look at the victims to see if you recognize them. Clarke has identified them as the men from the bar the other night."

Her legs buckled, and she reached out to the table for support. "What?"

Trent scanned several photos before he selected two from the stack and slid them in her direction. Clarke figured he was searching for photos that weren't overly graphic. Aimee glanced down and flipped through both images before placing them back on the table facedown.

Her face paled as she sank into the chair. In a low murmur, she confirmed what Clarke had already stated. She stared at the evidence board, wringing her hands in her lap.

The need to comfort and protect overrode his brain. He stood and moved behind her so he could grasp her shoulders to remind her she wasn't alone.

R ELIEF FLOODED AIMEE'S BODY when Clarke provided a reason for them to leave the station. She didn't know if she could stomach dinner, but they'd agreed to order sandwiches to go from PB&S Café. The crisp evening air surrounded her as they walked toward the restaurant; she was thankful she'd worn a jacket.

A riot of thoughts pummeled her brain. She'd barely survived her marriage that had torn her life apart. That black night, stained by red, white, and blue flashing lights, would be forever branded on her heart and soul. Her husband had been the worst kind of evil, and she'd been in the center of it. Her father had been murdered. She'd barely escaped.

A shiver wracked her body not because of the cold air, but those memories. When the café's door opened, she welcomed the distraction from her thoughts. Inside she saw Micah, the town veterinarian, waiting on his order. Clarke moved to the counter to place their orders.

"Aimee, how are you holding up? I was stunned to hear about the fire," Micah said. His face conveyed his concern. "Clarke, good to see you."

Aimee appreciated the kind words. "All right, all things considered."

"If you need anything, let me know," Micah replied. He turned to elbow Clarke in the gut. "I heard you made Irene happy. She's told practically everyone in town about how you helped her with all her Halloween decorations."

"Oh God, it's not that big of a deal. It was only a few boxes," Clarke said, waving his hand dismissively.

Aimee pointed at Micah's shirt. "I love that place. It's the coolest place in Seattle with its Prohibition-style space and the menu."

"Right, even the whole secret-password-to-open-the-hidden-door thing is over the top. Lucky for us, we can't complain too much, considering we have amazing food in this town," he said.

She clasped her hands in front of her chest. "Absolutely, but I'd love a hidden bar to hang out at after a long day. I miss that place so much."

Clarke draped his arm across her shoulders, jumping into the conversation. "What the heck are you two babbling about?"

She laughed up at him. "Sorry, you aren't cool enough to know."

Her throat constricted when she realized her mistake. Why was she so freaking stupid? She'd jumped right into this conversation without thinking because she'd been born in Seattle, Washington. Now she had to come up with an answer that didn't start with the phrase before WITSEC...

Micah jumped in and updated Clarke. "It's a local bar and eatery in Seattle. They're known for craft cocktails and locally sourced ingredients. It's a foodie paradise for locals."

"Oh, when were you two there? Clearly you had to spend a little time to know this deep state secret," Clarke asked, glancing between the two of them.

All she had to do was stick to her damn script and be her new identity. But no, she couldn't even do that. What she did excel at was screwing up her life. When would she learn? Tears threatened to spill down her face as her heart hammered against her ribcage. She hated having to lie.

"I'm an alumnus from the Washington State's College of Veterinary Medicine," Micah responded easily and then dropped his hand, indicating it was Aimee's turn to fill in the blanks.

"Micah, your order is ready," one of the restaurant staff hollered.

"I'll catch your answer next time." He nodded at Clarke and Aimee before he headed to the counter to collect his food.

Clarke squeezed her shoulder. When she lifted her eyes, his lips were pressed into a flat line. She hated that she'd upset him. Luckily, their order had been called, interrupting the moment building between them. Bag in hand, when he returned, he pressed his free hand against the small of her back, guiding her out of the building. They walked in silence to her truck. Why could silence be so loud?

"I'll meet you at home," Clarke said, then handed her the bag of food.

He'd retreated to his motorcycle when the first tear slid down her cheek. Relief swamped her system, and she'd have some time to force down her emotions before they returned to his house. Why couldn't she keep the lid shut on her memories when Clarke was around? Now, she had to gather her strength to prepare for the conversation that would inevitably come once the garage door closed at his house.

He was the reason she'd gone to her favorite place today, to bask in the beauty of the forest and clear her mind. It had become her solace. Normally, those trips reminded her that beauty still existed in the world and that her problems were small compared to the bigger picture. But today, it had been the opposite. She'd forced herself to remember why her life no longer existed and that she didn't deserve a second chance.

When his motorcycle parked alongside her truck in the garage, she pressed the clicker to lower the door. She exited her truck; Clarke still sat astride the bike. His dismount was a fluid motion, all his muscles bunching and straining against his jeans and olive-green Henley. He strode toward her, stopping at her truck to run his hand across the dusty hood, leaving a clean spot in its wake.

"Seriously? Now I'll have to wash it tomorrow," Aimee grumbled, then sighed.

She trailed him into the house. He moved to the kitchen sink and washed his hands. The wide expanse of his back flexed with his movements. When he finished, he turned around, wiping his hands on a dish towel. The intensity of his stare equaled that of a laser beam trying to penetrate her defenses until he could see inside her soul. His face didn't betray his thoughts, but if she were to guess what he was thinking, it was probably where to start with his growing list of questions.

Clarke tossed the towel on the counter and exhaled. "One day, I'd like to hear about Seattle, but not until you're ready to share that piece of your past with me."

"No...that's..." Her eyes snapped shut briefly at her botched reaction.

When she opened her eyes, she looked toward the ground. Anything to avoid the look of disappointment written all over his face. Damn it, she wanted to drop her walls and share that story––but she couldn't. A lump formed in her chest from his continued patience and unwavering support. He made her want to blurt out the truth. To share all those parts of her life with him, but that was the problem. Those stories didn't exist anymore. They weren't hers to share, and in time he'd just resent her avoidance.

"It's okay," he said. "Right now, there are bigger problems we need to discuss."

Aimee's head snapped up. "What does that mean?"

Clarke spread his feet and grabbed the counter behind him. "Where did you go earlier?"

Her heart beat a little harder in her chest. "I told you, to clear my head. Why does that matter anyway?"

"It matters because people care about you, and you worried them. No one could reach you, and you didn't return one call," he answered in a low, even tone. His silence finally implored her to provide more information.

"I went to Rayna Outpost to buy a few things, got a salad to go from the diner, then went to Tale Peak. I pretty much spent the day there. Afterward, I decided to take the longer route—Courier Pass—back home. I didn't realize when I turned off my phone that everyone would need to reach me."

"There's a silence feature on all phones," he said. "When did you listen to the messages?"

"Reception is hit or miss in the mountains, which is why I waited until I reached Outlook Point. When I heard Trent's message, I headed toward the station. Looking back, I should've called, sorry."

Clarke ran his hand over his face. "Where's your gun?"

"What the hell do you care? Are you upset because I didn't call you first? What the hell does that gun have to do with anything?" she snapped.

"Where is it, Aimee?" His voice vibrated down her spine.

"The nightstand in my room," she answered.

"We need to get that gun," he said as he walked toward her. "Tell me the truth, did you have that gun with you today?"

She whipped around to face the man who'd just pushed her last button. Heat bloomed across her chest and cheeks. "No, I haven't touched it since I put it there the other day. I find it ironic that you ask for complete trust, yet you've given me very little in return. You want to tell me why you have a framed picture in your desk drawer? That's a great place to hide a family photo."

His eyes flared for the briefest second then recovered. He grasped her elbow to direct her toward the bedroom. "They were killed. Displaying the picture became this constant reminder of what I'd lost. So instead of avoiding the room, I put it inside the desk drawer."

Now it was her turn to look surprised; that wasn't what she'd expected to hear. Stopping in her tracks, she turned back and touched his heart. "I'm so sorry. I wish I could say something that would make a difference. I understand that guilt. What happened?" The air between them thickened from the unexpected exchange of grief they both had in common.

Clarke cleared his throat. "I'll tell you after we finish talking about today. That's the priority. Did you have anything to do with the deaths of those three men?"

She slid open the drawer of the nightstand and pointed to the gun. Her body went cold as she registered his words and where this conversation seemed to be headed. "No."

Nodding, he closed the drawer. "I believe you, Aimee. Your body language at the station told me that, but I had to hear it from your mouth. The circumstantial evidence is compelling. The majority of the day, you couldn't be reached. Your truck is dusty from the road that passes the campsite where the men were found. One is the man from the bar. All three died from wounds inflicted by the same caliber handgun you have in your possession. You have no clear proof of owning a gun because you purchased it at a gun show with cash. You see my concern?"

Her legs wobbled. Instead of letting her hit the floor, Clarke scooped her up in his arms and carried her toward the family room. He put her in the middle and took a seat next to her.

The energy that had coursed through her system dwindled, leaving an emptiness that scared her. "I swear...I didn't kill them. I hate guns. My father was killed by one."

When his arm wrapped around her shoulders she leaned against his body. She laid her head on his hard pecs. The light scent of fabric softener mixed with wood filled her senses. They sat in silence while she listened to the strong beat of his heart.

Being in his arms gave her a strange sense of hope in her otherwise bleak world. "What should I do now? Does Trent think I did this?"

He cocked his head to the side to see her face. "At this point, we need to bring Trent up to speed. You need to tell him about the gun and Tale Peak. He can help you more from inside the circle of knowledge. Plus, you know he's on your side."

When she acknowledged his statement, he continued, "I think it would be best to offer your gun for ballistics testing to rule it out. That, combined with the official time of death from the autopsy report, will exonerate you. In this case, you're cooperating and getting ahead of the circumstantial evidence."

"Okay, but that won't make me a suspect, right?"

"Nope, just a lead that'll be dismissed once the evidence is reviewed," he said.

"I'll text Trent tonight. Will you come with me tomorrow to drop off the gun?" Her mind raced with additional questions to ask, but she decided to start with the obvious one. "What do you do for a living?"

"Law enforcement, deep undercover assignments where I infiltrate criminal organizations—you know, like drugs or weapons. The assignments can vary from months to years, depending on the job. Not having a family makes me a prime candidate."

"Are you CIA? Is your name even Clarke?"

The corner of his lips curved up. "No, I'm not that cool, but there are layers of protection in place to safeguard my identity when I'm on assignment. Yes, that's my given name."

"Wow, this just turned into a pinky-swear moment. You might be new to this level of secrecy, but you're supposed to enter a special handshake before you reveal anything." She linked her pinky finger with his and shook on it.

"You remind me of my sister. She loved secret handshakes and Wonder Woman." He shifted his weight to rest his legs on the coffee table.

"I'd love to hear about your family."

His chest expanded. He gulped down a big breath and held it for a second. His voice lowered as he spoke. "I haven't spoken about my family in a long time. Don't get me wrong, they were amazing, and I loved them. It's just the pain from that day, mixed with my profound loss, haunts me. My parents shared a deep love. My relationships with both my mom and dad were solid and filled with happiness. Even my little sister, Sidney, who was the bane of my existence, kept me laughing and wrapped around her finger."

"That sounds a lot like my family, without the sister. I was an only child," she shared, not caring that she'd divulged more than she should have. In this moment, it felt right to contribute.

"Hell, even my friends loved to hang at my house. Then, the day of my high school graduation, my parents and sister were killed by a drunk driver while heading home to host my graduation party. I'd bailed on them to hang with my friends for a few more pictures. I should've been in that car with them. Or, if I'd asked them to wait for a bit longer, they might've missed that driver altogether."

"The fault belongs with the driver who chose to drive impaired, not you," Aimee said, rubbing his chest.

"That night shattered the bubble I had lived in during my youth. Everything I thought I wanted in life changed in the blink of an eye. To survive, I needed control. I reevaluated everything, right down to my desire to have a family. It's why I chose my profession. I poured all my grief and anger into helping others live out their dreams because I wanted the world to be safer. But it doesn't always happen that way, does it?"

"That's quite a burden to carry," Aimee whispered, moving her head back to his chest.

"No, you have to live forward, but the past should only serve as two things: memories and lessons learned. Okay, enough about me, what happened to your father?"

She processed his statement for a minute. Deciding she owed him an answer, she provided the pared-down version. "He was shot and killed by a man for no reason. I'm sorry, this isn't a topic I'm comfortable discussing." Her throat constricted around the words.

He lifted her face with his index finger. "I'm sorry. Is his murderer in jail?"

She nodded.

His eyebrows drew together, a serious look on his face. "Good, that saves me from hunting that bastard down."

Overcome by emotion, she trailed her hand up his muscular torso until she cupped his face. The kiss she pressed to his lips was soft, but full of respect. "Thank you for having my back. Knowing I have your support means a lot to me."

This man exuded a dominant mix of confidence and virility, drawing her to him like a moth to a flame. It also didn't hurt that his tattooed bad-boy vibe was sexy, from his bald head to all those muscles. Oh yes, her girl parts approved. She longed to trace her fingers along his tattoos, learning why each one adorned his arm. So much intrigue was wrapped into that sinful package, which included his grumbly, sarcastic, and overprotective behavior. What he did show her with each interaction was that he cared about her, and that made her feel special.

She was about to move away from him when he palmed the back of her head, keeping her close. His gaze darkened, and those sensual, full lips crashed down on hers. Never had she'd been kissed so thoroughly or with so much emotion. Her hand lowered, fisting a handful of his shirt. Desire flowed hot and heavy in her body. This moment she wanted to savor, so she matched his intensity, pouring everything that she couldn't tell him into every touch.

A warning bell sounded in the farthest recess of her brain. She moaned into his mouth as his hand moved under her shirt to palm one of her breasts. He stroked her nipple over her lacy bra with his finger, sending a pulse of arousal straight to her core. Man, she was in over her head and had to shut this down. She backed out of his embrace and licked her lips.

"Uh, dinner, we should eat," she announced.

He held himself back, which she appreciated, but knowing she affected him unleashed wicked desires deep within her body. Maybe it could work between them since neither wanted anything permanent. Her dreams of becoming a mother and raising a family had died the moment she learned she'd married a monster. A thought for another day.

The pressing one now was if she should report the recent information to her DUSM. Lyndon could be a bit intense, and she didn't need him jumping to any conclusions. She wasn't sure why those men were dead, but she hadn't been the one who'd pulled the trigger.

Six

A FEW DAYS HAD passed since Aimee had delivered her gun, along with a few strands of her hair, to the sheriff's station for processing. Having Trent on the same page helped, and Clarke was pleased that she'd agreed. What bothered him was why the dead guy had a fistful of hair in the first place. His need for answers deepened.

Eager fingers hovered over the enter key with her name typed into the search field. He'd been down in his bunker, hunched over this stupid keyboard for twenty minutes, deciding if he should execute a background search. Releasing a frustrated sigh, he jammed the delete key down repeatedly until the cursor remained. Betraying the trust he'd just started to earn by doing a search behind her back made him a jerk. Maybe his reluctance was due to the mind-blowing kiss they'd shared. God, she'd caused his mind and body to go haywire.

He pushed back from the desk to head upstairs as his home phone rang. He hurried his pace, closing the hidden door, then sprinted toward the phone. He heard Aimee's voice in the den speaking with whomever had called first thing this morning.

She had her back to him as he approached the room. He could only hear one side of the conversation, but her tone was clipped and mocking. "Of course he has the number. I'll let him know you called."

Who the hell had called and ruffled her feathers? His immediate thought was Trent had gotten the analysis back from forensics.

"What happened?" Clarke asked as soon as she ended the call. He leaned against the door frame in the den.

"Damn it, Clarke." She spun around. Her eyes narrowed, and her chest puffed up. "I'm going to put freaking bells on your shoes. I thought you were gone, which is why I answered the phone."

He hooked his thumb into the belt loop of his jeans. "Stealth is an occupational hazard, sweetheart, but I'm not trying to startle you. As for answering my phone, I have nothing to hide, so who has you upset?"

Her nostrils flared, and her eyes narrowed with indecision. "I...I thought we were...I don't know, connecting. I mean, building, gah!" She pinched the bridge of her nose and closed her eyes for a moment. "Do you have a daughter?"

Her reaction had his hackles raised, but the question surprised him. "No, I don't have a daughter. You know that from our conversation the other night. Having a family would make me vulnerable, among other things. Who called saying I had a daughter?"

"I know...and that wasn't fair. That call was bizarre. Just never mind, I'm sorry."

This fiery and complex woman had corroded a small layer of his resolve with her bright hazel eyes and auburn tresses. Her admission warmed a spot deep inside his body because she was correct, they were building something together. What, exactly, was still being explored and defined.

"It's good to know that assuming the worst in people isn't a character flaw. Now, who called?" he asked, then winked.

"Someone named Jane. She said you hadn't sent in the authorization form that had been sent to you. And that you need to sign the field trip permission form if you want Lizzy to go to the pumpkin patch," she relayed.

He let out a deep rumble of laughter. "I can certainly see why you jumped to that conclusion." He stepped toward her and placed his hand on her shoulder. "Lizzy is my aunt, Elizabeth Pickle, who's in a memory care center. I need to send in her annual flu shot authorization form and the permission form for that field trip."

"Which is why you have the number," she mumbled, her cheeks stained a reddish pink.

He nodded and smiled. "Your penance for throwing me to the wolves, should you approve, is to come with me to visit my aunt in Boise. She's a wonderful woman and would love visitors. Not that she gets many anymore."

The smile she gave him lit up her whole face. "I'd love to meet her, but I'll drive, because I don't want to ride a motorcycle that far. And for the record, that's not a punishment at all."

"Fair enough. I'll even take you to my favorite burger joint. They cook your burger to order, but you're in charge of loading it up at the toppings bar. They have so many choices it's mind blowing." Clarke winked. "Oh, and I'll find another way to collect so don't worry."

Her mind raced with all the possibilities of how he could collect, and her body reacted with a warmth that burned hot right at her core.

"Let me grab my stuff and we're off," she said.

The drive to Boise was pleasant. They chatted about sports, movies, and music and shared many laughs. He liked it when she let down her guard and said whatever was on her mind or in her heart. After lunch, he directed Aimee toward his aunt's home. He went through the check-in process, signing them in, and then asked to see Jane so he could sign the various documents. On the way back to Lizzy's room, he played tour guide.

"Some days are better than others, so we'll have to see how it goes," Clarke cautioned and rapped on his aunt's partially open door. "Hey, Lizzy, how are you today?" he asked, then wrapped his aunt up in a big hug. "I'd like you to meet my friend, Aimee."

Lizzy's face conveyed her happiness with the unexpected visit. She held her hand to Aimee and motioned for her to come closer. "You're very pretty. How long have you two been together?" She patted Aimee's hand. "He's never brought a girl to meet me."

Clarke shook his head at his aunt, who looked good today. Her silver-and-black hair was styled in soft waves around her face. She'd always been in shape from being a flight attendant and all the activities she loved to do. The hardest part of Alzheimer's was he never knew what he'd get when he visited her. Some days were like old times, but others were filled with anger or indifference because she barely recognized him. Today was perfect. His aunt was present in mind and body, so he'd focus on that gift.

Clarke smiled at her and Aimee. "Mom would tell you to not embarrass me in front of my friends."

"Like hell." Lizzy harrumphed. "Trust me, if my sister were here, she'd be sitting right next to me, giving her son the fifth degree. I can count the number of times you've brought a woman home or to visit family on one hand."

He grumbled mostly to himself but added for Aimee's benefit, "Sorry, my aunt's a bit of a free spirit."

Aimee covered Elizabeth's hand with her own. "It's nice to meet you. I can appreciate a direct woman, but he's right, we are only friends. I'm staying with him while my studio is being repaired from fire damage."

He took a seat and watched his aunt dote on Aimee. Lizzy reached for one of her photo albums and sat with Aimee on the bed. She reminisced and shared stories from several of her adventures in various countries. Not once did Aimee seem to fake her interest. Her face radiated her ease and happiness. Not only that, she also engaged with his aunt, encouraging her to share more stories. To his horror, his aunt even told embarrassing stories from his youth.

Clarke held up his hand and interjected to slow Lizzy down. "Hold up, you're making me sound like a wuss. I only ended up inside the house at my own 'campout'-themed slumber party because I was worried my *little* sister would be afraid I was outside of the house."

"Oh, hush." His aunt's elegant hand waved off his complaint. "You were scared when that owl started to hoot. Your parents confirmed those events."

Female laughter broke out in the small room at his expense.

"You must tell me more stories about Clarke. This is awesome." Aimee's eyes sparkled with mirth as she encouraged his aunt.

"Well, let's see, one time he locked himself inside my bomb shelter—"

Okay, that was not a story he wanted shared, or the fact he had a secure room. "Enough. If you tell her all my stories on her first visit, there won't be a reason for a second one. Plus, it's almost time for dinner. How about we walk you to the dining room?"

Elizabeth patted Aimee's knee. "You can come and visit anytime you'd like."

She gave his aunt room to maneuver about the small space. "I'd like that. Plus, I'd like to hear about the other cool places you've visited. I've always wanted to travel and experience different cultures and foods."

Clarke held the door so the women could exit. They headed down the hallway toward the large dining room. After meeting every resident along the path, he extracted Elizabeth's chair at the assigned table. His aunt sat at the same place each meal with three other residents. He and Aimee exchanged amused looks every time his aunt introduced Aimee as his *special* friend. Oh, how his aunt loved to stir the pot with her big heart.

Once his aunt was seated, they both said their goodbyes and headed toward the parking lot. He'd enjoyed today, the camaraderie, his aunt's cognitive state, and being able to share all of this with Aimee. The whole experience seemed normal, like adding another building block to their relationship—friendship.

She interrupted his thoughts as she drove toward Mill Creek. "What did she mean by bomb shelter?"

He couldn't believe he didn't have any qualms about telling her about his safe room. He wanted to. Sidestepping that question would have been easy, all he had to do was blame his aunt's condition, but he didn't want to lie to her. Sharing another layer of his life was what felt right, and just maybe, she'd reciprocate. After all, they were building upon a friendship and deepening their bond, whether she'd admit it or not.

"She built a bomb shelter into her home. My aunt had a little doomsday-style paranoia flowing through her blood. She thought it important to be prepared for any contingency. When I was a kid she was too cool for words."

"Like a zombie apocalypse?"

He couldn't remember a day where of late where he'd laughed so much. "Exactly, but to her, it was an actual bomb event."

Aimee giggled and checked her side mirror. As they continued driving down the highway, they discussed dinner ideas. He liked that she wanted to make chicken enchiladas. He loved Mexican food, and Mill Creek needed to add it to its amazing list of restaurants. He'd missed home-cooked meals and having a companion to share dinner. It was a nice change of pace from his everyday routine.

"Thanks for today. I enjoyed Boise and doing something different. I'm getting to know the man behind. " She paused and moved her hand in a circle around him. Your cantankerous and stubborn exterior leaves me wanting to know more. You're a good man, Clarke."

"I aim to confuse and please, another one of my many curses. And don't forget to add in my need to control."

She shot him a quick glance. "Trust me, I haven't forgotten. Besides, naked and exposed is so much better than clothed and disguised any day."

"Are you flirting with me?"

She laughed. "Not on purpose. What I was trying to say came out jumbled."

He wanted to probe into that statement because he'd bet his paycheck it represented her past. God, he hoped that someday she'd just tell him what had happened. His goal now was not to be one more person on her list who'd let her down.

"I got what you meant. It's just fun to bust your chops," he answered.

They sat in companionable silence. He was taking in the scenery when her cellphone rang from the cup holder. Glancing down, he saw it was Trent.

She tossed her phone to Clarke. "Will you answer it for me?"

He swiped the bar to answer. "Hey, Trent. Aimee's driving so she asked me to answer her phone. You're on speaker. We're headed back to Mill Creek from Boise. The reception might get spotty in a few places."

"Everything okay?" Trent asked.

"Absolutely. We visited my aunt and took care of some business there."

"That's good. Hey, I got the results and wanted to share them. Ballistics came back negative. Has that gun ever been fired before, Aimee?"

"Nope, I only bought it for show. I don't know, someone may have before I bought it, but I was told it was new."

Clarke turned in his seat with the phone in his hand. "And the fibers?"

"The hair in the victim's hand matched Aimee's sample."

Her ragged intake of breath had Clarke reaching out to cover her hand. "I don't understand how he had my hair. He never had a hold of my hair. That's just weird."

Trent asked, "Are you sure he didn't grab you by your hair during that altercation? You may not have registered it due to the adrenaline rush. Was your scalp sore at all?"

Aimee moved her hand absently and went to her head. "No, not at all."

Trent continued with his update. "The time of death, based on the rigor and temperature, was deduced to between twelve and eighteen hours before the bodies were discovered. The autopsy came back with what we expected, except for one key fact. GSR was found on one of the victims, indicating that he pulled the trigger. That would make our scene a murder-suicide."

She interjected, "If you had a gun, why did I have to bring mine to the station?"

"Smart girl," Clarke said. "You never found a gun, so are you thinking the scene was contaminated before you arrived?"

The sound of pages being flipped came over the line. "That's the million-dollar question, but it doesn't seem likely. My working theory is we have an unidentified suspect," Trent said.

Clarke nodded. "I agree."

She flicked on the turn signal. When the intersection cleared of oncoming traffic, she entered the market's parking lot looking for an open spot. "Does this mean I can return to work on Monday?"

"Absolutely. I've been lost without you keeping me organized." Trent's enthusiasm came over the line loud and clear.

"Good. See you then, boss," Aimee replied and pulled into an empty spot. She unfastened her seatbelt, and when Clarke ended the call, she beamed. "Today keeps getting better. I think it might be a two-bottles-of-wine night. I need to grab a few items for our dinner. Do you want to come or wait here?"

"Lead the way," he said, opening his door and heading to grab a cart.

He processed the information he'd just heard while they cruised down several aisles. What a clusterfuck that had been, but he was relieved the evidence pointed another direction. Not that they deserved death, but those pricks wouldn't be harassing anyone else.

AFTER THEY RETURNED TO Clarke's house she helped him put away all the groceries and then started to work on dinner. She loved being able to cook again. Today had been so much fun, and for the first time in a very long time, she felt like a normal person. Not a woman in the WITSEC program. Even better, due to Trent's news, she didn't have to worry about whether to report all of this to her DUSM.

She planned to celebrate tonight and focus on all the good they'd shared. The electronic beeps of the oven being set to pre-heat filled the quiet space in the kitchen.

"Consider me your sous chef. What can I do to assist?" he asked while he opened a bottle of wine. "Red seems like a good choice."

"Works for me. Okay, you want to chop garlic or onion?" When he answered, she tossed him the onion.

The sound of knives chopping on wooden cutting boards mixed with more conversation. The moment the garlic and onion hit the melted butter to sauté, her mouth watered from the heavenly smell. Next, she took the rotisserie chicken out of the container to shred. Clarke came up behind her, his body heat warming her backside as he stole a hunk of chicken to eat. She lightly raked her teeth on his fingers when he offered her a bite. She didn't miss the low groan that escaped his mouth.

"Will you grab my phone and select a playlist? We should have music while we work." She loved music but needed a distraction from all those hard muscles. Her body flared with excitement and awareness at his proximity. He was all male and intoxicating.

He selected a list that contained her parent's favorites. To her, he couldn't have picked a better set to listen to. She swayed and danced at the stove as she added the chicken to the onions-and-garlic mixture and a third of the enchilada sauce. She turned to face Clarke, who now had his long-sleeved shirt rolled up to his elbows, exposing his powerful forearms.

"Want to work out those muscles and grate the cheese?" she asked while she pulled the brick from the refrigerator.

"Sweetheart, you butter me up like that, and I'll even do the dishes," he replied, flinging the dish towel over shoulder.

She pulled the pan off the burner and set it on a hot pad. Then, she opened the package of tortillas and spread out several. The spoon she grabbed went to work adding a layer of chicken to each disc.

"Okay, your job is to sprinkle the cheese on top when you're finished. Then we roll these babies up and place them in that pan."

Together, they worked in tandem, assembling their dinner, drinking wine, and listening to the music. She liked how the two of them clicked—nothing forced or fake. Once they finished, she put the casserole dish into the oven for twenty-five minutes. As she turned, she met his gaze. He didn't hide the fact that she'd caught him staring at her, or how his gaze slid down her body and back up to her face.

"I want to investigate your ink," she responded and moved closer to him, her wine glass in hand.

Deep in her gut, she knew every tattoo on this man represented something important to him. He didn't do anything half-assed from what she'd seen. These designs were a road map to his soul, and she wanted to navigate each mile of him. She reached for his arm to start her journey. Just like the man, an intricate masterpiece covered his flesh.

Lightly, she traced her finger over one that caught her eye. Goosebumps pebbled his skin in the wake of her touch. The meaning behind the three tombstones—the top portion of a heart encased all three with a sunrise peeking out from the center point—on the inside of his elbow were an homage to his family. It was the image that covered the pulse point on his wrist that gutted her. Wonder Woman's symbol with angel wings framing the letters had been etched on his skin.

She tapped the spot. "This one's for your sister?"

She rubbed small circles over the design. The symbolism spoke volumes for both the man and the meaning. A strong ache stabbed at her chest. They shared an understanding about gut-wrenching loss. It left a hole in a person's soul that would never be filled.

Her gaze lifted to his. "I love how you honored your family. It's perfect. Will you help me design something for my parents?"

She couldn't describe the intensity of the moment, but through it they'd become even closer. She'd never shared anything this strong with her ex-husband, even when they'd been dating. This man exuded strength and power, but he'd also shown her his softer side. He'd given her his trust by exposing something he held dear. The enormity of this moment moved her.

He answered with actions instead of words. He ran his thumb over her pulse point then pressed a kiss to her palm, making her melt into a puddle of goo. She just reacted to the moment with no concerns or what-ifs; she did what felt natural.

She rose on her tiptoes and lifted her chin. "Kiss me, Clarke."

His deep voice rumbled against her ear as he spoke. "I'll give you anything you need."

Tiny shivers of need and want wracked her body at the raw desire radiating from his orbs. To see her effect on this potent man infused her system with confidence. "I don't know what I did to deserve you, but having you by my side makes me stronger. Thank you, for everything."

He gripped the back of her head, tilting it upward. His lips mere millimeters away from hers, he paused. "You're dead wrong. You're strong all on your own. It's one of the things I admire about you."

To punctuate his point, he lowered his mouth and devoured hers. He took what he wanted and left her panting for more. Tingles of awareness caused her skin to pebble. Her core clenched with need while her skin vibrated with lust and longing. The hard ridge of his erection pressed against her abdomen. Knowing that she had caused that reaction in this virile man made her drunk with pleasure. A ferocity to devour this man overwhelmed her senses. He was driving her to want anything and everything in only seconds.

The timer sounded on the oven, interrupting the moment but not diminishing the surge of emotions that ravished her.

Reluctantly, she stepped out of his embrace and moved toward the oven. Maybe she should stop fighting herself and let this attraction play out. They were both adults. Limits could be established up front, a friends-with-benefits scenario, but nothing more. She couldn't give anyone more because that part of her heart had to remain closed off to survive. Besides, he'd mentioned countless times that his occupation didn't allow him to have girlfriends or family, so this could be a win-win.

The only question was, could she learn to compartmentalize her feelings and emotions to make this work?

Seven

WHY COULDN'T CLARKE HAVE chosen an easier girl? One who didn't frustrate him on so many levels. Or one who didn't make him ponder the merits of being a family man. He'd even gone as far as creating a mental decision table listing the pros and cons. His career was the wild card, especially since his last assignment. Hell, he didn't want easy—he wanted Aimee. She challenged him with her evasive and cryptic ways, and he looked forward to uncovering her mysteries.

She held his interest even without sex. He'd certainly have fewer cold showers, that he knew for sure. The fact remained his body electrified around her, and life held more promise. That knowledge excited and terrified him. His life had been neatly planned until he'd met Aimee Lang. He raked his hand over his face as he sat on the edge of his bed.

The sunlight filtered into the room between the cracks of his blinds. His mind worked over what he had to accomplish today. It was Saturday, and he couldn't believe a week had passed since she had come to stay with him. He'd given Irene a week to sort her Halloween decorations. He planned on seeing if Aimee wanted to join them in hauling the remaining ones to the library so Irene could decorate there too.

After showering and dressing, Clarke headed toward the kitchen. Aimee's voice drifted down the hallway, and the scent of coffee filled the air. Her hands moved a mile a minute as she chatted on the phone, making plans for breakfast. After a minute, she ended the call and stuffed the phone into one of her jeans' back pockets.

A smile crossed her face. "Morning," she said. "I made coffee and cinnamon rolls, but Maggie just called, and I'm going to meet her for breakfast."

Clarke filled a coffee cup, disappointment creeping into his stomach. He enjoyed spending time with Aimee and because of that, he didn't want to share her today.

"That should be gossipy, maybe like a Mill Creek soap opera?"

Aimee rinsed her mug out at the sink then placed it in the dishwasher. "Gossipy? Spoken like a true man. I'll be sure to not share a single thing I find out when I return home. Also, don't slander great television. You should watch one for a week before you jump to conclusions. *Genoa City* is awesome."

He held up his hand. "I don't know where *Genoa City* is located, but I'm not going to watch one, so get that thought out of your head. As for gossip, you must share. How else am I supposed to rib the guys and appear worldly?"

"I don't even know how to respond to you." She shook her head and rolled her eyes in mock exasperation. She snagged her phone from her back pocket and answered, "Hey, Trent. What's up?" A pause. "Okay, thanks for the update... Yup, I'll tell him now."

Clarke stared right at her, waiting for the update.

"The fingerprints on the Molotovs came back as a match to the dead guy. Mason received the results late last night and is closing the case today since the suspect is dead. You were right about that guy."

He sipped his coffee and swallowed before saying, "I'm glad he's no longer a threat to anyone. You okay? That's a lot to digest."

She cocked her head and sighed. "I guess I should feel something more, but all I feel is relief. I know that sounds horrible. I mean, that man lost his life."

"You're human, and there's nothing wrong with that response. That man made some poor decisions, and they cost him." Clarke rubbed the back of his neck. "What time do you think you'll be back? I'm off to help Irene transport her Halloween crap to the library. It shouldn't take more than an hour or two."

Aimee walked past him and patted his arm on her way to the garage. "And to think you two were mortal enemies. I'll catch up with you after breakfast. Have fun."

"You too," he replied right before she closed the door to the garage.

Silence blanketed the kitchen after she left. It was funny how a person could miss another when they made you happy. He demolished a cinnamon roll and finished the last of his coffee before heading over to Irene's place. He'd barely knocked on her door before her smiling face appeared.

"Right on time." She welcomed him into her home with a big sweep of her arm. She held a clipboard in her hand. "I've made a checklist of everything we need to take and the items that need your assistance with setup. I've also packed snacks to ensure you stay hydrated, fueled, and focused."

He groaned inwardly. Man was he a sucker. "Uh, I just can't say thanks, because that sounds a little compulsive and over organized," he complained.

"Nonsense, it's called efficient," she said, tossing in a wink for good measure.

Clarke lifted his brows and smiled. "Whatever. Show me what you want to take so I can figure out how to pack your SUV."

The next several minutes were busy with show and tell while Irene chatted about how she envisioned the library being decorated. Her genuine excitement reinforced his decision about offering to help. A simple task for him, but this really mattered to her.

He dutifully carried each box and figurine to her vehicle and reported back so she could cross off every item on her list. When he finished loading the last box, he accepted a glass of lemonade and a homemade granola bar.

He smiled. This lady was really a kind woman. Maybe he was wrong, but it certainly seemed as if she had been working on lots of new recipes. Perhaps it was a coincidence, but he liked the sheer enjoyment that radiated from her when she presented her treats.

"Wow, these are great, Irene. You may need to bring an extra one with you. All right, you ready to roll?"

Today, she had her hair braided, leaving her face free. Her crystal-blue eyes sparkled with life. He even liked her old-school flat-top sneakers. She never ceased to surprise him with her mixture of style and sass. She truly was a gem.

She tossed her keys to him. "Yes, but you drive. That way I can interrogate you on the ride over."

He effortlessly snagged the keys midair and grimaced at her. "Or we could listen to radio? It's a written rule that interrogations can't happen on Saturdays." He held the passenger door open for her.

Once she was inside, he closed the door and made his way to the driver's side. He adjusted the seat and mirrors and had just started the engine when she hit him with her first question.

"How's Aimee doing? She tries to keep everything bottled up. That isn't good for a person."

Clarke put the vehicle in reverse and pulled out of her garage. "Not usually, but she's a tough one."

"So, I hear you two are an item now?" she countered, sliding him a sidewards glance. "Don't deny it. You've been flirting with her for a while now."

He slanted a wide-eyed look at Irene. "We are not discussing this topic."

"Oh, come on. I have another bet with Maggie because she's such an easy mark to take money from. Plus, if I have any say in the matter—"

"You don't, and it's not nice to take money from people. That makes you a shark." He pulled into the library's parking lot and maneuvered her vehicle so they could unload as close to the door as possible.

Irene twisted in her seat and put her hand on his arm. "It's so much fun to watch you squirm. Now, give an old lady her say. You both deserve to find happiness. Together or not, but I happen to think you're cute together and make a perfect match."

"Cute" probably wasn't the word he'd choose, but he lifted a brow. "You're meddling, Irene, but I'll humor you. Why do you say that?"

"That's what old women do, Clarke. Why? It's so simple to me. You're running from your future, and she's running from her past—two puzzle pieces coming together to create the perfect now. Don't you see it? All right, open the hatch. We've got stuff to haul."

He saluted the woman sitting next to him and got to work. He carried the boxes while she unboxed and started organizing everything into piles. When he finished unloading, she directed him on how and where to place various ghosts, pumpkins, and bats.

Sometime later, he flipped his wrist to check the time. It was not bad—it had been just over two hours, and they had everything unloaded and set up. The front entrance of the library resembled a mini-haunted house. The rest of her decorations adorned the inner library, which looked festive and fun. The children would love it.

As he'd worked, he'd mulled over Irene's thoughts and had come to a decision. The time had come to talk to Aimee about this attraction that sizzled between them. They complemented each other. He could only image how hot they'd burn together. In fact, he found himself waiting to see what came next, and that scared him because it went against everything he'd established for his life. What that encompassed or how far he'd be willing to go, he hadn't a clue, but he was willing to see. She was worth that risk.

LAUGHTER AND CHATTER FLOWED from the booth Aimee shared with Maggie at Knotty Pine Tree. She'd missed her best friend. The heavenly scents of bacon, coffee, and baked treats filled the air. This town bustled with energy, and its residents were lining up to eat on a busy Saturday morning.

"So, how's life with the Trent these days?" Aimee asked.

Maggie sighed and clasped her hands to her heart. "I'm living my dream with the sexiest pain in my ass. His protective side is still in overdrive since my ordeal, and if he keeps it up much longer I may have to smack him. I love the man, but he's going to force me back into therapy for an entirely different reason."

"Well, there's no doubt about how much he loves you."

"No, there is not, and I wouldn't want him any other way. We went through a lot, and it's still very fresh." Maggie sipped her coffee and wrinkled her nose. "Enough about me. How are things going with Clarke? Trent mentioned you two have been tied at the hip."

"Yes, it's been fun, actually. He's a good man. In fact, he took me to see his aunt in Boise the other day."

"Okay, ladies, I have two orders of waffles, bacon, and sausage," Sally said, dropping off the orders. "Now, scoot over. I distinctly heard a bit of conversation that sounded like we were talking about you and Clarke. What's up? Have you two done the deed? Are you dating? Still playing hard to get? What?"

Aimee slid over, making room for the owner of the diner, and took her plate with her. "Wow, is my sex life the current topic of town gossip?"

Sally elbowed her. "Did you tell her about the C & A pool we created right here inside the diner?" Aimee's eyes went wide, and Maggie burst out laughing before Sally put Aimee at ease. "I'm totally kidding, but young love is so awesome to watch. The Clarke and Aimee gambling pool would sell out in minutes. Those squares would jump like hot potatoes. This town loves a good romance."

Aimee slathered butter across every inch of her breakfast. "Sally, what am I going to do with you? A pool, really? And, for the record, we aren't dating."

Sally shrugged and winked at Maggie. "Well, I guess we'll have to move on to the baby pool instead for Maggie and Trent. So, what's new in the classroom?"

Maggie's whole face glowed with happiness. "I'm down with that and will even buy a few myself. Oh, I love my fourth graders. They're a handful, but full of energy and questions. As for the baby pool, you might want to wait until we get married, but the practice part of it is quite amazing."

Aimee and the others laughed, then Sally added, "Oh, I have it on good authority Clarke is helping Irene decorate the library for Halloween."

"He is, and I think it's awesome," Aimee said.

Sally smiled. "Oh, it's perfect and says quite a lot about that man. In the past, Irene went all out for every holiday, but that stopped after her husband passed. The next time I see Clarke, I'm giving him a hug, because he's unknowingly made my friend very happy. That was something special she and her husband did together for the town. You should plan a field trip to the library and see it."

Maggie chewed her bite and swallowed. "I'll talk to the principal on Monday. That would be fun."

Sally stood, pulling a pad out from a pocket on her apron. "Thanks for the chitchat, ladies. I've got to run and take some orders."

Both Aimee and Maggie mumbled their goodbyes around mouths full of food. They shared a companionable silence as they ate the remainder of their breakfast. Never in her life would Aimee think a small town could have this much great food. When she'd arrived, she'd immediately loved the town's charm, from the decorated storefronts to the pots of fresh flowers that hung from the streetlights or sat on the sidewalks. This town was clean, bright, and festive. She'd found a treasure in this mountainside community with its residents and her friends. Calling Mill Creek her home made her heart swell with pride.

"What if I told you I was thinking about having a fling with Clarke?" Aimee whispered across the table.

Maggie's eyes widened, and her mouth formed an O for several seconds then transformed into a smile. "I'd tell you to go for it. You're both adults, and I know you've secretly been crushin' on him."

Aimee shrugged a shoulder. "Well, he is insanely hot, but beneath all that alpha male hotness, he's a decent guy who has a heart of gold. I don't want or need a relationship, so it would be just sex."

"Like booty call on speed dial?"

"I'm not sure speed dial is accurate. I mean I am staying at his house. God, that sounds horrible." Aimee groaned.

Maggie cocked her head. "Have you thought this through? It's not like you'll never see him again."

"Yes, and I think he'd agree. He's mentioned that he's not into emotional connections. So, it could be a thing just between us for as long as it lasts." Aimee dropped her head and covered her eyes. "I don't know, it sounded better in my head."

"Why? I mean, you like him, so keeping emotion out of it seems unrealistic. You've never spoken about your past, and that's okay, but I had hoped at some point you'd open up with me. I don't understand why you put so many limits on your life. You're young and beautiful."

Aimee rolled her neck, exhaling while she thought about her response. The waffles she'd finished were heavy and uncomfortable in her belly. She wanted to unburden herself because living in the shadows sucked. She trusted Maggie with all her heart, but Aimee feared that telling her story might put the people she cared about and the town at risk. Her ex-husband had so many enemies and allies who would love to see her dead. If no one knew anything about her past life, then there was no reason to hurt them if all hell broke loose.

She had to keep her guard up. "My ex-husband is a horrible person and lied to me our entire marriage. That kind of betrayal scars a person permanently. It's all in the past and a topic I don't like to discuss."

Maggie grasped Aimee's hand, her support and love stamped all over her face. "Don't let that jerk-faced loser control your whole life. Your bravery and strength brought you here—don't forget that. Take back your life. Give yourself permission to live. Trust me on this last part. I had to learn to do that for myself. Life is unpredictable, so you must live in the moment."

Aimee's gaze slid toward the window as a memory stabbed at her heart.

That damn night, she'd naively run toward those flashing red, blue, and white lights. All those officers and detectives weren't her salvation—they were her damnation. Guns had been drawn as she'd been ordered to stop and lie face down on the grass with her hands and legs spread. When two of the officers approached her prone form, one patted her down and placed her in handcuffs while the other listed the offenses for arrest: drug trafficking, money laundering, and accessory to murder charges. Then they hauled her up like trash and finished with her Miranda rights. Her pathetic pleas to help her father were cut short when she'd been shoved unceremoniously into the backseat of a patrol car.

When Maggie squeezed Aimee's hand, those thoughts disappeared. A lump formed in her throat, a reminder of the limitations she had to live by so she didn't bring harm to others for her past sins. Her resolve snapped into place. "I'm so glad you're my friend, Maggie."

A smile lit up Maggie's face. "I'm glad you're mine." Her phone chirped on the table from an incoming text. "Trent wants me to bring him lunch on my way home."

"Well, I'll let you place your order. This was fun," Aimee said, pulling out a twenty for her portion of the bill. "I'm going to head over to the library to see if Clarke and Irene need help finishing up."

She found the library parking lot empty. Just to be sure, she parked and tried the door, which was locked. Her head spun with thoughts about Clarke and those from her past. Being arrested and losing her father haunted her. She needed to clear her head and figure out what to do about Clarke and her growing attraction to him. Decision made, she left the lot to go to Tale Peak, the US Forest Service's observation and radio tower. She loved it up there because it had become her happy place. A place that helped her put herself in a better frame of mind.

Her truck bounced and chugged up the dirt road until it parked in its normal spot. Standing, she absorbed the breathtaking views, which gave her the impression that she was on top of the world. She stretched her arms and inhaled the scent of pine and sunshine. Today, she opted to sit on the big rock. It had become a place of solitude for her to escape and recharge her batteries.

This was where she could get away and process her thoughts and feelings. To witness the beauty and simplicity of nature. All of this reminded her that, at the end of the day, her issues were important but small compared to everything happening in the world. It helped to put things in perspective. She loved to lie in the bed of her truck and just watch the clouds form in the sky while the wind whistled through the trees. Even the sunsets were so beautiful. All the bright orange and blue colors stained the sky.

Oh shit, the sun had started to set.

As usual, she'd lost track of time, but it was Saturday, so who cared? She'd made a decision regarding Clarke Dragoon and had even come up with an idea for dinner. It was time to head to town, refreshed and ready to lay out her plan.

She pulled over on the outskirts of town, where she knew her phone would have reception. She'd missed two calls from him earlier in the day and winced as she dialed him.

"Aimee, where you've been? Maggie said you left the diner hours ago. I have to admit I was a little worried." Clarke said.

"I'm sorry, I should've let you know as a courtesy that I decided to head up to Tale Peak. I'm not used to people being concerned about me or even wondering where I am. How about I buy pizza as a peace offering? You order it, and I'll pick it up. I'm about twenty minutes away from PB&S."

"You're cared about. I'm just glad you're safe, and yes, I'll order the pizza. Fair warning, I can't promise I won't grumble about this again when I see you. You can do whatever you want, but just let me know so I don't conjure up horrible images of you in danger or hurt."

"I think that's called overprotective, but I agree, I should've called. I'll see you soon." While the waning sun warmed her face, his kind words warmed her heart.

An hour later, Aimee steered her truck into the garage and headed toward the kitchen. She preheated the oven and placed the pizza on the stone. That would keep everything nice and warm while she took a quick shower. A thin layer of dust and sweat covered her skin.

A loud thump had her spinning on her heels toward the laundry room. "Clarke?"

"Yeah, it's me," he replied before appearing in the kitchen.

"That sounded like you closed a trap door." Her hand flew to her mouth. "Oh my God, is that where you always are when I can't find you? Is that the location of the secret bomb shelter?"

He shook his head, a crooked smile covering his lips. "I can't confirm or deny that information. However, I can confirm I'm starving."

"Can you hold out fifteen minutes longer so I can wash this stink off me?" she asked.

Clarke's heated gaze roamed over her body. "I happen to like you dirty, but the clock is ticking."

She didn't respond except to turn tail and dash toward the bathroom giggling to herself. World records could've been shattered. She'd reentered the kitchen in exactly ten minutes and thirty seconds. Her wet hair piled into a messy bun on the top of her head, she wore a pair of yoga pants and a pink V-neck T-shirt. She could tell by his expression that she'd surprised him with her haste.

"Did you use soap?" he teased. He slid on the oven mitts and retrieved the pizza. He'd already set the table and had hot pads in the center. "I'm not a wine-and-pizza type of man. I'm having a beer."

"On this, we agree. Ice-cold beer is the best," Aimee said. The hiss and snap of two caps being removed filled the air.

"Hungry" might've been an understatement. He plowed through four slices to her two. As they ate, he filled her in on Irene's decorations and how she'd created a haunted house the kids would love. Aimee adored his compassion and how he supported Irene. God, this man was nothing like her ex-husband. Her image of this man was that Clarke did what he wanted because it felt right to him, not because it would score points with someone or further his cause down the road. To her, that was beyond sexy.

"I'm sorry I missed seeing it. I stopped by after breakfast to help, but you two were gone. At breakfast, Sally shared how much decorating means to Irene—it was something she did yearly with her husband. Apparently, they had big displays for every holiday."

He nodded. "You should stop by sometime this week and have Irene give you the tour. I think it would make her day."

Aimee put the last slice of pizza on his plate. "I'll do it."

"So, tell me, is Tale Peak magical or something? You seem to go there a lot," he asked right before he took a bite.

"Yes, it's beautiful and peaceful. You can see the whole valley un-obstructed in all directions. Plus, it's a great place to see the fall colors or watch storms develop. You can just relax or solve life's problems. I love it there."

"Were you solving any problems today?" he asked, his gaze snap-ping to hers.

This was her moment. She could either hide or go after what she wanted. Well, a portion of what she wanted, because a relationship wouldn't work. He had a career he loved, and she was only a short-term type of girl.

If they established grounds rules for this romantic entanglement that they both agreed upon, she could get this man out of her system. The only risk would be if they couldn't remain friends after.

Aimee took a deep breath and dropped her napkin onto the empty plate. "Yes, because I want to have sex with you. Several times, in fact, but not a relationship. You know, friends with benefits, but while we're benefiting together, we're exclusive. These are my terms."

He practically choked on his beer. "Run that past me again, sweetheart?"

"You heard me loud and clear," she countered. "The only long-term relationship I can give you is friendship."

His gaze was so intense her skin burned under his scrutiny. She could only assume he was processing her indecent proposal. It hadn't occurred to her that he might think her idea was slutty. As the silence dragged on, her stomach tightened with dread. Maybe she'd already destroyed their friendship by her request.

"To be clear, you want to fuck...exclusively...and several times."

She swallowed, her heart beating against her chest. "When you put it like that, it sounds vulgar. But, yes, that's the gist. Oh, and still be friends afterward...ideally."

He sat back and crossed his arms over his chest. "Why?"

"Isn't it obvious?" she replied, her cheeks heating. "Oh, never mind. This all sounded better in my head. Just forget it."

"Hell yeah, I'll have sex with you. You drive me wild with lust. The part of this that I can't promise is not developing deeper feelings. I don't even know why I'm saying this, but you're different from every other woman. In the past, not one of them has held my attention beyond sex. You and I haven't even had sex yet, and I find myself wanting to spend time with you. I don't even care what we do as long as it's together. You're a survivor of life who doesn't put up with my shit and isn't afraid to knee a man in the nuts if needed. I admire that about you."

Man, this was not how she'd thought this conversation would go. "I can't give you more than a fling, and not if it costs me our friendship. I just thought with your career, this arrangement would make sense. We can continue for as long as we want or end it after the first time without awkwardness. If you don't want to, that's okay too."

"Wanting you isn't the problem. I agree we need to put all the cards on the table. Sex and emotions kind of go hand in hand when it's a person you care about. I can't promise how it'll end, but I hope we'll always be friends. I won't give you less than the truth," he said, his voice solid and deep.

"I know, and I appreciate that you're being open with me. Uh, just so you know, I've never done this type of thing before," she replied, her voice softer than usual.

He reached across the table. "Okay, but I have two conditions of my own. One, while we're in this arrangement, we sleep in the same bed. Two, there has to be honesty between us or this won't work."

"Agreed," she said.

In a sense, she'd just negotiated a new lease on life. As long as she kept her heart out of it. Nothing would make her happier than to call him her boyfriend and to see where this romance could lead. However, that wasn't possible, so this was the next best thing. Maybe this whole idea was convoluted and crossed too many lines or boundaries, but it gave her an out.

She straddled his lap. "Now, kiss me."

No more words needed to be said. He cupped the back of her head and devoured her mouth. He tasted like ale and oregano. Her need for him pulsated throughout her body. Even her blood ignited, leaving a warm trail of tingles and sensations in its wake. It was a delicious feeling that made her drunk with pleasure.

Desperation tore at her resolve. Longing and want fueled her actions as she worked her fingers underneath the hem of his shirt. She lifted it and pulled the shirt over his head. The moment she touched his skin, his muscles contracted under the tips of her fingers. His skin was warm and contoured as she moved over his abdomen.

Wanting more she ground down on his erection that grew beneath her and rocked her hips. God, she needed more. She wanted him naked and deep inside her.

Standing, he lifted her in his arms in one fluid motion. Cradling her against his hard upper body, he pulled free of her mouth and groaned. "I'm not fucking you on this kitchen table. It'll happen, but not our first time. I hope you're rested because I don't plan on letting you get any sleep."

As shiver ran down her spine at those promising words. She'd waited a long time too. When the time came to terminate their arrangement, Clarke Dragoon would be purged from her system. Maybe not her soul or heart, but she'd face that problem another day.

Eight

CLARKE SHOULD BE THE happiest man on the planet. This was a fucking dream come true. She wanted him. He wanted her. It was sheer bliss, until she'd built even taller walls by negotiating a sex-only agreement. That was a first for him and not what he expected. She'd delivered a sucker punch straight to his gut, leaving him stunned and gulping down air. He also saw through her façade. This arrangement was more than friends with benefits, but he'd go along with it for now.

Her offer stung, if he were being honest, but he wasn't willing to miss this opportunity. Instead, he'd focus on the here and now, which meant he'd have his hands full with Aimee Lang. This deal gave him time to figure out what the hell he wanted in life because the carefully laid plan he'd developed after he'd graduated from high school didn't seem to be aligning with him anymore.

He kicked the bedroom door closed, keeping her pressed to his torso before depositing her onto the bed. He loved how her breasts bounced and her eyes widened with excitement. Needing to admire this beautiful woman, he stepped back, raking his gaze over every inch of her body. This was the ultimate present he'd just been given, and he wanted to savor unwrapping it. Aimee had been his fantasy for so long that he planned to fulfill each one with this flesh-and-blood version.

This arrangement she concocted only confirmed his assumption–she wanted him just as badly. He planned to use this time to knock down every wall she'd erected and show her that there wasn't anything they couldn't face together.

The smile that tugged at her lips made his ego soar. Her eyes had darkened with desire, and her skin was flushed. Months of yearning for this woman made him itchy and ready to explode all at once. She'd torn the lid off his lust, and every day since had been torture. He'd never been this hard or needy. He could blame that on a lack of sex, but he knew it had more to do with the woman on his bed.

"Open the nightstand. Grab the box of condoms and place it on the pillow," he said in a low growl.

She moved onto her side, giving him a great view of her ass in those tight pants. One that would get even better once she undressed. She did as he asked then shot him a brazen smile over her shoulder. "Oh, the jumbo pack. Seems like someone's confident."

"Oh, I have zero doubts, but I do like to be prepared. Now strip because I don't know how much longer I can wait."

Her eyelids fluttered at his command, but she dutifully rolled onto her back. Her eyes locked onto his as she hoisted her knees toward her chest. She gripped the waistband of her yoga pants, thrusting them down her legs and over her knees. Once they were bunched at her ankles, she performed a foot shimmy to remove them entirely. Efficiently, she whipped her shirt over her head, leaving her in a white lacy bra.

He sucked in a sharp breath at the bounty of supple skin and generous curves laid out before him. Grasping her ankles, he tugged her toward the edge of the bed, prepared to diligently commit every touch, taste, and caress of this night into memory. He nibbled and kissed his way down each leg, alternating his touch and the pressure of his bites as he traveled downward until he reached the arch of her foot. Then he repeated the process on the other leg. The guttural moans she made deep in her throat kept him exploring.

"Gorgeous and so damn sexy." His voice simmered with wild desire. He trailed one hand up her body, enjoying the goosebumps dotting her skin and stopping momentarily to tug down each lacy cup to expose her breasts. "I'm not sure I can restrain myself long enough to accomplish everything I want to do with you."

"Lots and lots of time," she whispered. Her hands immediately went to work to disengage the button on his jeans as he leaned over her body. The hiss of his zipper came next.

"All this and brains too. Damn, I'm one lucky son of a bitch." His voice was husky and deep.

His cock strained against his boxers, demanding release. She tugged the material toward his knees. When she freed him, his erection bobbed in front of her face. The erotic picture of him leaning over her almost-naked form, legs spread with her bra bunched under her bared breasts, would become a treasured painting in his mind that he'd take to his grave. Her tongue darted out to lick her lips. When she palmed his erection, he almost lost the last of his control. A sensation so exquisite and erotic made his length surge in her hand and his toes curl.

"No," he barked and backed off the bed. "Give me a minute, I'm on the edge here. I've waited too long for you to rush our first time.

He stepped out of his pants. Then he climbed over her body, nudging her back until she lay supine. Planting one hand on the left side of her face and the other on her right, he pressed a series of kisses across her forehead and down the bridge of her nose, his sole intent to show her how much she meant to him. When he claimed her lips he poured his soul into the kiss.

He liked how they both gasped for air when he ended the kiss. "Before we go any further, are you sure you want this...er, me?"

"Yes, I want you. I've never been more certain about anything in my life," she panted out.

Her words circled his heart and made his chest expand. When her legs wrapped around his waist, he palmed her back and moved them both toward the headboard. His body hummed with arousal. He kissed her lips gently, and then rained another series of light kisses across her face, paying attention to the shell of her delicate ear. He nibbled his way down her neck until he reached the sensitive junction where her neck and shoulder joined. Her whimpers and moans fueled his appetite, and he was starving.

He sampled her soft flesh then laved the tender spot with his tongue, pleased when her skin pebbled under his ministrations. He repeated the same process on the other side of her body. The smell of her lotion, coconut and vanilla, would forever remind him of her. When he reached her breasts, he kneaded her soft flesh. A sense of urgency drove his movements because he needed to mark this woman as his.

He tormented each nipple with his fingers until they were cherry red. Slowly, he lowered his lips to lick and suck on the tender buds.

Her soft moans filled the room, asking for more. "Oh God, you're driving me insane. I need... Clarke."

"I've got you." His voice was husky and full of promise.

At that moment, he bit down hard on her tight bud and slid his fingers down until he reached her slippery core. He choreographed a seductive dance with his tongue and finger as he moved downward until he found her little bundle of nerves. He was determined to fine-tune his masterpiece until she came undone beneath him. Circling her pearl with his finger, he lapped and nipped, eliciting a series of moans from deep in her throat. When her back arched and fingernails dug into his shoulders with her pleasure, he plunged two fingers deep, dragging them back and forth against her sensitive skin repeatedly. The blush that stained her cheeks and upper body darkened as her body clenched and exploded.

"Your orgasms belong to me now," he whispered against her mouth. He claimed her lips as he reached over her. Saying those six words ignited something fierce and protective deep inside him.

"Only you," she agreed. The evidence of her arousal still echoed in her tone.

THE CRINKLE OF THE condom wrapper released a burst of excitement and apprehension deep in her gut. Wanting Clarke was not the problem. She'd meant what she'd said earlier. Her concern was that she didn't have much experience with men and none had made her burn hotter than him.

His hand cupped her face, rubbing his thumb against her lip. "Hey, look at me. It's okay if you're having second thoughts."

"No," she rushed to say, not wanting him to misunderstand her.

That was the last thing she wanted him to think. The intensity of his gaze, combined with his concern and compassion, tugged at her heart. This big beast of a man who missed nothing had once again put her needs first.

She stammered to find the right words. "I—ah, I don't have a lot of experience and don't want to disappoint you."

"Sweetheart, you're perfect in every way. There is no way you could disappoint me. That I can promise you. I need you, Aimee."

He stroked his erection from base to crown. His gaze never leaving hers, he then rubbed it through her folds until the head rested at her opening. He took her hands, entwining their fingers, and moved her hands up until they framed her head. "You ready?"

"Always," she said, curling her legs around his waist.

When he thrust forward in small, measured strokes, her eyes practically rolled into the back of her head. A wicked burst of pleasure zipped through her body, causing every nerve ending to roar to life. Had she ever experienced anything this mind blowing? He stopped between each burst to allow her body to adjust to his size. True to his word, he waited for her signal she was ready for more. She watched the muscles in his arms flex under his movements until he buried himself deep inside of her. His washboard stomach flowed into the tight muscle of his torso right down to where they were connected. A sheen of sweat covered his skin, but his concentration was zeroed in on her.

Her body hummed with need and hunger. A fullness she'd never felt before overtook her senses, firing up nerve endings that surged her body to life. Her stomach fluttered, and, in its wake, hope bloomed deep in her gut. A thought that fit the moment but also scared the crap out of her.

"You're incredible," he ground out, his eyes dark from his arousal.

He picked up the pace, shuttling in and out of her body, creating a delicious friction that tingled down to her toes. She raked her nails across his back, digging in to bring him even closer to her body. Heat licked across her skin. Jolts of pleasure ricocheted throughout her body, ending right at her core. Even her toes curled when her muscles clenched tight trying to keep him deep inside her. His rhythm and pace drove her toward the precipice.

I had no clue sex could be like this.

"Let go, sweetheart. I'm not going to last much longer."

She licked her lips and whimpered in nonsensical statements. His controlled movements became hastier as his pleasure increased. Her hips undulated before she clamped down and saw stars. His strokes were constant, the friction between their bodies building even as she detonated. His frenzied pace slowed until he thrust deep and hard, emptying himself inside the thin latex barrier. Ragged breaths filled the silence.

When he collapsed on top of her, he pressed her firmly into the mattress and even deeper inside of her body. "Sorry, I don't want to crush you," he replied and maneuvered his frame to the side.

She immediately missed his weight and hated the emptiness that followed. He disposed of their protection before climbing back into the bed. She turned into him and sighed when he wrapped his arms around her body.

Instead of keeping her at arm's length, like he seemed to do with others, he'd given her a glimpse into his soul over these past days, and she wanted more. She liked that he'd made himself vulnerable to her.

"You, Aimee Lang, may never leave my bed. If I die tomorrow, I'll have died a happy man."

She elbowed him in the side. "Don't say things like that, ever. Besides, you couldn't because we haven't even used a quarter of that box yet. I didn't believe sex like that even existed."

"Good point, but please tell me more about how this sex was the best of your life," he said, his tone provocative as he kissed her temple. "My ego could use some heavy petting. Plus, the night is young, and now you've raised the bar. Ah, the possibilities of what I should do next."

Oh yes, she'd live in the moment and enjoy every second. All of this was just about sex––amazing, sweaty, mind-blowing, best-of-her-life sex––and it could never be anything more. That was what she had to remember.

C LARKE HAD LOST COUNT of the number of orgasms he'd happily given to Aimee last night. He carefully disengaged himself from her sleeping form, whose warm skin touched most of his body. Her hair was a riot of tangles from a night of hot sex. He sat on the edge of the bed and wiped the grit from his eyes. Her phone's ringing ripped into the silence, causing her to twist her body to snagged it off the nightstand.

She glanced at the caller ID. "Hey, boss, what's up?"

So much for his plans for waking her up with his lips trailing down her silky, smooth skin. He eased off the bed and headed toward the bathroom until he heard her next words and returned.

"Yeah, he's here. We were just having coffee." She grimaced at Clarke, shrugging. "You're on speaker now." She clutched the sheet in her fist, covering her naked body as she scooted closer to him. Her modesty made him smile, considering everything they'd done last night.

"I've got an update," Trent said. "We've had another murder. The scene and MO are consistent. The only variances were the location.

The sheriff's office received a call from a camper just after one AM this morning. The forensics team has the body."

"So, are you thinking serial killer?" Clarke asked.

"Possibly, but it's the hair we found in the victim's hand that troubles me. If it matches Aimee's sample, that complicates things.

"W-what does that mean?" she asked, fidgeting with the edge of the cover.

He slid his hand over her and entwined their fingers, sensing her unease and wanting to reinforce she wasn't going to face any of this alone. "That puts you at the scene, evidence-wise, of two murders."

"Exactly, in less than a week," Trent added. "It makes these murders seem personal and would make you a suspect. Off the record, I don't consider you a suspect, but I must do my job."

Her hand went cold in his grasp. "Okay, what do you need from me?"

"I have the ballistics and DNA results from last time. I'm going to email you a picture of the victim to see if you recognize him. Does the name Jeffrey Chase mean anything to you? I'm also going to need a timeline of where you were and with whom. Then, I'll interview those people to corroborate your account. If you have any receipts, that helps too."

"Email the pictures to my cellphone. She doesn't need that in her inbox," Clarke directed as he leaned back and grabbed his phone.

She twisted toward Clarke and opened her mouth then closed it. After a moment she sucked down a deep breath. "That name doesn't sound familiar. I left Clarke's house to have breakfast with Maggie. I went by the library to see Irene and Clarke but missed them. Instead of heading home, I decided to go to Tale Peak and was there all afternoon. I called Clarke on my way back to town to let him know I was coming home. Then, I stopped by PB&S to pick up the pizza he ordered, and I've been here ever since."

The distinct *ting* of mail delivering had Aimee looking at Clarke's device. He opened his message program to reveal one from Tamara, which was marked urgent, and the other from Trent. He tapped the screen to make the image larger, pleased it was a DMV photo instead of from the crime scene.

Aimee looked at the picture with the man's personal information redacted. Out of habit, he studied her reaction, which remained neutral. "No, he doesn't look familiar. Have you notified his family?"

"Not yet. I'm going to do that in person since he's from the area," Trent answered.

Aimee crumbled in front of Clarke's eyes. Her shoulders shook, and tears streamed down her ashen face. He wrapped an arm around her and held her. This entire situation rubbed him the wrong way. Not because he thought she was guilty, but because the crime scene was strange.

Clarke took over the call for her. "We good for now?"

"Yes, I'll be in touch when I have more information. Oh, and Aimee, I think it's best to take an extended leave with pay until we understand why you're linked. I don't want to put you at risk."

On that, Clarke agreed. He'd decided he'd become her personal protection until this crap was sorted out with the perp behind bars. She was strong, but a person could only take so much shit. "Agreed, keep us posted."

He opened Tamara's message while holding Aimee. *My sister's due date has been moved up two weeks. I have openings on Monday or Tuesday of this week if you want to meet with me. If not, you'll have to meet with one of my colleagues because I'll be out of the office through the middle of November. Let me know ASAP.*

Great, bad news all around. He sucked down a big breath and exhaled slowly, his muscles taut. His plans for the day had blown up in his face. Instead of enjoying Aimee, his mind raced in several directions.

"What's wrong? You just tensed up. Are you worried you've slept with a murderer? I didn't do it, Clarke..." Her voice trailed off, muffled from being pressed against his chest.

He tugged her chin with his finger so he could see her eyes. "Stop being silly. I don't think that at all. But I do think it's time to trust someone with your past. This situation is serious. Do you think there's a possibility any of this is tied to what happened to you?"

Her pupils flared briefly until she masked her reaction. Yes, she had more to share, but she tried to keep everything locked down with all her might. A strategy he understood because he'd mastered it after his family had been killed. The downside was it ate away at his heart and soul every day until he feared nothing would be left. Maybe if he encouraged her to rip open those wounds by exposing himself, she'd reciprocate like she had the other night.

Her shoulders dipped, and in a voice devoid of emotion, she said, "No, I think it's just some strange coincidence and a lot of bad luck on my side."

Time for a heart-to-heart. "We need to talk." He scooted back against the headboard and patted the bed next to him.

She crawled up against him without hesitation, and he covered them with the duvet. Sometimes, the best place to talk was in bed.

"I don't believe in coincidences, so I'm calling bullshit on your declaration. I'm worried about you because I care, but also because these murders are serious. I don't like that you're the common denominator. I'll stand by your side and fight with you, if you let me, but I have to do it from the inside. I can't stand by on the sideline."

She didn't race to offer more details. He figured that when she placed her head against his chest, she needed time to process what he'd offered.

"Just so you know, I'm not going anywhere. When you're ready, let me know your decision. Since I'm prying into your life, I figure it's only right to give you something in return. I'm trusting your discretion to keep this between us. Technically, I'm not authorized to speak about my assignments outside work. It could put a lot of folks at risk, including yourself."

She raised her head, her brows knitted together in curiosity. She started to nod, then abruptly stopped. Instead, she linked their pinkies together. "I pinky swear," she answered.

That was good enough for him. "I understand demons and how difficult it is to move past them. I told you about my family and its impact on my future. I haven't shared what happened during my last assignment with anyone except my boss and what I recorded in my report. I discharged my service weapon to take down the main threat but severely misjudged his wife's judgment. She dove in front of the bullet to protect her husband, and my shot killed her and her unborn child. A baby boy, who the mother had already named Dillion, didn't even get a chance to be born. My second shot killed her husband. I think about that innocent body and mother who died every damn day and what I should've done differently."

Her hand moved up his chest and stopped over his heart. "Did that man threaten to kill you?"

"Yes. He didn't want to be taken into custody, so he thought killing me would remove that threat."

"I think mothers would have an innate instinct to protect their child."

He covered her hand with his own. "That's what I thought, but that situation went south quickly. I failed that unborn boy and his mother."

"Maybe his mother failed him when she acted selfishly," Aimee countered. "The whole situation is sad."

Clarke kissed the top of her head. "The husband failed both, but that doesn't change the outcome. I still took the life of an innocent child and its mother. After my parents were killed, I vowed to help make the world a safer place. I failed miserably for that little guy."

She twisted until she was on her knees and framed his face with her hands. "What it makes you is human and a man who focuses on taking down evil. You have a pure heart, Mr. Dragoon, and those qualities are rare."

She plopped back down and snuggled against him. "My story is different. My ex-husband was a controlling and abusive man. He didn't start that way when we met in college. He swept me off my feet, but after we got married, he let his psycho flag fly. He used my desire for family and children to keep me in line over time, when that tactic wasn't as efficient, he expanded his torment to include my father—whom I adored—to keep me in line. You see, my poor decision-making cost my father his life."

His stomach twisted in disgust. "Did your ex-husband kill your father?"

She sucked in a sharp breath, giving him the answer. "Yes," she whispered, her voice cracked from the unshed emotions, she tried to keep at bay. "That's my burden for the rest of my days."

His heart lurched at her statement. She spoke a language he understood. If her ex-husband weren't behind bars, he'd pay him a visit to balance the scales of injustice. He had more questions for her but had to proceed cautiously. He wondered if that asshole could orchestrate his revenge while incarcerated. It wouldn't be the first time Clarke had seen that happen. That gave him a place to start digging while Trent worked the investigation. His gut told him something was off, and his concern was that Aimee was in danger.

Nine

A IMEE FINISHED HER SHOWER, then lathered on her favorite coconut and vanilla lotion. She'd styled her hair into a loose braid and slipped on a pair of jeans and a lightweight purple sweater. She missed the office and activity around town and was bummed she couldn't go into work today. On the upside, it gave her plenty of time to spend with Clarke. Unused muscles were deliciously sore from their weekend activities and, true to his word, they'd depleted the box.

This morning, she needed to share a little of her past with Clarke. A warmth deep in her chest bubbled to life with this idea. She dug around in her bag until she found the box that contained her treasures. She grabbed what she wanted from the contents and padded toward the kitchen. Opening a tiny portion of her heart to Clarke by sharing glimpses into her previous life had liberated and energized her. It made her feel human, and reminiscing about her parents caused her heart swell with pride. She loved them and missed them every damn day.

In a way, she wasn't deceiving Clarke in every aspect of her life. It was the rest she'd keep locked away as dictated by the requirements of WITSEC. He believed in her when she hadn't believed in herself. Whatever time they had together, she wanted to be as open as possible while making the most of it.

He sat at the table, his thumbs tapping against his phone in a flurry of activity.

"Morning," she greeted, then moved toward the aroma of freshly ground coffee. She filled her cup with the dark liquid, cream, and sugar. The clink of her spoon filled the room. After her first sip she settled into the seat across from him.

He put his phone down, his gaze intense. "How'd you sleep?"

"With my eyes closed," she sassed. "Warmth wasn't a problem, either, since I had this rather enormous and naked man behind me all night."

His smile just about melted her panties right off her body. "Good, that's what you can expect in my bed every night...naked, warm, and exhausted."

She'd sign on that dotted line any day. She slid the photos across the table and dug the rings out of her pocket. "I retrieved these from my apartment that day after the fire. These are my parents' wedding rings and some photographs of us."

He inspected each ring, then studied the photos. "You were a heart-breaker when you were younger, weren't you? Wow, you look just like your mother but have your father's eyes."

Her heart burst with joy at his comment. "Yes, but I wished I'd gotten her musical talent. At night when she practiced, my father and I danced instead of sitting next to her to learn."

Clark stacked everything neatly on the table. "Thank you for intro-ducing me to your family. That means a lot to me. If you'd like, I can scan these pictures to a flash drive so you'll have a backup copy. Now I understand what you wanted to retrieve that day."

"That's a great idea. I'd be devastated if anything happened to them. My parents—they would've liked you."

His eyes brightened. "Leave those here, and I'll get them copied."

"So, do you have any plans for today, besides stopping by the drugstore?" she asked, flashing him a coy smile.

He sat back and crossed his arms over his chest. "You know, it's the first time shopping has ever been on my to-do list. To be safe, I think I'll buy several boxes. My appetite around you seems to be never-ending. How about we hit one in Boise?"

She cocked her head to the side and bit her bottom lip. "Are you embarrassed about us?"

He raised his eyebrow at her. "Seriously, I'd parade you around naked and put a sign on your back declaring you my woman, but that would be crass. Besides, the only person who gets to see you naked is me. I'm a selfish and possessive bastard where you're concerned."

Her cheeks heated from his blatant statement. She liked knowing she belonged to him, even if their time together was limited. "My day is wide open." She made a semicircle in front of her. "Oh, gosh, is your aunt okay?"

He sat up and shook his head. "She's fine. This trip has to do with me. And my offer is self-serving because I would like your company. Long story short, a requirement of my job is psychological evaluations. You don't go back out on assignment until the shrink approves it—the goal is to eliminate insanity. In my line of work, an agent's tenure isn't long, due to stress and environment. I've been dodging this one, but your insight the other night has altered my perspective."

"I'm guessing your shrink has his hands full with you as a patient," she tossed back, suppressing a giggle. "I'd be happy to escort you to this appointment."

"Great, we should hit the road, because *she* wants to see me at eleven." He turned off the coffee pot and dumped the filter in the trash.

Her cellphone chirped with an incoming text. She swiped her phone off the table and walked to her bedroom to grab her bag.

Halfway to her room, she stopped dead in her tracks. She looked at the screen again to make sure she saw the text from the bank: *"Wire transfer of $25,000 received."* She sidestepped into the den and punched in the number to the bank.

"Good morning. Thanks for calling Mountain Creek Bank. This is Eileen Peters. How may I assist you?"

"Hey, Eileen, it's Aimee Lang. I think there's a mistake. I just received a text about a wire transfer I'm not expecting. Maybe the wrong account number was listed?"

"Surprise money is always the best, but let me pull up your account."

Not in Aimee's world. She heard a series of clicks while telephones rang in the background. She paced the small room as she waited, looking at all the travel books that lined the shelves.

"I see twenty-five thousand deposited into your account. Give me a minute to look into it."

"Okay, thanks." Aimee turned when she heard Clarke clear his throat. She pressed the mute button so she could talk to him. "Give me a second—I'm on with Eileen at the bank. There seems to be a mix-up with a wire transfer that was deposited into my account. We can take my truck. Grab the key on the hook in the kitchen. You can drive, since you know where we're going. I'll be out in a minute."

He nodded then disappeared down the hallway.

A minute later, Eileen came back on the line. "Aimee, I can't access that information at the moment. The system went down. Can I call you back later?"

"Sure, that's fine. Thanks, Eileen."

Dammit, Aimee didn't want to wait to get an answer. She just wanted to get this settled and return the money to the rightful owner. Her mind snapped to one thought that made her stomach drop. Maybe DUSM Lyndon had decided to move her to another place because he found out about the two murders. When she moved to Mill Creek originally, the United States Marshal Service had deposited a large sum of cash into her account to get her started. *Shit, shit, shit!* She didn't want to move and start over again; she liked her life here in Mill Creek. She liked Clarke.

She dialed a number she'd been forced to memorize. One she'd been told was secure. One she never wanted to use.

He answered on the first ring. "Have you been compromised?" Just like that, he'd blurt out the scariest and worst scenario, making her skin crawl. That was the last thing she wanted him to think.

"No, but did you wire more money into my account?"

"No, what's going on?" Lyndon countered, his tone cautious and reserved.

"It's nothing. I've already spoken to the bank about the error. They're researching it now. I just thought I'd check with you."

His long pause made her cringe. "Well, you saved me an extra step because I needed to call you anyway with an update."

Her phone chirped with an incoming text from Clarke, who sat in her truck waiting for her. *U ok? Need me back inside?*

She quickly tapped out her reply as her heart lurched at his concern. *No, a bit longer, and I'll be out.*

Lyndon took her silence as his cue to proceed. "Your ex-husband's appeal has been granted—"

"Already?" she choked out.

"Yes, his case has been put on the docket, and a date is forthcoming."

She rolled her eyes at the absurdity of that statement. That bastard should not have a chance to get out of jail. He should rot in that hellhole. Her father didn't get the chance for resurrection.

DUSM Lyndon, not one to provide any type of emotional support or platitudes, continued like he'd just told her it would rain tomorrow. "You may have to testify, which means you'll be moved to an undisclosed safe house until that time. We'll cover all those specifics once the new evidence is disclosed and dates have been set."

"Any other good news?" she said. The marshal didn't deserve her ire, but she couldn't seem to help herself.

"Actually, the investigators have uncovered another warehouse in Seattle, Washington. The title is under your maiden name, but the facility was empty when they searched it. The purchase date was two years ago. Any knowledge of this property or its use?"

Aimee pinched the bridge of her nose and inhaled to try to stop the room from spinning. Her day didn't need another curveball, and losing her shit wouldn't help anything. "Why are they still investigating? I thought that ended with his arrest. And for the record, I haven't a clue. I know you think I was complicit in my husband's schemes and criminal activity, but I assure you that couldn't be further from the truth. I have zero knowledge of this warehouse or why my name is on the title."

"You know the answer. If the portion of missing money and drugs ever surfaced, that would help to corroborate your claim. The government doesn't like it when four hundred million dollars of evidence and money vanish—gives the appearance of an insider. If the forensic team uncovers anything additional, I'll be in touch."

She listened to the line go dead and closed her eyes. A prickly sensation worked over her skin. Maintaining power over her life had become essential, and the last few days had unraveled some of that control. That knowledge both scared and unnerved her because it echoed experiences she had in the past. There were days when she thought she'd never be free of her ex-husband and his crimes.

When they got to Boise and Clarke went to his appointment, she planned to use the time to find her center and regain her balance. He'd thought his appointment would last no more than two hours, so that gave her plenty of time to clear her head.

On the ride to town, she told him about the money but buried her frustration from her call with Lyndon. She couldn't share any of that with him anyway. *God, whoever took that money and drugs, please return it. I'm so sick of dealing with all of this.* Yeah, like that would happen—she'd have better luck and odds if she took care of it herself.

THEY'D FINALLY RETURNED TO Mill Creek later that afternoon. Clarke's meeting had taken longer than he'd anticipated. On the drive home, they decided to have a guilty-pleasure dinner and stopped at the Knotty Pine Tree before heading back to his place.

"Pass the ketchup, please," Aimee asked Clarke before she popped a french fry into her mouth. She added a few squirts of the red stuff to her plate next to her ranch and blue cheese dressing. "Yum, I needed a fix of greasy delight."

His laughter filled the diner as he stared at the train wreck of her dinner. She'd ordered onion rings, french fries, fried mozzarella, and wings. "You could scare a man with that type of craving."

"Please, we've covered that issue." She snickered and slid a wing through the blue cheese before chomping down on it. Wing sauce and white dressing slid down the corner of her mouth.

He automatically reached out to swipe the mixture from her lip and sucked his finger clean. She stared at him the entire time. "Maybe I should ask Sally if she has another of those plastic bibs they give people who eat seafood."

"Bite me," she challenged. "Like your dinner is any better, burger boy."

He took a bite of his cheeseburger and chewed. Then he popped an onion ring into his mouth. He loved how her throat flexed as she swallowed, bisecting her delicate neck. It didn't matter what she did, he found her sexy and witty with jumbo-sized heat. His thoughts drifted to his meeting with his psychologist, when he'd admitted he might be interested in an assignment change after he'd purged his conscience regarding the clusterfuck of his last job.

"Hey, Aimee, Clarke. How are you two?" Daniel asked as he stood in front of their table.

Clarke raised his head and nodded at the hardware store owner.

"We're good. How are the repairs coming along?" Aimee put her half-eaten mozzarella stick on her plate.

"I planned to call you today to discuss a potential delay. Long story short, Lana and me would like to take advantage of all the insurance work being done and pay out of pocket to replace the remaining windows and upgrade the roof. We're going to do both at the same time. The downside is, it'll delay you moving back into the studio for about a month."

Clarke dropped the fry he was about to bite into. "Aimee can stay at my house for as long as she needs."

She nodded. "That's fine with me. Thanks, Clarke. I can't wait to see the upgrades, Daniel."

"Oh, that's perfect, Aimee. I'm glad that works for you. I was worried about where you'd stay. Sorry for disturbing your dinner."

She waited until her landlord moved away from their table. "Seriously, that's a long time. If you want your space, just let me know."

"Nope, not a chance," Clarke answered. Over his dead body was more like it, but he kept those words to himself. She'd always have a place to stay at his home.

They ate the rest of their meal in companionable silence, another thing he liked about her. She wasn't the type of woman who had to fill in every second with random chitchat or gossip. When their waitress dropped off the bill, she lunged for the slip of paper like she'd been a previous slapjack champion.

"My treat for my temporary landlord with benefits." She sucked one finger into her mouth before wiping her hand on the napkin. "Damn wing sauce gets everywhere."

His reply was cut short when Trent strode into the diner, making a beeline to their table.

She greeted him and placed two twenties onto the table. "Hi, Trent. Clarke and I just finished. Did you survive the monthly budget review meeting without me?"

"Hell no. That meeting gets worse every month. I have an update, but give me a second to grab an iced tea. I'll meet you two outside."

Clarke's gut twisted. He didn't want or need any more curveballs tossed their way. His hand nestled against the small of her back, guiding her toward the exit. Instinct drove his actions. He laced his fingers through hers and squeezed. This amazing woman by his side had turned his life upside down. He'd do whatever it took to protect her.

Trent exited the building and closed the gap between them so they could talk privately. "Forensics has determined that the hair fiber recovered at the scene is a match to your sample. Again, ballistics didn't match. No prints were recovered, and no witnesses have come forward. The coroner established TOD around twelve hours, based on body temperature, which places your mountain trek in the middle of that window. So, I need to do my job and validate your alibi."

"Do you have to, Trent? You know I didn't do this. I'll be officially listed in the system regarding these cases," Aimee pleaded in a panic.

"I do because it's procedure and will look better if I didn't extend any special treatment or favors. If I thought you were guilty, we'd handle this differently."

Clarke gripped her shoulders. "He's right. What's next?"

Trent sipped his tea. "I'm going to grab a tower dump of her cellphone, which should be sufficient to show the call she placed to you and that she has no connections to the victim."

"Do you think there's a connection between the two cases?" Clarke asked, his mind pumping with questions and scenarios. "I get the link between the first crime scene and her hair, but the second doesn't make sense. There must be a connection between those men."

"Agreed, and I've asked our resident guru to do me a personal favor. Noah is doing a deep dive into these guys' backgrounds. He's back in Washington, packing up his office and condominium to move out here, but he's taking advantage of all his FBI toys to help us."

"Awesome, I knew I liked that guy." Clarke grabbed Aimee's hand. "She's going to be glued to my side for the foreseeable future."

"I'm not judging, but it looks like that's already happening." Trent looked at their joined hands.

Aimee rolled her eyes. "I don't need a big brother. I can handle myself just fine."

"Yes, she can, and I'm not putting my family jewels in danger if you know what I mean," Clarke said to Trent.

Trent shook his head and headed for his vehicle.

Clarke tugged her toward her truck. "I have an idea for tonight. I'd like to teach you backgammon. I haven't played since my mother used to whoop my ass."

"How do you know I'm not a master of that game already? Maybe my brilliant father, who was an aerospace engineer, taught me how to play?"

He belted out a deep laugh. "Are you shitting me? I learn something about you every day. Game on."

He tucked her inside the truck's passenger side and shut the door. He hadn't missed how her muscles had bunched tight underneath his hands after she shared that tidbit. His determination and resolve to figure out his favorite puzzle fueled his thoughts. She might not see those events as a risk to her safety, but in his experience, it screamed the opposite. He slid behind the wheel and turned over the engine, listening as she spoke on the phone.

"Hi, did you find out who made the deposit?" A pause. "Oh, what does that mean?" She was silent for a moment as she listened. "Okay, yes, please cancel it. Thanks for that information."

Clarke glanced sideways at her. "What did Eileen say?"

"She didn't have much information. It's a bank she doesn't know much about, but she's canceling and returning it. Whoever made that mistake will be happy to have their money back."

He pried her hand open so he could hold it. No words were exchanged as he drove the short distance home. She disappeared for a bit after they got home. It didn't take him long to find her because she was in the kitchen, staring out the window. He refused to let her hide. To crawl inside herself and pull away from him. They'd shared too much.

He walked up behind her and enveloped her with his arms. He pressed a kiss on her hair. When her head fell against his chest and she sucked in a deep breath, he smiled at her silent acknowledgment. She felt safe and trusted him. They stayed locked together for many long minutes until their heartbeats and breaths melded into one.

He lowered his head and whispered against the shell of her ear, "Why did you tense up earlier when you told me about your father?" He almost regretted asking when she tried to twist free from his grasp. He tightened his hold. "Stop. You can't keep running from questions you don't like. I'm not judging you, and I'm not going anywhere. I want to know you, all of you, the good and the bad."

"I tensed because it's been a long day, and I miss my family. You, of anyone, should understand that emptiness."

"No, you're deflecting because you're scared. The fact that you're the center of both crime scenes is troublesome, and we need to identify the link. Tell me more about your ex-husband and your family. I think this might be connected to him, and that's why you don't want anything reported, because it'll draw attention."

She jerked from his hold. "There's nothing more to say. I don't know those men, and my ex is locked up. He's not behind any of this, and even saying that is ridiculous. I can't provide an answer as to why any of this is happening, but I'm innocent."

"I agree, but the facts tell a different story. Even the timing of this wire transfer is bizarre. Something is happening, so talk to me. Let's figure this out together."

"I don't want to spend our limited time together talking about this crap. I'm tired and going to my room," she informed, stomping her way past him until he halted her exit by snagging her arm.

"We have an agreement, which requires you in my bed. That doesn't mean anything has to happen other than sleep, but those were our agreed-upon terms. Are you nullifying it?" He didn't like that she viewed their time together as temporary.

"Seriously, that's your play? Fine, I'm going to *sleep*, in *your* room as agreed."

He was hopeful that she didn't immediately jump to ending their agreement. When he'd pushed her on that point, he'd didn't want that to be the outcome. A draft of air washed over him from her hasty retreat. The next sound was his bedroom door slamming shut. He scrubbed his hand down his face and exhaled in frustration. Pissing her off hadn't been his endgame. She'd pushed his buttons, and he'd lost his temper. That wasn't acceptable, and he'd have to apologize later. He needed to give her time to cool off before he headed to bed.

What should happen next was crystal clear in his mind. He strode toward his bat cave, intent to dig deep into her life. The first place he planned to start was with her ex-asshole. This wasn't about going behind her back. It was about identifying and assessing her threats. Thank fuck he had access to amazing search tools, compliments of the United States Marshal Service to perform a rigorous search into her background. He'd deal with the fallout tomorrow.

Ten

HOURS LATER AND BLEARY-EYED, Clarke's frustration strangled him. He signed out of his computer program and shoved his keyboard away from him. He tapped out a text to Trent that the two of them needed to meet first thing tomorrow. Pounding the pavement to expel his negative energy with a long run sounded good, but leaving Aimee alone at night wasn't happening. Not that Clarke thought someone would storm the house, but until he had a better understanding of these bizarre murders, he'd side with caution.

Since running was out of the question, the next best option was to head to bed. He paused at the door, steeling himself for whatever came next. He cracked the door open, groaning at the sight. His alarm clock produced a soft blue light that illuminated the beauty in the middle of his bed. The scents of vanilla and coconut surrounded him. Her black lashes dusted her cheeks, while her auburn tresses were splayed across the pillows.

He shucked off his shirt and pants but left his boxers in place since she'd chosen to wear one of his T-shirts to sleep in. He headed toward the bathroom to hit the head and brush his teeth before crawling into bed. Her subconscious knew what she wanted, even in repose, because she wrapped herself around him. The heat of silky flesh warmed his skin. Something in his upper body tightened from the simplicity of this intimate moment.

He closed his eyes, determined to review the proposed plan he'd present to Trent tomorrow.

A soft, groggy voice penetrated his thoughts. "I'm sorry I pushed you away. I guess that's my go-to move, which isn't fair to you. There's so much I want to tell you because I do trust you, but I just can't. I know that's asking a lot, so maybe I should leave, because hurting you is the last thing I want to do."

A pang of regret slammed into him, but at the same time, that statement couldn't have been more honest. He believed her with every fiber of his being. It wasn't a calculated response to win his favor; it was raw and factual. He didn't want her to leave.

There are times in life you had to give the benefit of the doubt and believe in someone, and he believed in Aimee. "You belong where you are, by my side. Sometimes it takes time to unburden your soul, and when that day comes, I'll be ready to listen to every word. Bad things don't just disappear. They have to be purged by action."

"Why couldn't I have found you first? I'm tired of all the shadows. Please make me forget all the bad things."

She crawled on top of his body and straddled his hips, placing her core on his hardened length. Her body heat enveloped him. She undulated on his rock-hard cock while she lifted her arms to remove his shirt. Her breasts bounced free, and her nipples tightened from the cool air circulating in the room. There was no need for more words. They came to another understanding while strengthening their bond.

He traced his hands up the sides of her silky skin, tickling the underside of her breasts with his thumbs. He rolled with her and pinned her back to the bed and sat astride her body. Skimming his hand down the middle of her body, he eased back on his haunches.

Tears streamed down her cheeks. Her mind had gone back to whatever thoughts haunted her.

"Tell me how you survived," he whispered against her neck. Then, while he waited for her to decide how they'd proceed, he ran his hands up and down her arms.

Finally, in a small voice that wobbled she said, "I met my ex-husband in college. He seemed so nice and devoted to me. We shared the same interests, and we were both driven to be successful in business. We wanted a family and had plans to travel the world. Soon after we married, he changed into a person I didn't recognize, and my dreams shattered. He developed this love of guns seemingly overnight and had so many of them. When I voiced my disapproval and dislike, he used that against me. He liked the power a gun gave him. I truly think he got off on other people's fear."

She grabbed Clarke's hands, entwining their fingers. "My ex found new ways to exact his torture while he ensnared my loyalty and life. One night he had one of his men forcefully bring me downstairs to his office, where a man I'd never seen before kneeled before him. My ex pointed to a tray of guns and told me if I didn't pick up each one and aim it at the man that he'd kill him. His life was in my hands. I'll never forget how that man begged for forgiveness from my husband. In the end, it didn't matter that I complied, because he pulled a gun out of his side holster and killed him anyway."

The hopelessness and desperation in her tone undid Clarke. "You did what you had to do to survive. That man's death is not on your hands. It's on your ex-husbands. He wasn't going to let that man live either way."

She stiffened. "The day my father was killed, he made me promise that I wouldn't let this define me. That I'd make something out of my life and never look back. I'm failing him—my promise." Her voice cracked and ended in another sob.

"You're wrong, sweetheart. You're a fighter because you survived it all. We all make mistakes; the difference is if we let them define our future too."

"Then that applies to you, you know." She turned, pushing him to the side, then rested her chin on his chest.

Clarke rubbed her cheek with the backside of his hand. "I believe your father told you that because he knew his end was coming. He didn't want you to blame yourself."

No more words were spoken as they lay together and drifted to sleep. He awakened sometime later to a hand stroking him. She'd moved her hand inside his boxers and worked his flesh from base to crown––definitely not a wet dream. A decadent treat that drove his erotic fantasy to another level. He awoke to the delight of her delicate hand working his shaft with precision and determination as pleasure pulsed in his veins. She knew his body and worked her unrelenting magic to drive him even higher. No woman had ever felt so good, so perfect.

A frenzy of action had him tugging his boxers down his legs, allowing his cock room to lengthen. This reality was better than any wet dream he'd ever had. His cock was hard and ready when her tongue licked around his crown and down his shaft. The warmth from her mouth and the suction added to the sensation. She alternated between sucking him deep and working his shaft with her hand. He watched her beautiful face as her mouth sucked him deeper. When she glanced up to look at him, the interplay of her emotions took his breath away.

He skimmed his hand over her backside until his fingers found her slippery center. Her excitement peaking wasn't due to what she had received from him, but rather, what she'd given to him.. He circled her clit until her arousal coated his finger. Her moan of pleasure added to the eroticism of their scene. He slid his finger inside her tight channel before adding a second. Loving the way she greedily clung to him. Her body telling a story that matched her actions. His other hand alternated between tugging her nipple and rolling the tight bud between his thumb and forefinger. Oh, this woman had forever changed him. She'd reached inside his soul and held his heart prisoner. Her muffled groans grew louder, and her hips ground down on his hand. Pinpricks of ecstasy had his balls tightening from the delicious rhythm her mouth created.

Life with Aimee would never be dull. He couldn't wait another second to be inside her. He tugged her up his body and claimed her mouth. Outside the bedroom, they were perfectly matched, but in the bedroom, they created combustible masterpieces. Sex before Aimee was good, but being with the right woman had altered his expectations and desires.

He nipped and laved her bottom lip, encouraging her to part her lips so he could deepen the kiss and claim the woman he loved. The shock of his internal declaration didn't scare him, it rejuvenated him. His heart soared. This woman had changed him irrevocably. She'd always own a part of his heart and, hopefully, his future.

When he broke off the kiss, he reached for a condom from the box on the nightstand and rolled it down his length. "I need you right now, sweetheart." He tucked her under his body and aligned his cock at her center. Her slippery heat welcomed him. He gripped her hips and slammed himself deep, desperate to be home. "Oh, Jesus...you're perfection."

She matched his intensity, which drove him insane. He increased his strokes until he pounded deep inside her. He held her tight so she didn't slam her head against the headboard as he released his inner beast. Her insides gripped his cock, milking him with every thrust. That was his girl—she took what she wanted. Her body quivered, and her skin flushed a deep red.

"Riding the edge?" he asked, his tone raw and breathless.

"Clarke— God...yes, don't stop."

He slowed his pace, dragging his entire length through her slick folds over and over until she exploded.

"I'm unraveling, Clarke." She moaned and writhed underneath him.

The pressure of her tight flesh, combined with a rush of her slick heat, caused him to detonate. Sweat ran down his back as he drove into her again and again until his balls emptied everything he had to give her. He collapsed on top of his woman, moving slightly to the side so he didn't crush her. He laid his cheek against her breast and smiled. Nirvana was the only word that came to mind. It was the only word that made sense because what they had just shared altered his universe.

"You've ruined me for all other women," he mumbled against her flesh.

"I'd have to agree with you, no other man would ever compare to you."

Damn straight, since he never wanted another man to touch her. She belonged to him, and somehow, he had to persuade her to stay with him. He rolled off the bed to dispose of the condom. When he returned, her soft snores filled the quiet room. He hauled her against his body. The time had come to text his boss to discuss his career progression.

"RICHARD, IT'S DEAN. I just returned from the courthouse, and I have good news. The written brief I submitted has been reviewed, and our request for oral arguments has been approved. Our court date is the fifteenth of December, so we don't have a moment to waste."

Richard closed his eyes and smiled, taking a few seconds to enjoy this news. "Excellent, and I'm ready, too. I've already ended things with Alice, which means everything is now in full motion. I'll see you tomorrow for our planned meeting. Then, I'll focus on the final leg. It won't be long until the FBI has a treasure trove of new evidence, forcing a total unequivocal exoneration."

"That can't come fast enough. I'll see you then," Dean replied, terminating the call.

Richard sat in a chair on his small patio, kicking his legs up on the glass side table. A cool breeze that smelled of fresh water tickled his neck. Exhaustion claimed his body after two long years of working to free the only man he loved and considered family.

He closed his eyes and inhaled slowly through his nose, holding his breath for several seconds before exhaling. He repeated this several times while the pitter-patter of raindrops pelted away his tension. His mind drifted as the scent of wet earth reminded him of the day he'd been saved.

Long gone were the days when he was the scrawny boy everyone beat up and then stole his measly possessions. He'd been transferred from foster home to home more times than he could count. The last one had been the worst with him ending up in the hospital. Then on a rainy Sunday afternoon, after he'd been released, he'd landed at another new home that would change his life. It was where he'd met Alex Chubb, and for reasons Richard had never understand, that boy had protected Richard and shown him that he mattered.

They'd forged a strong friendship in the unlikeliest of places, which had morphed into something deeper over the years. Brothers by choice, not blood, they'd been inseparable ever since. Through Alex, he'd met Dean, who'd also spent his youth in the foster care system. Together, they'd daydreamed about starting a business. Although Dean had gone a separate direction than Richard and Alex once they'd aged out of the system, they'd never lost contact. The three of them had remained close, sharing a common understanding of how cruel and transient the world could be.

Finally, they'd reconnected later in life to make their dreams a reality. The three of them were a lethal combination in business because each man brought a different skill set to the table. Dean's legal prowess never ceased to amaze Richard.

Dean had become their personal lawyer, then had built a legal team to represent all facets of their distribution business. Alex could charm anyone and had been a successful pharmaceutical sales manager, learning everything about that industry. That knowledge fed his keen entrepreneurial vision for their business.

Richard's operational expertise allowed him to focus on formulating contingencies and strategies to enact safety measures to protect each man and the business. His role kept him behind the scenes and out of the public eye.

After Alex had quit his job, he'd created several distribution companies—a mix of legitimate and non-legitimate—to purchase and distribute generic pharmaceuticals to various hospitals and doctor's offices. The genius of the plan allowed them to launder the money between the shell companies and distribution companies while funneling a portion of the drugs through the black market.

Together, they'd been damn near unstoppable, until that fucking night had caught them off guard. Luckily, Richard had been able to mitigate most of the risk and exposure for the business, but not for Alex. That mistake would soon be rectified. What Richard had learned over the last two years was just how far he'd go for his family and how much dirt his hands could handle.

It boggled his mind that Alex would jeopardize it all when he'd met that woman. He'd brought her into the business and had put her in charge of the accounting—the very heart of the operation. Alex had guaranteed them she'd unknowingly provide another layer of protection, confirming the validity, for the business. That dynamic had caused Richard heartburn because he'd known their motivation and commitment, but she'd been an unknown commodity. He'd seen her intelligence, but his brother had assured them he had her under his control. That was when Richard had learned another life lesson—love made a man reckless.

Eleven

CLARKE'S PHONE RUMBLED IN his pocket. He pulled the device free while he stood at the kitchen window, staring at his driveway. Trent and Maggie should arrive soon. He needed to speak privately with Trent, which gave Aimee and Maggie time to connect.

"Hello," said Clarke, then flicked his wrist for the umpteenth time to check the time—right before eleven in the morning.

A familiar voice came over the line. "Between Tamara's psych-eval report and your text this morning, I'm getting the distinct impression I'm going to lose one of my best undercover deputies." The voice of Aaron Sanchez, his boss, boomed over the line.

"It's only Wednesday, so I still have a week and a half of vacation left before we have to deep dive this conversation, but a change in role seems right. What that means, exactly, I'm still working on, but I figured you deserved a heads-up."

"Appreciate it, and we'll talk more once you're back in November. In the meantime, I'll move the schedule around to accommodate those discussions. There are other temporary career options for you, like a three-to-six-month local assignment, if you want more time at home. Then, at the end, you can reevaluate and make your final decision."

"I appreciate that flexibility and you're not pressuring me," Clarke replied.

"Hey, I've done that job, so I understand the sacrifice and what it means when you question your commitment. It's not a nine-to-fiver, for it consumes your entire being until it's over. Why do you think I'm in this role now?"

He laughed. As far as bosses went, Aaron was one of the best. He had their backs without question, and if he had to give his team feedback, it was always behind closed doors. He also went out of his way to make their lives easier.

The man was fair, firm, and loyal to each of his employees. "Thanks, Aaron."

The crunch of tires on the gravel road leading to Clarke's driveway had him ending the call and pocketing his phone. He strode to the front door and hollered to Aimee that Trent and Maggie had arrived. The second after he opened the door, a flash of auburn hair dashed past him to pull Maggie into a hug.

The corner of Clarke's mouth twitched as Trent ascended the stairs after his wife. "I'm not hugging you, but now I know your definition of 'morning' is broad," Clarke complained as he ushered everyone into his home.

Trent slapped him on the back. "Some of us have to work, asshole, and it's still morning. If you wanted my presence earlier, you should've been more specific."

Clarke grumbled under his breath, "Touché. Aimee, Maggie, we'll be downstairs if you need us."

"Oh, the secret spot," Maggie said, her eyes practically sparkling. "Have you shown that area to Aimee yet?"

Aimee grimaced. "Nope, but I heard about the bomb shelter. His aunt let that surprise spill out when I met her."

"Seriously, Clarke, show her the bat cave, it's so cool," Maggie said.

"We won't be long, and afterward, we can grab a bite of lunch," Trent replied and followed Clarke into the laundry room.

"You two make the plans." He lifted the trap door in the floor, revealing a flight of steps.

The girls' laughter filtered down the hallway as they moved farther into the house.

Once they were in his bunker, Clarke sat at his computer and motioned for Trent to follow with the other chair. "How much do you know about Aimee's background?" he asked.

Trent's eyebrows scrunched together for a second. "I remember it was clean. She doesn't really talk about it, but I assumed that was because she'd left a bad situation. I'd say that assessment is correct the more I've gotten to know her. You'd be the best measure of that statement. Why?"

"Well, it's too clean. I did a deep dive last night using my resources, and it's squeaky. Nothing is aligning, and I can't find any links to articles or anything to corroborate a word of her story. Granted, I don't have exact dates or locations, but still, it's odd. Then, you have her tied to two murders because of her hair. It gives me a bad feeling that whatever she was hiding from in her past has caught up to her."

"Yes, or a serial killer, which doesn't jive with the personal connections. I'm broadening my search of related crimes to other cities and states just to do my due diligence. I heard back from Noah last night. He found zero connections between the men at the two murder scenes. Just to be sure, I've asked him to look at wives, girlfriends, or other relatives."

"Her hair has been at both scenes, Trent. That's personal."

"I know, and both scenarios are bad, but have you spoken to her about this before you violated her trust and investigated her? We don't have a lot to work with on this investigation regarding her."

"Yes, and I've gotten her to open some, but she's careful. Again, she doesn't provide specifics, but I'm getting her to share more."

"What have you learned? I can't work on information I don't have." Trent leaned back in his chair and crossed his arms over his chest.

Clarke gripped the back of his neck. "Hey, that's her story to share. Getting her to tell me this much has been challenging, and I won't betray that trust. Let me speak to her to see if she is willing to talk with you. I have to be careful since I performed that background search earlier without her consent."

"You really do care about her, don't you?" Trent's rhetorical statement hung in the air between them.

"Did you regret leaving the FBI?" he asked, propping his elbows on his knees.

His friend studied him for a while before he answered. "The short answer, at first yes, but knowing what I gained with Maggie, hell no. The icing on that cake for me was being able to avenge Dalton's death."

"I'm considering a career change. I never thought I'd see this day come, but I can't ignore this uncertainty. It's like I need to pivot, but I don't like blind turns."

"When you find the woman you love, that's a side effect," Trent answered with a smile on his face.

He rolled his eyes at his friend. "Normally, I'd bust your balls over such a statement, but Aimee has become important to me."

"Enjoy the ride, my friend, but don't make my mistake. Be open with Aimee—tell her what you're feeling."

He snorted his disgust. "That's the tricky part. She's determined to keep our time together limited. She's doesn't think she can do long term."

"What does that mean—like, a casual sex type of arrangement?" Trent asked, his eyebrows bunched together.

Shaking his head in defeat, Clarke added, "Subterfuge is the correct term. What we have goes deeper than that, and she knows it. This is just her attempt at keeping some distance. If that makes sense."

"That sucks, man, but don't give up. Look at what Maggie and I overcame to get to this point. Then, the next thing you know, you'll be discussing which room in the house should be the nursery."

"Are you two expecting?" Clarke asked.

"Not yet. Right now, we're just practicing. After we get married that'll be my goal every damn day."

"Practice makes perfect, as they say. I'm happy for you, man. Enjoy it because life is too fucking short. Okay, enough of this personal touchy-feely bullshit."

AIMEE DIRECTED MAGGIE TO the family room and sat on one end of the sofa. "I can't believe you get a fall break. We didn't get that when we were in grade school."

Maggie curled up on the other end cushion to face the other. "I know, right? These kids get so much more time off. We were robbed of that enjoyment. Okay, I'm dying to know since our talk the other day—what's happening between you and Clarke?"

Aimee twirled a piece of hair around her finger. "I'm going to stay with him a bit longer since the renovation at the hardware store is going to take some time."

"Do not lie to me, Ms. Lang. I know you two are doing it. One, you're glowing, and two, you can't take your eyes off each other. So details, now."

Aimee's cheeks heated from embarrassment. She'd been an easy mark. "Okay, before you get too excited, we have an agreement. This thing between us has zero strings attached. He's not a boyfriend, just a friend." *Great, now, she was even lying to herself.* "When we're finished, we remain friends. The sex, though, is awesome. I've never, you know, had an experience like this before, like many in one night. My ex-husband sucked in the bedroom."

"Multiple orgasms rule." Maggie pumped her fist in the air. "Your ex is a douchebag. I'm so happy for you. You deserve to be all tingly and happy, but are you sure that's the only thing between you two? Clarke seems to really care about you."

"Oh, he's wonderful, and there's so much more to him than he lets people see. His heart is as big as the man himself. We have fun together, even outside the bedroom, but it's all I can give to him. I wish I'd met him first. Besides, this works for both of us since his job takes him away for long periods of time—so it's a win-win."

"Okay, but from where I'm sitting, I see two people who found happiness and complement each other. Are you sure you can't give this relationship a try? He makes you smile, Aimee, and he cares about you. I think you're being stubborn and letting your past dictate your future."

Aimee loved her friend, but she also disagreed with her statement. If Maggie knew the full story, she'd understand Aimee's reasoning. Besides, she'd already thrown a bit of caution to the wind by letting herself get close to Clarke, and she hadn't regretted that choice. She loved him, but those words would never be able to leave her lips.

God, I'm in love with Clarke Dragoon.

"It's what we need, and we went into this arrangement with our eyes wide open," Aimee replied.

Her phone chirped, alerting her to an incoming text. She swiped the device from the coffee table and read the message from Eileen at the bank: "*I've been watching your account. Since we canceled the first transfer, four additional deposits have been made, totaling one million dollars as of today. One is from the same account as before, and the three others are from different offshore accounts. Please call to discuss this when it is convenient. Thanks.*

Aimee's eyes widened, and she put her phone down. Dread pulsed through her veins. What the hell was happening? Could Clarke be right and all of this had to do with her ex-husband? How, she couldn't fathom because he sat behind bars.

"Hey, what's wrong?" Maggie asked, her concern evident in her tone. "You went white."

Aimee stood and grabbed Maggie's hand. "Come on, I need to talk to Clarke and Trent." She stopped at the top of the stairway in the laundry room and looked back at Maggie before Aimee announced, "Clarke, we need to talk. Can Maggie and I come down?"

His booming voice traveled up. "Be careful, the stairs are steep."

In a matter of seconds, she had descended into the bomb shelter she'd have to agree more closely resembled a technologically advanced bat cave with all the gadgets and computers. She had to think that maybe his aunt wasn't the only paranoid person in the family.

Against the back wall, there were two chain-link fences. One was empty, and the other held guns and other items. On her left, four large monitors hung two-by-two above a desk, with a computer, printer, and various other electronic devices littering the surface.

She shrugged off her surprise and turned to Clarke. "Eileen just texted me that four additional deposits were made into my account, totaling a million dollars. One from the same account, and the other three were different numbers."

"Let me guess, offshore accounts?" he asked, snagging Aimee's hand, and dragging her into his lap as he sat in front of his computer.

"Eileen from the bank?" Trent asked.

Maggie exhaled and moved over to where he sat, putting her hands on his shoulders. "That doesn't sound good. How could that have happened?"

"No, earlier this week I received a twenty-five-thousand-dollar deposit from an offshore account, which I cancelled. I don't know where this money is coming from, but it's not mine," said Aimee.

He cracked his knuckles. "I could have Noah look into this for you, but if this account has been established in a country that doesn't abide by FATCA, we won't find out who's listed as the owner."

Maggie's forehead crinkled with confusion. "What's FATCA?"

Trent smiled at his fiancée. "Sorry, Foreign Account Tax Compliance Act, governance to help keep transactions legitimate."

"Do it," Aimee answered. She craned her neck to face Clarke. "Do you have a pen and paper? I'll write down what Eileen has given me."

After Clarke gave her the items, Aimee scribbled furiously and handed the paper to Trent.

He took the proffered note and put it into his pocket. "I'll get this information to Noah."

"Thanks, Trent, I appreciate it. This is all getting a little out of hand." She moved out of Clarke's lap. "My stomach is a little upset at the moment. Can we have a raincheck for lunch?"

"Absolutely. I'm just sorry you have to deal with any of it," Maggie said.

Clarke turned toward Trent. "Another favor to ask. See if Noah can do this PDQ? Considering everything happening, the information can't come fast enough."

Maggie and Aimee exchanged hugs while Trent and Clarke shook hands.

"You bet. I'll be in touch," Trent answered, then followed Maggie up the stairs.

When they were alone, Aimee crossed to Clarke and hugged him, needing his touch to ground her, because everything else felt out of control. "I don't understand what's happening. This is bordering on absurd."

He rested his chin on top of her head. His presence chased away the chill of her own fear. The clean scent of soap and wood filled her nostrils, a smell distinctly his. Strong, capable hands held her tight.

Her immediate tension lessened, but dread sat heavy in her belly. "I don't want to discuss any of this right now. I just need a mental break from all of this. A person can only take so much crap in a day. You up for some backgammon?"

"Done. Just don't cry when you lose."

Eably the next morning, rays of light filtered through the window in the family room. Aimee sat on the sofa, nursing a cup of coffee. Her head throbbed. The two ibuprofen she'd swallowed earlier wasn't helping. The dread that had moved into her belly yesterday had multiplied overnight, leaving her with a sour stomach. Even the bath Clarke had drawn last night, followed by the sweetest and most sensual massage of her life, hadn't erased all her tension. She'd still tossed and turned.

Clarke came up behind her and rested his hands on her shoulders. "Head still bothering you?"

She nodded. A moan escaped her when strong fingers kneaded and rubbed her tense muscles. "Oh, that's wonderful. Please don't stop."

Never had a man been so attuned to all her needs, sometimes before she even knew. That thought both intrigued and scared her. It hadn't been until she'd spent time with Clarke that she realized even the good times with her ex-husband hadn't come close to what she had now.

He leaned down and kissed her crown a few times. "There's something I need to share with you. It's not bad, but you deserve to know what I'm thinking, and I don't want to keep things from you."

She turned in her chair to face him and steeled herself for the news she didn't want to hear. He'd finally had too much and was going to end their agreement. She couldn't blame him if that was his decision; it wasn't like her life was simple or close to normal.

He had a life to live, and all she would ever be was baggage. "Okay, what is it?"

"I've decided to take a temporary job assignment, which means I won't be leaving anytime soon for a long-term undercover gig. My perspective has evolved regarding my life, and what I want out of it. I won't deny that you're a big part of that decision. I want to spend time with you, not because of an agreement with an implied end date, but because we're good together. To see where this goes organically. I want the woman who dances when she thinks no one's watching."

Her heart fluttered wildly in her chest—excitement, affection, happiness—threatening to burst at his words. A future with this man made her giddy with thoughts of family and babies, growing old, and making a life together. Unfortunately, she wasn't free to have that dream. Her future would never include Clarke, and she could never tell him why.

She erected the mask she'd vowed to wear every day of Aimee Lang's life. "I can only dream in black and white; there will never be any color in my world. Don't throw your future away on me. I do care about you, Clarke, but I can't offer you any more than I already have. You are an amazing man." Her voice quivered as tears stung her eyes. The look of utter disappointment that covered his face gutted her.

"Now you know how I feel. You deserved the truth," Clarke said.

"So, are you ending our time together?"

He dragged his thumb along her jaw. "I can't."

She closed her eyes and inhaled, missing his touch when he dropped his hand. What he'd said meant the world to her. She thought about the possibility of amending their agreement, but he'd left the room when she opened her eyes.

About an hour later, she sat in the family room reading a book while she figured Clarke had gone to work in his office. She hadn't laid eyes on or heard from him since this morning. Her energy had been zapped, but at least her head felt better. She powered off her reading device and closed her eyes to nap when his deep voice penetrated her haze.

"Aimee, it's Trent. He just finished speaking with Noah," Clarke said as he entered the family room with his phone on speaker.

"What's Noah got?" Aimee asked in a tentative voice. Ready for the shoe to drop, so to speak, she sucked in a deep breath. All she wanted to hear was those deposits were another mistake because someone had transposed numbers or something equally silly.

"Lucky for us, the country where the accounts were opened are part of FATCA, so we could access the information. All four are in Switzerland and have the same owner, a Sara Brickley."

Nothing could've prepared Aimee for what Noah had uncovered. Her eyes widened. Her heart pounded against her chest, threatening to explode. Hearing that name sucked the remaining oxygen out of her body, leaving her dizzy.

"Do you know that person?" Clarke asked, his gaze missing nothing as he surgically sliced through all her layers, trying to reach her soul. She had to shut this shit down, now.

She dug deep to mask her emotions and to find the last ounce of strength she possessed to cover up her blunder. "No," she barked, taking the phone. "I'm just so relieved. I have no clue who that woman is, but now I can call Eileen and instruct her to return that money."

Aimee bolted from the room toward the den and placed her call. The second she hung up, she turned around and ran smack into Clarke. An immovable wall of muscle stood still, watching her like a hawk.

His gaze stripped away every layer of protection she had right down to her bone. "Are you sure you haven't heard that name before?"

Her mouth went dry. She swallowed, trying to find a little saliva somewhere in the recesses of her mouth to lubricate her throat. "I've already answered that question."

His eyes darkened and narrowed. "Your body contradicted your words. That is why I'm asking you again. Perhaps you remember that name now? Give me the goddamned truth. I think I deserve that much from you at this point."

Shit! How the hell was she going to sidestep this blunder? She couldn't tell him she knew that name. She had to push him away; it was the only answer. He didn't deserve this, but she had no other option. She jammed her finger into his chest. "I resent your accusation. Jesus, Clarke, we're just fucking, which doesn't entitle either of us to anything deeper."

Clarke grabbed both her arms. "Stop—"

Her cell rang, interrupting him. She wrenched free of his hold and answered her phone in a terse voice. "Hello." She turned away from Clarke and closed her eyes. Dammit, she should've checked the screen before she answered. Now she was stuck. If she told Lyndon it wasn't a good time, he'd read into that statement, and if she left the room, Clarke would read into that. Argh!

"Want to tell me why we've uncovered four additional warehouses—two more in Seattle and the other two in Miami and Los Angeles—all in your maiden name? That makes five total," Lyndon asked in a stern tone.

What the hell was happening? Her world was spinning out of control, and she didn't understand why. She tried to keep her voice level, but her frustration was making it difficult. "I've already told you, I have no idea. They have nothing to do with me."

"That's good, then it shouldn't bother you that we're securing search warrants for all of them."

"Great, maybe you'll finally get the answers you're seeking. Then, for once you'll believe I had nothing to do with any of it."

Clarke moved in front of her. *Who are you talking to?* he mouthed.

"I hope you're right. Now, for my last question. Why did DUSM Dragoon run an in-depth background search on Aimee Lang?"

"What?" Her gaze snapped to Clarke's, who watched her intently. "I have no idea, but he's a friend I've been staying with since the fire at my place."

Lyndon didn't hide his annoyance in his tone. "I'll put an end to his searches by reaching out to him through official channels. At least I know he can keep his mouth shut. Remember, your cover and new identity is only as strong as your commitment to protecting it."

"You know what? I'll save you the extra step. There are a lot of things I worry about, but Clarke selling me out is not one of them. Here. You can tell Clarke to back off yourself." Aimee tossed her phone at Clarke.

She stormed out of the den and ran to her bedroom, shutting the door with a decisive click. A fiery argument would consume them both later, but right now she needed space. It stunned her that he'd do such a thing. He'd betrayed her trust.

Anger and disappointment flowed white hot through her body until the tears started to fall down her cheeks.

Twelve

C LARKE CAUGHT HER PHONE and put it to his ear. Who the hell had she been talking to, and why did this person have his name? "Um, this is Clarke Dragoon. Who's this?"

"I'm Deputy Marshal Jake Lyndon, and Aimee Lang is my charge. You'll need to cease and desist immediately where she's concerned. Who have you spoken with about her, and do you feel any of your actions could've compromised her?"

Oh, fuck no, that DUSM prick rubbed him wrong in so many places with his pretentious and condescending tone. This jerk would learn quickly that he responded better when professional courtesy was used rather than accusations and attitude. They were on the same damn team at the end of the day. Everything surrounding Aimee snapped into place.

He couldn't believe he hadn't pieced this together earlier. "I realize you haven't worked with me before, so let me be clear about my expectations. I'll give you a pass this first time, but your next question should have a 'please' attached, and you should drop the attitude. We're on the same team, asshole. No, I haven't, nor would I ever. How long has she been in WITSEC?"

"Who do you report to, Deputy Dragoon?"

He pressed the end button to terminate the call. His expectations were clear, so that mistake was on Lyndon. It wasn't his fault his fellow marshal couldn't play nicely in the sandbox. He turned toward the hallway and strode to her closed door.

He rapped his knuckles on the wood. "Hey, thanks for the introduction to that asshole. We need to talk."

"It's unlocked," he heard a small voice answer from the other side.

When he opened the door, he pursed his lips and shook his head. Her red-rimmed eyes and blotchy face squeezed his heart. He wanted to pull her into his arms but hesitated because he wasn't sure if she'd allow him or punch him in the face. After they hashed all of this out, he owed her an apology for going behind her back and doing that search. He never intended to hurt her, but he would be upset if the tables were turned. Now, he hoped she'd at least hear him out and give him the chance to apologize.

He sat on the edge of her bed. "When did you go into WITSEC?"

"God, I didn't even know you were a marshal. I stupidly thought you were a DEA or ATF officer."

"I'm sorry, Aimee. I deserve your anger for going behind your back, but I only wanted to help. I wanted more information about your ex-husband."

"How could you do that? You said you'd wait until I was ready to share my story."

He cringed with the pain he heard in her voice, knowing he was the source. "You're right, I don't even know what to say. I—"

"You had no right. It's my life, Clarke, *mine*. You said you'd wait."

"I know, I fucked up, Aimee. It wasn't that I didn't trust you or thought anything negative about you. I did it because I truly wanted to help."

Aimee just stared at him. "Yes, I'm in WITSEC, and no, Lyndon doesn't like me very much. I think he thinks I'm guilty and behind the missing evidence. I do like his assistant, Supervisory Deputy Jenkins. She's always been very nice and supportive. Not once did she make me feel like I was a horrible person. I usually work with her, but of late it's been Lyndon. He listened as she decoded her life. "My birth name is Sara Brickley, and I was married to Alex Chubb. I was born in Seattle, Washington, and attended the University of Washington and graduated with a dual degree in Accounting and Business."

"Ah, that makes sense why you and Micah connected on that restaurant."

"Yes, which is why I had no clue about Michigan football. I wasn't very good at sticking to the cover identity."

A sense of pride filled him when he learned some of what she'd shared was real. She'd given him her trust by sharing true aspects of her life when she wasn't supposed to. Those kernels of truth had told him quite a lot. Everything she mentioned about her parents had been real. Now he understood why she tensed when she'd slipped and said her father had been an aerospace engineer.

Aimee sucked in an unsteady breath. "The worst part is coming. At my father's encouragement, I escaped that night, even though my husband leveled a gun at my father's head. I ran out the back door straight toward the police lights, thinking we'd been saved. I didn't know why the police were there. I ran as fast as I could and only stopped when a single gunshot split the air. Once I reached the officers, the FBI read me my Miranda rights and deposited me in the backseat of a SUV."

The story she shared stunned him. She'd been arrested by the FBI, who'd been investigating her husband's businesses. She'd been charged with drug trafficking and money laundering while her husband's charges were the same but included accessory to murder charges and murder. The interesting part was the missing evidence that was identified in the warrant—four hundred million dollars and a large sum of drugs.

"I'm guessing that because of your accounting degree, your husband put you in charge of keeping and cooking the books?"

Her voice wobbled. "Yes, I had no clue. I thought all his businesses were legitimate. I didn't catch on until about three months before I was arrested. That's when Alex went batshit crazy and forced my cooperation by threatening my father. I don't know anything about missing money or drugs. I told the FBI everything I knew and in exchange, they offered the Federal Witness Protection Program."

"Your husband was convicted and sentenced to prison on money laundering and drug trafficking charges? I thought he was charged with accessory to murder and murder?"

"Charged, yes, but the evidence was insufficient, so he was never convicted of those crimes. They never found the gun and couldn't link Alex to any of them."

"How did Alex perform all these illegal activities?"

"In the beginning, he worked at a pharmaceutical company and acquired his knowledge of the industry that way. Then, when he quit, he created several distribution companies—legitimate and non-legitimate—to launder the money then between those shell companies he managed the legitimate pharmaceuticals and funneled the rest via the black market."

"So, the one million dollars that was deposited into Aimee's account was made to look like you sent yourself money?"

"Yes, then I would be guilty because I have that missing money. I swear to you, Clarke, I have no clue who's behind those accounts, but it isn't me."

"I believe you, but this is serious because your husband could have enemies who didn't get paid and want their money. Or might want to hurt you to avenge your husband's arrest. We should share all of this with Trent. He won't betray your trust, but the sheriff needs to know what could be coming to Mill Creek. Plus, it'll be good to get his perspective."

"I trust Trent. I'm still pissed you did that search behind my back, but at least now you understand why I couldn't say more. Hey, about what you said earlier, I think ending our agreement is the best thing to do under the circumstances. I don't want you making life decisions because of me, and with all this happening, I can't put you in the middle of my mess. We weren't meant to be."

Clarke wanted to argue with her, but his phone interrupted the moment. He glanced at the screen and shook his head in annoyance. "Hey, boss, I take it you heard from DUSM *asshole* Lyndon?"

"As a matter of fact, I did, and he had many glowing words to describe your conversation. Bottom line, did you meddle?"

"No, she's a friend who's had a rough couple of days. I had no clue she was in WITSEC."

"Okay, if I need to know more, I expect you to loop me in before I get my next call. Now sit down, because this will shock you, and I've already approved it. He requested you be assigned as protective detail, since you already have a relationship with her and can do it under the radar. He needs time to run down some leads."

"What the hell does that mean?"

"Don't know. I wasn't read in, but you're not to let her out of your sight for the near future."

"Understood, and thanks," Clarke replied and ended the call. He pocketed his phone and flattened his lips. "According to Mr. Asshole and my boss, I've been officially tasked to watch over you for the foreseeable future."

"Well, that's convenient. Are you okay with me staying here? It won't be for long once all of this gets sorted out."

"Of course, and now you're my job. Let me know when you want to meet with Trent."

Clarke turned and left the room. Fresh air and distance were what he needed now. It calmed him, knowing he was in charge of her protection. No one would take it more seriously than him. She might not be able to offer him more, but he'd give her the world.

AIMEE DECIDED IT WOULD be best for Trent and Maggie to learn about her past sooner rather than later. That update had to come from her. She would never forgive herself if something happened to one of Mill Creek's residents. This was one decision she could get right. After telling Clarke, he agreed and called the station to extend the invitation for dinner. Now, she stood in the kitchen preparing it, which was better than worrying about the epic failure her life had become again.

She'd already cooked the noodles and sausage. Now she was making her homemade marinara. The sound of metal hitting a wooden cutting board in succinct, measured strokes filled the room. She went to town on garlic—*chop, chop, chop*. Next were the onions—*chop, chop, chop*. Then, the basil and thyme—*chop, chop, chop*. Her eyes stung with unshed tears from the pungent onion. The watery purge came from her anguish. Bringing trouble to her friends was unacceptable, just like hurting Clarke broke her heart.

"Hey, what's wrong?" His deep timbre washed over her, concern written across his face.

"Onion and garlic, that's all," she lied, heading to the sink to wash her hands and splash cool water on her face.

He placed his hand on her back when she returned to the cutting board with containers of ricotta and cottage cheese. "We're still friends, Aimee, so don't shut me out. I'll do everything in my power to help you bring this to a close."

Her movements were clumsy as she plopped the contents of both containers into a bowl and mixed them. "You're right, and I'm sorry. I'm just confused and scared."

That was the truth because losing him in the end would gut her. The part that startled her the most—she wanted to try to build a future, but it would never work because WITSEC would never allow it. He couldn't live his life on the run. No, she had to do the right thing and let him go.

"What can I do to help?" he asked while he rolled up the long sleeves of his flannel shirt.

"There's a head of romaine lettuce in the fridge that needs to be washed and dried."

They worked in companionable silence. She assembled the lasagna in layers while he took care of the greens. When she finished, she set the baking dish aside and preheated the oven. Trent and Maggie would be here in just under two hours, so the timing was perfect.

"Next is the garlic bread. Will you grab the butter spread on the top shelf?" she said.

The knife sliced into the fresh loaf. Next, she grabbed two spatulas and handed them to him. She'd miss these moments in the kitchen as they worked together. In no time, they finished the preparations and had everything in the oven. She'd have just enough time to freshen up before her friends arrived.

At precisely six o'clock, the doorbell rang, and her oven timer had dinged five minutes earlier. The lasagna cooled on a trivet while the bread finished baking; everything was right on time. She and Clarke had decided to play her mother's music tonight during dinner. It was fitting to have her family close since, for the first time in two years, she didn't have to hide behind a cloak. She would remain Aimee Lang, but she'd be Sara Brickley tonight. Nervous energy stirred in her belly at how Trent and Maggie would react to learning the truth.

Aimee had a dish towel slung over her shoulder and was putting the finishing touches on their dinner when Clarke went to answer the door. When she heard their familiar voices enter the kitchen, she turned and hugged Maggie and then Trent. "Maggie, Trent, thanks for coming over on such short notice."

"Oh my gosh, your house smells delicious. I had no idea you could cook. Maybe you should move in with Clarke permanently since your studio doesn't have a kitchen."

Aimee hugged Maggie. "We can open the wine and get a head start on the men." Aimee pulled the cork free and filled two glasses with the red, fruity goodness. She handed one to Maggie and toasted her friend. "To good friends and getting to know each other better."

"Cheers," Maggie said.

They sipped their merlot and went to work placing the food on the table so everyone could serve themselves. Moments later, the table was full with the sounds of forks and knives scraping across the plates while laugher and conversation filled the in-between spaces. Not once had dread crept into Aimee's belly due to the anticipation of exposing her lie to her friends. Camaraderie and warmth flowed easily between everyone in that room, and that soothed her.

"Mmm, this lasagna is amazing. You have to share the recipe," Maggie said around a mouthful.

"You may want to ask for a lesson to accompany that recipe," Trent teased.

She slapped his arm. "And maybe you can sleep on the sofa tonight."

He put his arms up in surrender and grinned at his fiancée. "I'm sorry, baby. You're the best cook, and I love you."

She snapped her fingers around her head in an exaggerated manner. "That's what I'm talking about. You have to set boundaries. Then, if necessary, punish them by withholding sex if they cross those lines."

"That, Clarke, is a trap. You want to respond, but the second you do, you're toast," Trent informed his friend and then put his arm around his fiancée's shoulder.

Maggie's smile widened as she winked at him. "It's hard work, but they are trainable."

Clarke shook his head. "Dude, pull your skirt up and put on a pair of pants."

Trent flipped Clarke the bird, then turned his attention to Aimee. "Sexist much? Anytime you feel like cooking, we'll be here. This is awesome."

Aimee refilled their wineglasses and grabbed two bottles of beer for the men. When she returned to her seat, she glanced at Clarke, giving him a slight nod that she was going to steer the conversation to the point of this dinner. He didn't miss a beat, winking his agreement. Then, to her surprise, he reached under the table and squeezed her hand.

"All right, there's something I need to share with you both. I guess you could tell we had an ulterior motive behind our dinner invitation. I hope you don't think less of me and can forgive me for deceiving you both. I'm--"

"Take all the time you need, Aimee," Maggie said.

"Okay, I'm ripping the bandage right off this sucker. I'm in WIT-SEC, and Aimee Lang is my identity."

Maggie's eyes went wide then narrowed. "Oh, Aimee, I'm sorry, but that actually makes perfect sense. Can you share your story, or is that still not allowed?"

Aimee nodded at her friend and over the next ten minutes, she started at the beginning and ended with her move to Mill Creek. "You know the rest, since you hired me in January."

"Best decision I've ever made, Aimee," Trent said. "You didn't lie. You assumed your identity and survived. I can't imagine how difficult it would be to act like all your memories and emotions never happened. Thank you for trusting us to share your story."

Maggie jumped out of her seat and threw her arms around Aimee. "You are so brave. Never for a second doubt my support. All of this only makes me love you more. Can we tell Kane and Annika when they return from Europe? They should know."

Clarke interjected, "No, the fewer who know, the better. It's the only way we can continue to keep Aimee safe. Everything that's been shared here today must remain in the strictest of confidence."

When her friend let go to take her seat again, tears stung Aimee's eyes for the umpteenth time in so many hours. Her emotions were raw, and she hoped this decision hadn't put anyone in this room in jeopardy.

Clarke laid his arm across the back of Aimee's chair. "It appears that her past is coming after her. We have that link from the four wire transfers that were made in her maiden name. Professionally, you had to know, Trent. That, mixed with the two identical murder scenes, makes this one clusterfuck. I'm not sure what those represent, but the timing is suspect, and I'm not a fan of the label 'coincidence.'"

Trent nodded. "So, does one million dollars represent anything to you? Maybe a wedding gift or an unpaid debt?"

"Not that I can remember, but there's something else I need to tell you. DUSM Lyndon has uncovered five warehouses recently with my birth name on the titles. The first one was empty, but he's getting warrants for the others--"

"That's new information," Clarke added. "It's interesting that it's not your married name. Did he mention anything else? I know a lot is happening, but all these details are important."

Aimee thought about that question for a moment. "Not that I can remember right now. Lyndon is the reason I was reluctant to report the other things. The marshal would move me out of Mill Creek if he thought my identity was compromised. That's the last thing I wanted to happen. I also don't get the feeling that he's my advocate, if you know what I mean. I'm pretty sure he thinks I'm guilty of murder and those wire transfers. Well, I did mention the first one, and he didn't seem to care. I haven't told him about the other four. I'm afraid if I did, he'd think I was behind the missing evidence—four hundred million dollars and drugs too, since they came from Sara Brickley."

Clarke leaned forward to grab his beer. "I've had the pleasure of speaking to him, and he's rough around the edges in a starched-collar kind of way. I'd put him more in the asshole category. That said, he shocked me by putting me in charge of her protection."

Trent's eyebrows scrunched as he seemed to work through something for several seconds. "Why would he put you in charge of her protection? Is that normal?"

Clarke rubbed his forehead. "Not from my understanding, and I got the same impression from my boss. According to Lyndon, he has to run down some leads."

"Maybe he's working for the bad guys—you know, trying to make it seem all natural, but he's betrayed her. You see that on television all the time," Maggie blurted out.

"Huh, I hadn't thought of that angle. At this point anything is possible," Clarke answered.

Aimee took a sip of her wine. "Did Noah dig into the accounts themselves?" Three heads turned her way with blank looks on their faces. "Creating a history and timeline of when they were established? Opening balances?"

Clarke nodded. "That's a good thought, Aimee."

Trent wiped his hand across his eyes. "I'm not sure. Our conversation centered around the name listed on the account. I'll reach out and see if he went deeper or has additional information."

The group spent another half hour reviewing different scenarios, ending with Trent increasing patrols on their street. When Trent and Maggie finally left to head home, Clarke cleared the table and loaded dishes into the dishwasher.

She floated about the kitchen, lighter than she'd felt in a long time. Being able to be herself for a night had been liberating. Everything else they'd discussed had scared her to death, but she'd tackle that tomorrow. She wasn't alone, which made all the difference in the world.

Thirteen

CLARKE'S BODY VIBRATED WITH restless energy. The sheets were crumpled and twisted around his legs from tossing and turning throughout the night. Aimee's scent lingered on the sheets. His frustration threatened to boil over. He glanced at the alarm clock that mocked him with bright numbers displaying 4:46 AM. *Fuck me.* His brain pounded against his skull from the onslaught of thoughts like mental aerobics.

A soft rap at his door, followed by her voice, snapped him back to the moment. He sat upright and had one leg over the side of the bed when his door cracked open.

"Clarke," Aimee whispered again before she gasped.

He could only image what had slammed into her brain as he sat on the edge of his bed naked, legs apart, and sporting morning wood. "Is everything okay? Did you need something?"

"Um...yes, to talk."

Well, it wasn't like she hadn't seen it all before, so he didn't rush to cover himself. He patted the corner of his bed, tossing the cover over his lower body. Even in the low light, he thought he caught a glimpse of her trembling.

"Lyndon just called. Supervisory Deputy Jenkins is dead. Someone killed her. He wanted me to update you and to reiterate that I'm not to leave your side. If I need anything, I'm to go to you in the meantime. His boss is reaching out to yours, and he'll call you later himself."

"Wow, that's quite an update for this hour of the morning."

She nibbled on her bottom lip. "I don't know what I feel anymore. I'm confused and angry and scared, and I really just want to go back to being Aimee, who has a boring life."

He threw his arm around her shoulders and tugged her into a hug, pleased she came willingly. "You have every right to those feelings; shit shows aren't supposed to be fun. You must keep moving forward."

She rested her head against his chest and exhaled. Against his better judgment, he kissed her crown, wishing it could be more but wanting to reinforce his words. He leaned his cheek on the top of her head, holding her for several minutes. He planned to fight for what he wanted, which was a future with her. Fancy words and phrases tossed around in his head until he realized being blunt was best. When her hand wrapped around his softening shaft, his head snapped up.

Instantly, his entire body roared to life with raw desire. His cock hardened, and every nerve ending in his body came alive with need. When she tilted her head to look him in the eyes, he saw her desire radiating in her orbs and acted on impulse. He lowered his mouth to hers in a heated duel. Taking the kiss even deeper, trying to show her how perfect they were together. That they were meant to be partners in love and life.

Her hand worked his length, driving him toward nirvana. Except his brain kicked into gear and doused him with ice water. In the deepest recesses of his brain, a warning light flashed. He broke off the kiss and scooted back from her.

She let out a breathy whimper. "Please, I need you. I never should've ended..."

That damn agreement, he hated it. The hypocrisy of his state-ment made him roll his eyes. He'd done the same thing with numerous women, only those so-called agreements had been one-nighters. "I meant what I said earlier. I want that woman who dances when she thinks no one's watching. I want all of you, not just the scraps you're willing to offer, for however long it lasts. I want Aimee Lang and Sara Brickley—all of you."

He knew her answer the moment her head bowed, and her shoulders slumped. "Why can't you be like other men and just accept what I'm offering?"

"I'm sorry. You've changed me, sweetheart. I want more than casual and quick." Clarke exhaled. "Please give us a chance, that's all I'm asking of you."

"Then we're at an impasse because this is all I have to offer. I can't promise tomorrow," Aimee said, turning toward the door.

"If you're up to it, I need to review my security system with you. Can you meet me downstairs in an hour?"

She nodded and disappeared, right along with his heart. Why did life have to be so difficult?

Forty minutes later, he'd taken care of the morning essentials plus a quick jack to release tension, or he might just kill the next person who pissed him off. That damn woman infuriated him with her stubbornness and this mirage of maintaining her distance. How could she not see what they had was worth fighting for and building upon?

When Aimee arrived, he handed her a coffee cup filled with her preferred morning concoction and motioned for her to sit next to him at his desk. He plopped down in his big leather chair and moved his keyboard closer. His hands flew across the keys and every so often he gripped the mouse to click on applications or open files.

When the aerial map of his property appeared on his screen, he stopped and turned to her. "I want to go over the security measures I have set up in and around my house," he said.

She gawked at him. "Are there cameras inside the house too?"

"Yes, but not in private spaces. I'm cautious, not a pervert."

"Are you sure you want to show me all of this? I mean, I've been accused of horrible crimes, Clarke."

"You're guilty, then?"

She bristled. "No, I didn't know anything about it until the end, then my ex-husband coerced me."

"Precisely. Have you ever thought about why the FBI made you that offer? They painted a picture and matched the evidence to get you to cooperate. They had to make you desperate with fear and preyed on your good qualities. You were the key to help them prosecute your husband and take down his illegal business," Clarke challenged.

"It's still embarrassing to be that naive and to have made all those poor decisions."

He ran his hand over his bald head, determined to get her to see the error in her thinking. "So, are you telling me that if your husband had been up-front, you would've turned a blind eye because you loved him that much and would've made the exact same decision?"

"No, I would've left him and never looked back," she snapped.

"Give yourself a break. You were conned by a man who knew what he was doing. That makes you a victim."

"You make that sound so easy. I think you were right when you were younger, when you decided to ensure you were always in control over your life. Being out of control is a horrible feeling."

Clarke turned her face toward him with his index finger. "Yes, it is, but I was wrong about control. I've always had it, but I can't control others, just like I can't guarantee safe outcomes. There was nothing I could've done to save my family. Okay, let's talk about security."

He spent the next thirty minutes explaining the type of devices around his property and how they worked. Then, he showed her on the map where they were located. He explained how he could have each device alert him when activated and send the captured images, heat signatures, or audio recordings to his server. When he finished and answered all her questions, he went on to explain the biometric security. He grabbed the device to capture her fingerprint so she could open his office and the weapons lockers.

"Holy shit, you're like that British spy, but I have to admit it's kind of hot," Aimee said.

"I'm just a humble man who loves gadgets. Let's head outside and look around so you can get a handle on the locations verses the map." He logged out of his computer right as Trent called. "You're on speaker," Clarke said.

"How are you today?" Trent asked in a serious tone.

"Good," Aimee said. "I just got a private tour of the spy's dungeon. It's kind of cool. I can see why Maggie calls it the bat cave."

Trent's laughter spilled across the line. "Be careful, or all that will go to his already big head."

"Uh, hello, I'm in the room with Aimee," Clarke grumbled.

"Noah got back to me. The four accounts have relatively small remaining balances, nowhere close to four hundred million. Two were opened about six months ago, and the others about two years ago. Does that mean anything to you, Aimee?"

"Not really, but let me think about it."

Clarke drummed his fingers on the desk. "Trent, we got an early call from Lyndon this morning. His supervisory deputy was killed. I think that answers why he wanted me to stay close to Aimee and help."

"Wow, I'm sorry to hear that. Hey, I've got to take this call—I'll talk to you later."

Clarke ended the call and turned to Aimee. "You ready to go see my gadget babies in person?"

"Gadget-babies, seriously?" she teased and elbowed his arm.

He playfully swatted her on the ass. "Do not insult my children, woman."

The tour continued in his yard, where he pointed out every device and its primary roles. After the security debriefing, Aimee headed toward the house to make sandwiches for lunch. His nape prickled with awareness, a warning he had never ignored but hadn't experienced before at this home. He spent several minutes scanning his yard under the guise of coiling up his hose and checking the garage door sliders, but nothing seemed amiss.

He made a mental note to check his camera after lunch. When he popped into the kitchen, two turkey and cheddar sandwiches were on the table, alongside a bag of potato chips. He scrubbed his hands at the kitchen sink before joining her at the table.

"I've been thinking about what you said earlier. I didn't mention the one-million-dollar deposit or the two murders to Lyndon. I wasn't trying to hide anything, but I didn't want him to jump to conclusions and do something hasty. Looking back, that makes me look guilty."

Clarke popped a chip into his mouth and chewed then washed it down with a sip of iced tea. "Maybe, but we'll keep that between us for now. You came forward to the sheriff, and that's on the record."

The house phone rang, and he sat still.

"Do you want me to get that?" Aimee asked.

"No, if it's important, they'll leave a message."

When the ringing stopped and then his cellphone erupted, she raised her eyebrow at him. "I'm thinking it's urgent."

Clarke sighed and answered his phone. "Dragoon."

"How many phones do I have to call to get you to pick up? I have quite a lot on my plate at the moment." Lyndon's tone was scornful. "Please update Ms. Lang that we've executed the search warrants and two of the warehouses were empty, but the other two were loaded with evidence that's being processed."

Clarke put his phone on speaker but placed his index finger across his lips. "So, give me some highlights."

"We seized a large sum of opioids, weapons, and documents, but most interesting are the two full sets of false identities with Aimee Lang's photo. That right there is grounds for me to bring her in, but if you give me your word as a United States Marshal that you'll keep her under lock and key, I'll let her stay with you for now. I need to sort through this evidence to see how current it is, assess the risk. My other problem is my time's being split with Deputy Jenkin's murder."

"Are you sure she was murdered?"

"That's the preliminary assessment, since she was shot in the back of the head and had no defensive wounds or any signs of a struggle."

"Shit, sorry to hear that. Do you have any actionable leads?" Clarke asked.

"Getting closer, but the situation is fluid, as you know."

Clarke leaned forward in his chair. "Good luck. I hope you quickly nail the person responsible. You have my word regarding Lang. Thanks for the update."

The devastation on her face at hearing the marshal's update had him up and out of his seat. He turned her chair and crushed her body against his as he crouched beside her. "Hey, we're a team. What we just learned gives us more insight into this threat. Now, we know where to start digging."

"This makes me look like I'm planning to run. I mean, why else would someone have fake identification? God, if Lyndon knew about the one million dollars, he probably would have brought me in."

"Lyndon doesn't know you like I do. This whole scheme is designed to make you look like you stole the money, invested, then waited until you could access it to flee. We need to investigate your husband. Someone may be loyal who's trying to help him or is pissed that he shorted them." Clarke took his seat.

She dropped her head back and blew out a breath. "I don't know. I didn't meet that many of his people. I mean, Alex didn't conduct much business at home; however, it was where I did the books. He had a few goons who followed him, none of whom seemed intelligent enough to create this plan, let alone execute it. The closest person to him I knew was his longtime friend and lawyer, Dean. I can't remember his last name."

"That's a start. Do you remember when the FBI spoke to you about the missing evidence? Did they ever specify the type of drugs?" Clarke asked.

"If they did, I didn't consider it significant then. Let me think about it. Maybe I'll remember something else."

"At this point, we need to focus on who may have taken the money and is trying to pin this on you." He didn't divulge his other hunch because it was a little farfetched.

The only part that tied to his idea was the fact that Aimee's involvement in the two murders was personal with her hair being at the scene. Did DUSM Lyndon have a mole within his team? At this point, Clarke thought it warranted a discussion with his boss to get his opinion.

"I have an idea for tonight if you're game. As you know, I love music, and now that I can be myself a little, I'd love to dance and blow off a little steam. I'd be safe with you and won't leave your side."

"I think it's a great idea," said Clarke.

"Deal." She slapped the table. "I'm going to go figure out what to wear. Be warned, Mr. Dragoon, your feet will hurt when I'm finished with you."

A small price to pay when her face brightened, and her eyes sparkled with excitement. That didn't mean he'd put her safety at risk. He punched in the sheriff's number, pleased the man answered on the first ring.

Trent answered in a monotone voice. "I'm beginning to dislike your calls because there's always bad news."

"Okay, I'll throw you a bone. How about a pick 'em. Good news or bad?" Clarke asked.

"Bad news—that way I can end with something happy. What's up?"

Clarke rolled his eyes and laughed at the sheriff and his friend. Then, he got down to business and informed him of Lyndon's latest update.

"Shit, that's quite a damning haul. The law enforcement side of my brain must ask you this question. Do you think she's playing both sides and could be guilty?"

"I can't fault you for that because I've asked the same question. It's hard to accept innocence between every event and piece of evidence collected. It's why I'm confident, from asking her outright and watching her reactions from the get-go, that's she's innocent. She's being set up to look like she's taken the money, but the crime scenes baffle me. Those are personal. However, if it turns out she's hoodwinked me, then she's one diabolical motherfucker."

"Okay, we're on the same page regarding our assessments. So, what's the good news?" asked Trent.

"You remember how you said after Maggie's ordeal that you wanted to run simulated drills as training exercises for your deputies?"

"Yes, but how's that good news?"

"Aimee wants to head to Two Stepping tonight to blow off steam. How about a last-minute threat with credible intel that an attack might happen there tonight? It would provide additional cover for Aimee just in case, and it gives you a chance to put your lead deputy in charge of this little simulation."

"I'll call the manager at Two-Stepping and get this simulation rolling."

"Thanks, man, I appreciate it."

A FEW HOURS LATER, Aimee vibrated with excitement as the band started its first set. She grabbed Clarke's hand. Once they reached the dance floor, she let herself go, her body moving to the beat and rhythm of the music. Dancing and Clarke could become her two most favorite things.

True to his word, Clarke matched her energy from song to song. His mother would be proud of him. When a slow song started to play, she figured they'd go to the bar and cool off with a drink. Instead, strong fingers snagged her and twirled her into a wall of muscle. The subtle scents of amber, bourbon, and vanilla from his cologne wrapped around her. She rested her head against his chest and enjoyed the simplicity of the moment.

A part of her wanted to try and see what would happen between them. It wasn't like he didn't know the risks of her life. It also meant he knew she'd be moved around, and that wasn't fair to him or a family. Hell, she didn't even know if she could have a relationship while in WITSEC. That would be a question she could've asked Deputy Jenkins, but she wouldn't ask Lyndon. It could make Clarke look unprofessional, and she wouldn't do that to him.

When the song ended, he leaned down and spoke against her ear so she could hear him. His words vibrated against her skin. "I'm thirsty, how about you?"

At her encouragement, he tugged her toward the bar and ordered a glass of chardonnay for her and a beer for him. They stood off to the side and sipped their beverages. No words needed to be exchanged as they watched the crowd and smiled at each other. She liked how they'd developed their own secret language. When she finished her drink, he placed it alongside his empty bottle on a high-top table.

Clarke extended his hand to her. "You ready to show these people how it's done?"

She suppressed a yawn and smiled. "Believe it or not, you wore me out. Thank you for tonight, but I have an even better idea. How about we go home, open a bottle of wine, and I'll beat you at backgammon a few times."

The lopsided smile that covered his face made him look downright sexy. "You're on, but don't think I'll go easy on you this time."

She playfully slapped his hand. She'd enjoyed dancing, but something about spending time with him at home seemed even better. Tomorrow, they could go back to dissecting her threat.

Fourteen

THE NEXT MORNING, AIMEE floated around the house. Last night had been nearly perfect, from dancing to winning two out of three backgammon games. The only thing that would've perfected it was to have woken up in Clarke's bed this morning. They'd polished off a bottle of wine and had spent the night talking about life and laughing. Maybe it was the wine, but she couldn't stop rambling about her childhood, her parents, and everything. It had been cathartic to share her treasured memories, and the fact that it had been with him had made it that much sweeter.

She wanted to share another experience with him instead of waiting for Lyndon to call with more news. She searched the house and found Clarke downstairs in his office, finishing up a phone call to Darla.

"Everything okay?" she asked. She didn't want to eavesdrop, but a twinge of doubt fluttered in her belly with everything happening.

"Everything's great. That was Darla from Mountain Gems. She's working on a project for me."

"Oh, well, I have an idea, but it requires us to leave the house. I want to take you to Tale Peak and show you my special haven. I thought with everything happening with the investigation, we could use a little of nature's therapy."

Clarke stared at her for a few moments before he answered, "I'd love to see this place you cherish. Since it's remote, I won't go unless I'm armed. Can you handle that?"

She pondered his question, finding that she had zero objections. "Okay. I think we should swing by the diner first since it's Saturday and bring a picnic lunch. We can eat in the back of my truck and enjoy a lazy afternoon."

"Sounds great. Let me grab my things, and I'll meet you in the garage."

In no time, she and Clarke were headed toward the diner, and then they'd be on the dirt road heading toward her favorite place. She glanced at the clock in her dash, pleased that they'd arrived in one hour and forty-five minutes. She backed her pickup into a cutout under a copse of trees that overlooked the valley on three sides, with Tale Peak behind them. The views were as breathtaking as the man who sat next to her.

"Jump out and take a look around. I'll get to work on spreading out the tarp and blanket so we can eat," she blurted, eager to see his reaction.

She set the emergency brake and hiked herself over the tire well into the truck bed. Afterward, she arranged the basket in the middle of the space and dropped the tailgate for him. She could dangle her feet off the tailgate while she sat and took in the views. The scent of sunshine, dirt, and pine trees filled her lungs. A light breeze rustled the branches, and big, puffy white clouds dotted the sky.

"This is amazing. I can see why you spend so much time up here. The views go on forever." The truck's shocks bounced when he hopped up onto the tailgate and sat next to her.

Learning back, she tugged the basket closer so it was between them. When the box of chicken was opened, the smell of seasoned, fried meat teased her nose. Next, she had the potato salad and coleslaw ready to go.

"I'm starving," she admitted, filling a paper plate with her selections.

He followed her lead and piled on the food. "This is spectacular. Thanks for opening your heart to me by sharing something so personal to you."

After she had eaten as much as her stomach could hold, she gathered up the containers and stowed everything back in the basket. Once the trash was collected, she tied the small plastic bag. "Now, this is my favorite part of the whole experience. Lie back and watch the clouds until you drift off to sleep. Sometimes, if you're lucky, you feel connected to heaven."

He lay on his back and stared up at the sky. When he grabbed her hand and kissed her palm, another pang of longing gripped her heart. "Have you ever camped?" he asked, letting go of her hand.

"No, that wasn't my father's thing."

"Well, when all of this is over, that will be my treat to you. It's as amazing as this, but with brilliant stars and a campfire. Hell, even if it rains, that's beautiful too."

She turned and propped her head on her elbow, her heart beating a little faster at the prospect. "That sounds lovely. I'd love to."

She rested her eyes and sighed. She drifted off to sleep somewhere between the peaceful tranquility and a full belly. Clarke's cellphone shattered the silence and startled her. Her eyelids were still heavy from sleep. How long had she dozed?

When he finished his call, he turned to face her. Tension filled the air between them, sucking out all the oxygen. His lips were pressed into a flat line for a few seconds before he gave her the update. "Lyndon has requested me to bring you to the sheriff's station for a deposition. I don't know more than that, but we've been summoned."

Her stomach cramped. She swallowed several times to force down the bile rising in the back of her throat. Her mind whirled with thoughts while her stomach worked hard to purge lunch. She hurried as she slid off the tailgate, hunched over to the side, and puked. The foul taste of acid, partially digested lunch, and fear made her heave once more.

Clarke's warm hand landed on the center of her back. He rubbed gentle circles while he handed her a wet napkin to wipe her mouth. She accepted the bottle of water to rinse her mouth. The compassion written across his face helped her regain her composure.

"I think it might be best for you to drive, sorry," she mumbled as she handed him the keys.

He didn't answer her with words. Instead, his strong arms scooped her up and carried her to the passenger's side. He opened the door and sat her down. Once settled, he stretched across her body and secured the seatbelt. He didn't balk or complain, just put her needs first and soothed her pain. He made her feel precious, and that broke the dam that held her tears.

When her cries subsided, she dried her eyes and put her hand on his thigh. "Thank you. I don't deserve you, but I'm so damn lucky you fell into my life."

He didn't take his eyes off the mountainous roads but dropped his hand to give hers a quick, reassuring squeeze. "Now you know how I feel."

She pulled her hand back. "I've been thinking, and this doesn't make any sense to me. Why now, after all this time? If someone had the money, why didn't they just take it and be gone? Why torment me now?"

"All good questions," he answered while he turned left into the sheriff's station and parked. "It's almost like two different people are coming after you with different motives."

His statement hung between them as they exited the truck. He immediately walked over to her, placing his palm on the small of her back. Always touching and reassuring her that she wasn't alone as he guided her inside.

Trent greeted them and motioned for them to join him in the conference room. "DUSM Lyndon contacted me after he spoke to you, Clarke. He wants me to be present as a witness. That's all I know. You ready for me to call him?"

Aimee stopped. "I need to go to the ladies' room first. Give me a second."

When she exited the conference room, she swung by her desk to grab the toiletry kit she kept in a drawer. If she was going to have more mud slung at her, at least she could have a clean mouth. She slammed open the restroom door and took care of her business.

When she finished, she stashed her kit back in her desk. She turned toward the conference room with fresh, minty breath and a new perspective. The sooner she heard what this man had to say, the quicker she could refute it and help Trent and Clarke figure out who was behind everything.

She opened the door and smiled. "Thanks, I feel ten times better."

The second she took her seat, Trent placed the call. A few minutes later, she was informed that they were on a secure line via video conferencing. Surprisingly the image was crystal clear with little lag time. When Lyndon's face came onto the screen, her stomach rioted and churned. That man had no love for her, that much was sure. She sucked down a deep breath. How much worse could this get?

"Everyone ready to begin?" DUSM Lyndon asked, moving his head to look at each person in the room through the video feed.

Aimee nodded alongside Clarke and Trent.

"This deposition is with Aimee Lang at the Mill Creek Sheriff's Station on Saturday, October 24, at 4:30 p.m. Please state your names for the record."

"Aimee Lang."

"Sheriff Jacobs."

"DUSM Dragoon."

"DUSM Lyndon," he said. "Aimee, you are a person of interest in the murder of Supervisory Deputy Jenkins. It's important to note that not all the evidence retrieved has been processed. The gun, ammunition, and shell casings are still being reviewed by ballistics. The coroner is finalizing his report, but the preliminary TOD is Monday, midmorning to early evening. Any questions on what I've shared so far?"

Trent made eye contact with them to confirm before answering, "No."

Lyndon continued. "We've obtained CCTV footage from the condominium where Jenkins lived. This image is of a person briefly appearing on the camera coming and going from the direction of her place, wearing a bulky raincoat, hunched over, with long auburn hair. Our crime scene analysts also found a few strands of hair on the shoulder of our victim. Imagine my surprise when the DNA on that fiber sample came back as a match to you, Aimee. A person in WITSEC starts with a clean slate, so how did your DNA get into the system?" He glowered at her.

Her tongue stuck to the roof of her mouth. Aimee spun toward Trent. "Can I get a bottle of water?"

Trent nodded, moved to the corner of the room, and opened the refrigerator. He twisted the cap loose and slid the bottle across the table. Removing the cap, she gulped down the cool liquid. She used these few precious seconds to gather her thoughts.

After a few seconds, she turned back to the screen and answered his question. "There were two recent murders in Mill Creek where my hair had been left at the scene."

"I'm aware of those, but your name has never been mentioned," Lyndon countered.

Trent cleared his throat and sat forward in his seat. "Aimee wasn't mentioned because she's not a suspect. I can send you the reports to review. Both murders have produced little to no leads with no witnesses. As to why her DNA is in the system, she volunteered a sample to compare it to the strands clutched in the dead man's hands. That same man had been identified as the person who'd gotten physical toward her without her permission. This same person's fingerprints also matched the Molotov cocktails used in the fire at the hardware store and her residence. If you'd like a copy of the arson report, you can contact Fire Chief Gerald Mason."

Clarke added to Trent's statement. "We didn't know Ms. Lang was part of the WITSEC program. That said, between everything that's happened in Mill Creek and what you're reporting, she might have a target on her head."

The disapproval that radiated in Lyndon's eyes worried her. She nibbled on her bottom lip, and her mind raced with what he planned to do based on the context of this meeting.

"Ms. Lang, there shouldn't be any more surprises from this point forward. You need to be transparent and disclose anything that happens to you. Are we clear?"

She blurted, "Remember that mistaken deposit I told you about earlier this week? Well, I returned that money after working with the branch manager. Then, four wire transfers totaling one million dollars were deposited into my account a few days later."

The deep inhale on the video screen made her pause as he feverishly scribbled something on a yellow pad.

When he stopped, she continued her update and braced herself for his heated response. "Um, those four offshore accounts were also opened in Sara Brickley's name, but I don't know them."

"How would you possibly know that information unless they belong to you?" Lyndon challenged in a condescending tone.

She squirmed in her seat at how bad all of this sounded. "I—"

"Watch the tone and check your attitude," Clarke warned in a low growl. "She knows because it troubled her, and she did the right thing by bringing it to me and the sheriff."

Trent said, "I contacted a colleague in the FBI who researched it for me. Thanks to FACTA, she has the information."

"I'll need you to send me the information on the four accounts. When did this happen, Aimee?"

"On Thursday. Should I email the information or give it to you now?"

"You've had plenty of time to update me. Email is fine," Lyndon said. He scribbled more notes on his yellow pad. "Aimee, where were you on Monday, the nineteenth of October?"

"Um...was that the day of your appointment?" She turned to ask Clarke. When he confirmed, she continued, "Spent the morning at Clarke's house. Spoke with the bank about the first mistaken deposit. Then, I called you. Afterward, we left for Boise around 9:15 AM for Clarke's appointment at eleven in the morning. On the way back to Mill Creek, we stopped for lunch and one store."

Lyndon tapped his pen on the tablet. "How long was Clarke at this appointment? Were you with him the entire time? If not, where did you spend the time? Where did you eat lunch, which store—I need all the specifics."

Clarke leaned forward. "Two and a half hours, and I'll scan and send you the receipts for lunch and the drugstore."

Aimee provided the rest. "I wasn't with him. I strolled over to the park. When he texted me at the conclusion of his appointment, I walked back to the building and met him at my truck."

Lyndon sat back with his elbows on the armrest, fingers steepled. "I'll get this deposition finalized and send it over for your review and signature. If you think of anything else pertinent, contact me immediately. Aimee, you're to remain with DUSM Dragoon until further notice. I should have ballistics and more information regarding the warehouse soon. Normally, I'd bring you in, but under the circumstance, it's better for you to stay with him. Don't make me regret that decision."

Aimee nodded at Lyndon then moved her gaze to Trent and then Clarke. The video line went black when Lyndon disconnected the call. "That didn't sound very good."

Trent raked his hand through his hair. "No, but he did his job. I do see your point. Lyndon either has a bad disposition or isn't a fan of Aimee's. What isn't clear is how she would benefit from killing Jenkins. It's all disjointed, so what are we missing? When was the last time you even left Mill Creek before you did with Clarke?"

Aimee propped her elbow on the table, resting her head in the palm of her hand. "Not once since I arrived this past January."

Clarke rubbed his hands up and down his face and groaned. "She didn't have a raincoat or gun when I left her. That means she would've had those items stashed or has an accomplice who brought them to her. Next time we speak to Lyndon, I'm going to ask him the distance between the condominium and park. If she had to take a taxi or ride share, there would be video evidence of that ride. I want to do something, but if he perceives I'm interfering, he may take Aimee into custody."

"I'm screwed. There is so much piling up it makes me look horrible." She sighed heavily, resting her forehead on the conference table.

Clarke put his hand on her back. "Hey, the evidence isn't true, so we have to poke holes in it. The next time we speak to Lyndon, we're going to question him and see where his team is with the investigation."

Trent stared at the empty screen. "I think it's time to hire an attorney. There's so much evidence already, but it seems more is coming out of the woodwork every day."

"What about my identity? I made an agreement when I entered WITSEC to protect it. Would I be breaking it?"

Clarke shook his head. "You'd be protected under client-attorney privilege, and I agree with him. This is about protecting you."

Trent glanced back to face them both. "I'll call Kane and see if his friend and lawyer Larry Behr has any recommendations in Boise. His firm in New York has been expanding, and they might even have an office there now."

"Sounds good, thanks, man," Clarke said and nodded toward Aimee. "You ready to head home? We've had enough fun in the sheriff's station for one day."

Aimee stood. "Give Maggie a hug for me, and thanks for not thinking I'm some crazed, money-loving murderer."

"Talk to you both soon," Trent replied, pushing open the conference room door and then stepping aside to allow Clarke and Aimee to exit.

Fifteen

Typically, Sundays should be fun days, or at least the lyrics from a popular eighties' song told her, but Aimee's current situation made that impossible. Instead, she decided to wash her truck. It had so much dirt on it you could draw pictures on the finish. She'd left her truck in the driveway after they'd returned from the station yesterday. The garage had everything she needed, and she'd snagged the dish soap from the kitchen on her way. After the garage door opened, she squirted the soap into the bucket and filled it with water at the hose bib.

The sun shined bright, and a light breeze fluttered her hair, sending several strands into her mouth. The subtle scent of pine and dirt surrounded her while the warmth from the sun heated her skin. It was warmer than normal for a late October day. The sound of her ringer had Aimee dashing back into the garage so she could grab it off the workbench.

"I'm so sorry. Trent told me last night about the deposition. What can I do?"

"Hey, Maggie. Thanks, but there's nothing that can be done. At the end of the day, it's all my fault for agreeing to marry my ex-husband. He's the gift that keeps giving."

"That's bullshit. None of that is your fault—he manipulated you."

"I had to allow it, right?" Aimee replied in a matter-of-fact tone. She turned toward the house door and sat on the cement step. "It's not a favorite topic, because I have so much guilt over what I should've done. You know, the whole hindsight is a twenty-twenty thing."

Maggie huffed. "Do I need to smack you upside the head? Life continually moves forward, and since no one owns a patent yet for a real-time pause or do-over button, you do the best you can in those moments."

"So, what are you and Trent doing today?" she asked, stretching out her legs, wanting to hide from this conversation. Talking about her wasted life and shattered dreams only served to depress her. Sometimes in life, one doesn't get do-overs, and this was one of those times.

"Not much. Trent is working on paperwork. How are you two lovebirds doing?"

Aimee cringed because that wasn't a subject she wanted to discuss either. "We're good, but we ended the 'benefits' part. It ran its course. Now we're just friends."

"Uh-huh, and I'm an Olympic gymnast. Why did *you* end it?"

"He has a career he loves, and having a relationship with me probably isn't great for his professional image. Plus, I can't do long-term or commitments. My husband ruined that for me."

"You know I love you, but you are so frustrating. Clarke lusted after you before he knew the truth, and now that he does, he still cares about you. You're afraid to open your heart again, and everything else you spew is smoke, so you don't have to see the truth."

"He deserves better than me, and I want him to be happy."

"You make him happy," Maggie shot right back. "Open your eyes and live. Of anyone, Clarke can help you navigate WITSEC, and I don't see him tucking tail and running."

Aimee didn't respond right away because her friend's statement made sense. The problem she faced was opening her heart without giving Clarke the power to destroy her. What if things didn't work out? Could she pick up the pieces and move forward? "All right, you made a few good points, so I'll consider it. That's the best I can do now."

"That works. Okay, I'll go pester Trent and leave you to your day. We'll talk soon."

Aimee ended the call and stood to grab the bucket and get to work. Could she and Clarke make this work? She dunked the sponge and brought the sudsy brick to her hood when her hand froze. What the hell was on her windshield? The sponge splashed back into the bucket, shooting water over the edge.

She frantically dried her hand on the hem of her T-shirt. Shaking fingers plucked the wedding picture of her and Alex from under the wiper blade. It had been torn in half. *What the hell?*

Her throat constricted as she stared at the photo. She whipped her head up and scanned the yard. When she flipped the photo over, a number was scrawled across the back with a warning. *If you tell, he'll be next. You've been a pain in the ass from the beginning.*

"A IMEE." CLARKE'S VOICE BOOMED louder the closer he got.

She whirled around, and a scrap of paper flew out of her hand. "Jesus, Clarke, I've told you to announce yourself. You scared the crap out of me."

He crouched and snatched the photo from the ground. "I did, but you didn't hear me. What's wrong? Is this your wedding picture?"

"It was on the windshield. I-I don't understand how it got here. This is all... You're not supposed to know. Please, Clarke."

He gripped her hand, dragging her inside the garage. He thumbed the button to close the door. Whatever the fuck was happening didn't need to take place in the open. Well, now they were getting somewhere because her tormentor had finally stepped forward.

"Go downstairs, and I'll meet you there in a minute," he said. When she didn't respond, he turned her to face him. The color had drained from her face, and her body trembled. "You are safe, and we're going to figure this out, but I need you with me." When she acknowledged him, he smiled then kissed her on the lips. "Now, head downstairs, and I'll be there in a minute. We'll work the problem together."

When she entered the house, he put the photo on the workbench. He found a pair of gloves to wear and snapped pictures of the front and back. Then he called Trent.

Clarke barked into the phone. "We have a situation, and I need you to check for fingerprints. I'm going to review my security footage because Aimee's truck was in my driveway. I'll have a copy of that ready for you when you arrive."

Clarke could hear Trent moving around in the background. "I'll be over soon. If you get a good image, I can run it through facial recognition, unless she can positively ID."

"I'm going to text you the pictures of the photo, and I'll see you in a bit." Clarke fired off his text then locked the garage.

When he reached the control panel for his security system, he triggered the house alarm. Next, he switched the cameras and sensors to alert him if an event were captured. When it got to Aimee, she was sitting at his desk with her head in her hands. It irritated him that he couldn't solve this puzzle. Watching the woman he loved suffer was akin to a slow death. Whether she would accept his declaration didn't matter to him anymore. The simple truth was that he loved her.

"Who do you think left this for you?" he asked in low, even tone.

She lifted her head and propped it on her hands so she could look up at him. "I don't know, and none of this makes sense. I did remember something, though. A few days back, Lyndon informed me that my ex-husband's appeal was approved."

Clarke bent his head to see her entire face. He cupped her cheeks and lightly traced her cheekbones with his thumbs. "That's big news, and it's motive, Aimee. Everything that's happened makes you look guilty. I think now we understand why the money and warehouses have been discovered. The part that doesn't fit is the murders. They seem to have nothing to do with your ex."

"Okay, I don't follow. My ex is in jail. What are you saying, that he wants me to have an adjoining cell with him?"

Clarke removed his hands and nudged her to stand. When she vacated his chair, he sat, tugging her onto his knee so he could access his computer. "Revenge is what I'm thinking. That or he's trying to show he's innocent and has been wrongfully convicted. Now, we need to find out who's helping him. Let's see what we've got."

He swept his fingers across the keyboard and navigated the mouse pointer across the screen, alternating between clicking and typing. In short order, he had three cameras that were aimed at his garage, showing footage from last night until this morning on three different monitors. Minutes passed as the footage moved through the time frame he entered.

"There's the bastard—4:18 AM." He turned his focus on the other two cameras to zero in on that same image, hoping they'd get a clearer picture as the person entered his property.

"It's hard to see his face." Aimee squinted and leaned toward the monitor.

Clarke let out a frustrated sigh. "That's by design. He hid his face with a hoodie and goggles, so this guy isn't a novice. I'm going to check my perimeter cameras, but I'll bet he parked farther down on the road and walked in on foot. Do you recognize anything about him?"

"No, I don't have a lot to work with here," she muttered.

"We've got a closeup of his profile. I'm going to copy all of this and give it to Trent. I called him before I headed down so he can take the photo and run it for prints."

"There's a number on the back I need to call. He said not to let you know."

"I know," he answered as he looked at the alert sent to his phone from the driveway. He handed his phone to her. "Come on, Trent's here."

He greeted Trent at the front door and ushered him toward the kitchen. "I'll be back in a second. I left the photo on the work-bench." After grabbing the photo, Clarke reentered the house and heard Aimee's voice as he crossed the threshold to the kitchen.

"Hi, Trent. Would you like something to drink?"

"No, thanks. How are you holding up?" Trent asked, taking a seat at the table across from her.

"I wish that wasn't the primary question everyone asked me these days. I'm good, though, considering everything that's been slung my way. We saw the guy who delivered the photo, but you can't really see his face."

Trent sat back with his legs spread and his arms crossed over his chest. "I'm concerned it could get even worse before it gets better. There's one thing I know for certain—Clarke's got your back, so trust in him, no matter what else happens."

Clarke handed Trent the photo. "Okay, I've got it."

"Let's see what you've got." Trent unfolded his arms and reached into his cargo pants to retrieve a glove and evidence bag. After he had donned the gloves, he took the photo and studied it. "All right, I'll get this processed. I will also request the phone records for this number on the back."

"My money is on a burner phone," Clarke responded as he dug through a kitchen drawer until he found a notepad and pen. "Okay, Aimee, you ready to call the number? Ask open-ended questions to try to get him to talk. Go for the obvious information, and don't agree to anything."

His pulse quickened as possible scenarios stacked up in his mind, each worse than the last. The person making her life hell had finally stepped up their game. He wanted her attention. Now he had it.

The question that needed to be answered was what did they want from Aimee? Did this man work alone or have an accomplice? What was his endgame? He also planned to contact Noah himself. Clarke wanted to know every detail about her ex and whom he associated with prior to his arrest.

A IMEE GRABBED HER PHONE with trembling fingers and punched in the numbers. A knot lodged in her throat while her heart hammered against her chest. When the call connected, a rush of adrenaline surged through her body. She pressed the speaker button for the guys to hear and waited while it rang and rang. Finally, Clarke drew an imaginary line across his neck with his thumb.

She ended the call and looked up. "Why didn't he answer? Wasn't that the point?"

"Or, it was to get your number," Trent answered, his gaze locked on Clarke.

He leveled a hard stare her way. "Aimee, no matter what, do not engage with this number if I'm not with you."

Not even two full minutes after the attempted call, her phone announced she'd received a text from that number. *Can't talk at the moment—it isn't safe. I'll call back soon. He knows your identity. You aren't safe, because his reach is wide. I can help you, and I'll explain when we talk—don't trust anyone.*

"That was ominous and utterly unhelpful." She sighed and shook her head in disgust.

Trent stood. "Let me get this evidence filed and processed. I hate to bring this up, but shouldn't she report this to Lyndon?"

Clarke ran his hand over the top of his head. "Yup, we can update him after you get the information on the phone. Has he sent over the deposition?"

Trent gripped Aimee's shoulder and gave a light squeeze.. "Not yet, but I expect it anytime. I'll let you know when it arrives. Don't engage with that man without Clarke."

She nodded and sent her thanks to Trent as he left the kitchen with Clarke following him out. Not that long ago, she hadn't believed in love or happily ever after. She'd been burned. To survive, she had to learn that she couldn't depend on anyone else but herself. Now, here she sat with Clarke, trusting him with all her secrets and longing to build a future with him. She'd developed a new focus and wanted to hold on to it with both hands. Afraid that if she let go, it might just vanish.

S EVERAL HOURS LATER, AIMEE sat in the conference room of the sheriff's station with Clarke by her side. Trent had called to let them know that he'd received the deposition. She and Clarke had spent the afternoon going over possible scenarios and people who'd benefit from either her incarceration or Alex's release.

What became apparent to Aimee was Alex had kept her isolated from his business. She only knew a handful of people who'd come to the house. She hadn't even known the last name of his lawyer. He'd controlled her time and had chased off most of her friends over the years.

The torn picture was from their wedding day when they were cutting the cake. The missing half was the cake. When they'd gotten married, it had been a small ceremony. There were no bridesmaids or groomsmen, only her parents and two of his friends—his lawyer and some other guy whose name she couldn't even remember.

Alex had always said it was because they were best friends and lovers. That they only needed each other. At the time, she'd been happy, and her world had revolved around him, so those words hadn't alarmed her.

Trent opened the door and slid the document across the table. "Here's the deposition. Read every word, Aimee. While you're looking that over, I have another update. I called in a favor. The phone is a burner, and now that group is working to identify where its International Mobile Equipment Identity number purchased it."

"How long?" Clarke asked.

"A lot faster if I could've had Noah do it, but he's on the road driving his moving truck from DC to Mill Creek," Trent answered, flashing Clarke a middle finger.

Aimee scanned the document. "I think it's good, but before I sign it, will you two review it?" she asked Clarke, sliding the document his way. Afterward, he gave it to Trent, who read each page.

"Everything looks correct, so sign and date the back page. I'll scan it back now, then ship the original to Lyndon," Trent said, handing the document back to her.

"I'd like a copy too. The lawyer might find it useful," she said.

He nodded and winked at her. "Good thinking. Normally, I have the greatest assistant of all time helping me get all these details right, but she's out of the office right now."

She laughed and rolled her eyes. "Well, you should give her a raise when she comes back."

"Duly noted," he answered. He initiated the video conferencing program and dialed the number. In another few seconds, DUSM Lyndon appeared on the screen.

"Did you find an error in the document?" he asked in lieu of a greeting.

"No." Aimee held up the deposition and showed him the signature page. "Something happened earlier that you need to know. Someone left half a wedding photo on my truck with a phone number on the back. When I called the number, no one answered, but shortly afterward, he sent a text with a warning that my identity is compromised and I'm not safe."

Trent lifted a document. "Clarke and Aimee called me to pick up the evidence to process for fingerprints. I've checked into the phone, and it's a burner. My team is still working on identifying where it was purchased. Clarke's surveillance picked up the male image who left the note at 4:18 AM this morning, but he wore a hoodie and googles."

Lyndon turned in his swivel chair and rummaged through something behind him until he turned back around with a file folder in his hand. He flipped through the contents and removed a pad of paper to scribble a few notes. "Noted. As of right now, I don't have any further updates. I'm going to send a marshal to Mill Creek. I want them to look at the photo and review all the evidence and case notes."

Clarke rocked back in his chair and cleared his throat. "Why not use me, Lyndon? I'm already here. Plus, you've cleared me to watch over her for. If you bring in someone new, you might scare this person away. We can loop you in if contact is made, and the sheriff's office will back me up."

Trent nodded. "We already know the area and its residents. A new person would stand out."

"Okay, I can see the wisdom, but you don't act alone. I want to know what's happening before it does. I'll have my boss reach out to Sanchez."

Clarke cupped the back of his head. "We have some theories we'd like to discuss with you regarding the investigation." He then asked the one question that bothered him the most about the missing evidence—why wouldn't whoever had it disappear? "Why toy with Aimee after all this time and increase the risk of exposure or discovery? What was the purpose of killing Jenkins? That makes zero sense because what would Aimee gain? The other problem is I know she didn't have a gun or raincoat in the truck. Where did she pick one up? Where would she have stashed the raincoat and gun? So, that leaves an accomplice. Have you pulled Aimee's phone records to see if she's been talking to anyone outside of her circle of friends?

"Lastly, have you calculated the time between the park and the condo to see if she could've made it back and forth on foot? Would she have had to take a taxi or ride share? Have you checked the driver's route logs for any pickups and drop-offs around those two addresses? Most vehicles have cameras these days. Since Aimee isn't a sociopath, nothing about any of it fits together."

Lyndon stretched his neck from side to side and sighed. "I have a marshal who's dead. As you know, Dragoon, that makes people itchy to find the culprit and lock them up. When the gathered evidence seems air-tight and emotions are running high, it's hard to challenge their view to see past the minutiae and compare it to the bigger picture. I can share that walking between the two would not have been possible. I'm still digging into the taxi and ride-sharing options."

"I do understand, and I appreciate that you're working outside of the evidence box," Clarke added, then pressed his lips into a tight line.

"I should be getting ballistics back anytime now, and what that produces will dictate our next move. There's also a resident who lives next door to Jenkins. He's been on a wilderness unplugged retreat. According to his family, he should be back tonight. I'm hoping he might shed some light on anyone who might've been visiting or if Jenkins seemed off lately."

"Do you think there's a chance you have a mole within your team?" Clarke asked.

"When I know more, I'll contact you."

Aimee watched the screen go black and turned toward the two men. "Does he not know the phrases 'hello' or 'goodbye?'"

Male chuckles followed briefly before Trent turned his gaze to Clarke, who shared a knowing look between them. She hated that secret language. "Okay, what aren't you two telling me?"

"That Lyndon is hard to read," Clarke answered. "He's keeping his cards close to his chest with the exception of the few tidbits he gave us. The other is that he told us, without using the words, that he's getting pressure to wrap up the investigation quickly. That means going against the evidence to look at other possible suspects is not going to be widely supported."

"Great, I guess that means I'm the sacrificial lamb," she surmised. "I guess if I were in their shoes, I'd think I was guilty too."

"Okay, I need to head home to Maggie. She's cooking dinner tonight." Trent's sardonic smile made her giggle. "Call me if that guy contacts you, no matter the time. He just might be our key to figuring all of this out."

Sixteen

THE NEXT DAY PROGRESSED at a snail's pace as Clarke waited for something to happen. He'd taken Aimee to lunch at PB&S Café to break up the monotony of waiting. Now, it was three PM, and the jerk from the photo still hadn't called. Neither had Lyndon with the additional information he'd promised to provide.

When Clarke had taken Aimee to lunch at PB&S Café to give them both a change of scenery, it had also offered him an opportunity to pick up the locket he'd commissioned for her. Luckily, she readily agreed to stay in the truck because she didn't feel like being social. That statement tugged at his heart. Afterward, they'd stopped at the market to pick up supplies, and he'd insisted she accompany him. The main reason was that this stop would take longer, and he wanted to ensure her safety, but the other was to get her out and about.

The clatter of pots and pans drifted to his office. She loved to cook and had wanted to make them dinner. Having home-cooked meals most nights reminded him of his mother. Meals had been the nucleus of his family, and he had so many good memories of eating together. Having Aimee in his home felt natural and warmed his heart, and damn if he didn't want to hear the thunder of feet from their children as they played. He planned to give her the locket tonight.

A rush of future hopes rotated across his brain like a viewfinder—weddings, births, Christmas, Easter, etc. God, if she didn't come around, he might have to go back out on long-term assignments because this house would never be the same. It would always remind him of Aimee. Life could be wild and unpredictable; two months ago, he'd been satisfied to be a bachelor for the remainder of his life. Now that thought depressed him.

He flipped his wrist again to check the time. Only forty-three minutes had passed. He busied himself with completing his report on Aimee since she'd been placed in his custody. He'd decided to document his conclusions and theories based on her movements in conjunction with the evidence presented by Lyndon. Having another objective marshal to provide insights and challenges on this investigation couldn't hurt. He'd just started the closing paragraph when his cell rang. After glancing at his screen, his gut clenched with what would come next when he saw the name displayed.

"Dragoon," he answered. "Did ballistics come back?"

He heard Lyndon shuffling paperwork on the other end of the line. "More, and it's not good news for Ms. Lang."

Clarke grabbed a pad of paper and pen to take notes. Tingles inched down his spine. "Okay, I'll get Aimee."

"No, I need to cover this with you first," Lyndon said. "I received the outstanding ballistics reports for the warehouse and Jenkins's murder. I'll start with the warehouse. The gun retrieved was linked to the murder of Sara's father, Brian Brickley. It's a perfect match to the casings and bullets recovered from his crime scene and body. That gun is registered to Alex Chubb, but the prints pulled from the weapon matched Sara Chubb's fingerprints from when she was booked. I had to request access to those files because they're stored on a secure server due to her WITSEC status."

Clarke dropped the pen and rested his head between his hands. Every word Lyndon spoke was like a punch to his gut. The sheer volume of evidence stunned him.

"Moving to the gun recovered from Jenkins's home. It, too, came back as a perfect match to the bullets and casings recovered from the scene and body. Fingerprints were matched to Sara Chubb, a.k.a Aimee Lang. The team also matched this weapon to multiple crime scenes located in Mill Creek."

"Are you bullshitting me?" Clarke asked.

Could it be possible that he'd misread her this whole time because he'd allowed his heart to overrule logic? Her alibi for those two murders was not rock solid. Shock waves pounded his gut until one thought emerged. She hated guns, and her reaction to them had been raw and honest. His reaction was as unwanted as it was ridiculous; there was no way Aimee was guilty. He'd stake his career on it.

"Death is not a matter I joke about," Lyndon said in a tone that grated his nerves.

Clarke wanted to punch the bastard. "Is that it?"

"No, the other items were in relation to the documents recovered from the warehouse. My forensics team validated that the bulk of drugs recovered was recently purchased using funds from a bank in Switzerland. It matched to one of the four accounts she gave me the other day. Those drugs were set to sail on a cargo vessel—according to the bill of lading—last Friday to Stuttgart, Germany. The drugs were packaged under bags of coffee beans. The team also recovered fake identification and travel documents that were packaged in an overnight carrier envelope set to be mailed today. A plane had been chartered in Boise, Idaho, to pick up a solo passenger, Mindy Redding a.k.a Aimee Lang, to fly to Belize."

Clarke didn't say what he was thinking, which was, *holy fucking shit, that's a crap-ton of evidence.* Instead, he decided to state what bothered him the most. "That's a tidy case, every loose end coming together so perfectly to frame Aimee. You must admit that all of this seems over the top and too good to be true."

"Our jobs are to follow leads, collect the evidence, and process it. I don't control the story that the facts prove," Lyndon countered.

Clarke gripped the back of his neck and closed his eyes in frustration. "No, but we can control the narrative until we've exhausted every reasonable and logical option, witness, and data point. Again, I have to ask, why would she put herself at risk now instead of just disappearing?"

"You understand the expectation and pressure surrounding a team member's murder, and the evidence concludes that Aimee is linked to it," Lyndon said.

The unspoken words from Lyndon came through louder than the ones he'd uttered. "So, what are you not telling me?"

Lyndon cleared his throat. "She did not take a taxi or ride share the day of the murder. Also, that burner phone was purchased at the drugstore across the street from Jenkins's condominium. Last night, I spoke to the neighbor who's been on vacation. He mentioned that our marshal had a male over numerous times over the last six months but really couldn't describe him because he always wore ball caps, kept his head down, and often walked hunched or curled into himself. The neighbor said, and I quote, 'When I look back, his behavior did seem suspicious.'"

"What's next?" Clarke asked as he jotted a few notes from this conversation. Deep down, he already knew the answer.

"I've issued a warrant for Aimee Lang's arrest based on the evidence collected to date, and her false identification makes her a flight risk. I have no way of knowing if she's procured additional identities or has withdrawn or stashed away money. I've also frozen all her accounts. Since she's in your custody, I'll need you to bring her to the sheriff's station. I've already emailed the arrest warrant to Sheriff Jacobs and copied you. I plan to arrive in Mill Creek by seven to transfer her into my custody and process her in Boise."

"She has a lawyer, and I'll inform him what's happening," Clarke said.

"That's smart. I'll see you two soon," Lyndon replied before he terminated the call.

Clarke slammed down his phone, then immediately snatched it back up and pressed Trent's number, pleased when he answered quickly.

"I just opened the email from Lyndon and was just about to call you. Does she know yet?" Trent asked.

"No, Lyndon called me first. Did you hear back from Kane regarding lawyers? We need one pronto. He plans to be here tonight to escort her back to Boise for processing."

"I'm texting him now. What else did Lyndon say?"

Clarke spent the next several minutes updating the sheriff on all the evidence that had been shared, which included the marshal's doublespeak. Aimee would be distraught when he told her. He made a mental note to grab his go-bag because he planned to stay by her side the entire time. If he had any say, she would not endure this nightmare alone like she had the first time. He'd also pay for her legal expenses. Together, they'd clear her name.

"Wow, just wow. I don't even know what to say; it's overwhelming," Trent muttered. "Hey, Kane just responded. Larry Behr will be her lawyer. Kane's ordered the company jet and hopes to depart as soon as possible. In the meantime, tell Aimee to avoid answering any questions. Inform Lyndon that her lawyer will arrive later tonight."

Clarke glanced at his phone, realizing he'd missed an alert while he'd been speaking with Lyndon. He went to work on his computer to bring up his camera feeds to scan his property before heading upstairs. "Okay, text me Mr. Behr's contact information and let him know that all costs are to be routed through me. Give me about an hour to meet you at the station." He paused then growled, "Holy shit...get here now, we have a problem. That man's made contact."

AIMEE HAD CARVED UP the tri-tip into small chunks and had the meat in the pan with the onion and garlic. She adored Hungarian goulash and hoped Clarke would too. This had been one of her mother's favorite dishes, which she'd learned from her grandmother. She discarded the leftover meat scraps and fat into the overflowing trash can. Music didn't fit her mood today; the melancholy that surrounded her had gotten worse as the day progressed. She grabbed the remaining ingredients, adding them to the pan, that needed to simmer for a few hours.

The dough was the next step in her preparations so it would have time to proof and rise. The dinner rolls melted in your mouth and were one of her mom's favorite recipes. As she kneaded the sticky ball, her father's words weighed on her mind. *"Don't let this define you. Make something out of your life—no matter what, don't look back."*

She cringed at how she'd behaved toward Clarke's admission of wanting her forever. Fear was a horrible way to live a life. Maybe they could be together even with her in WITSEC. It wasn't like he didn't know what he'd be getting into, and he still wanted her. How often in life did you find a man who was honorable, compassionate, and so damn sexy?

She didn't owe him an apology—she owed him the truth about how he made her feel. Why was she afraid to work toward the future with him? If he could accept all her baggage, it was time to stop looking in the rearview mirror and take a risk. It wasn't like she'd set out to find this perfect man—he had fallen into her lap. Tonight, she'd put it all on the line and see if they still had a chance to move forward together.

She extracted a white trash bag from the box in the pantry and snapped it open. When she removed the filled bag from the can, she tied the strings into a knot and carried it outside. Two big plastic bins for trash and recycling sat on the side of the house by the garage. After she had heaved the heavy bag into the bin and closed the lid, a man's voice caused her to jump. Her heart seized in her throat as she clutched her chest.

"You startled me, can I help you?" she croaked out, looking at a lanky man with freckles and reddish-brown hair who stood between her and the house. A sense of déjà vu seared her brain.

"Don't you remember me?" he asked condescendingly. Darkness crossed his eyes, turning the bluish color to midnight. He reached inside his parka and removed the other half of the photo, presenting it to her.

A shiver worked down her spine. "Who are you, and what do you want?" She glanced to the right, cursing herself for closing the kitchen door. She sucked in a deep, calming breath as she remembered what Clarke had told her about his security. Slowly, she turned, taking a few steps toward the garage with him right on her heels. His fingers dug into the flesh on her arm, halting her next step. She hoped she'd gotten close enough to capture whatever was about to happen on that camera.

He frowned at her. "We have much to discuss, and I don't have a lot of time. I've risked everything to warn you, but you must accompany me. Right now. Trust me, it'll be easier if you do."

"Who are you? I'm not just leaving with you. If you need to tell me something, talk."

"I'm one of Alex's closest friends, Richard Parker. I was there that day you married him alongside our other friend—"

"Dean Walter, his lawyer," she finished. She'd finally remembered his name. "I remember you now, but I've never seen you since. Why weren't you around if you and Alex were so close? I mean, no disrespect, but he's never spoken about you." As soon as that statement popped out of her mouth, she winced. Maybe antagonizing this man wasn't the smartest plan.

"That was by design for the business. I remained in the background and managed the safety nets, one might say. Then, Alex met you, and his infatuation with you made him lose focus. You, Sara Brickley-Chubb, became his biggest mistake, putting all three of us at risk."

She bristled. "How long have you known him?"

"Alex may not be my blood brother, but he's my brother in every other way. He's rotting in a jail cell because he was wrongly accused of crimes you committed. You must pay for those sins."

The hard press of metal jammed against her side. "Just remember, I tried to do this without forcing you. Let's go. You're coming with me."

Her stomach heaved with revulsion. "You're not making any sense. I don't know what you're talking about. I haven't done anything except marry a man who manipulated me."

His mouth twisted into an evil smile. "Do you remember the day your dear old dad died? That was the day Alex had you pick up four different guns from a silver platter and aim them at a man's head. To up the ante, he told you if you didn't cooperate, he'd give the command to have one of his goons kill your father. Then, after you obeyed, you panicked and ran—unknowingly toward the authorities—which sealed his fate. Any of this ring a bell?"

Hot tears streamed down her cheeks. "You bastard, my father was innocent."

"No, he was a witness and loose end. Those guns were necessary insurance to help free Alex down the road when Dean filed his appeal. Just like your hairbrush, which gave us fibers to spread, linking you to all different people and places. That night, after you ran, they saw the red and blue lights, so Dean gathered up the items in his briefcase and escaped out the back of the house before officers established a perimeter. Come on, let's go."

Richard forced her forward and had her walking down the driveway toward a vehicle parked behind several bushes by Irene's house. He opened the driver's side door and had her slide across then sat behind the wheel.

After starting the car, he steered with one hand and held the gun on her with the other.

Blood pounded in her ears. "You killed those men at the campsite, didn't you?"

His pompous smile and gleeful attitude made her stomach lurch. "That night, you fled, caught me off guard, but the contingency plans I enacted enabled me to move four hundred million dollars before the government seized those assets. I also redirected a rather large drug supply, so we didn't lose that product or the revenue. I've been running the business in Alex's temporary absence. Being out of sight and mind all those years gave me an edge."

This was her life, and she could either sit back and let it happen, or she could control some of the outcome. She lunged for his gun, pushing on the muzzle. The car swerved and skidded off the dirt road and into a ditch as she wrestled with the lanky man who had surprising strength to keep the end of his gun pointed away from her. He squeezed the trigger and blew out the side window. Her ears rang from the deafening blast.

Headlights approached the vehicle. "This is Sheriff Jacobs. Exit the vehicle with your hands up."

Aimee shouted, "Trent, Richard has a gun!"

They continued to struggle until Richard tore the gun from her grasp. In the next second, he had his arm around her throat, dragging her toward the door. Once they exited the vehicle, he held her arm and pressed the gun to her temple with his other hand and addressed the sheriff. "You will back away, or I'll kill her. This was not supposed to happen. Get back in your vehicle. Drive away right now. Alex needs me to deliver her so he can be released."

"Okay, Richard. If I drop my gun, will you lower yours so we can talk? You can tell me your terms, so I know what you need."

"Agreed," Richard answered.

A million thoughts should've been racing through her mind, but only one hurt her stomach. She would never get the chance to tell Clarke she loved him.

Seventeen

C LARKE QUICKLY CHECKED EACH camera and sensor on his property to see if the man had come alone. When his phone rang again, for the third time in a row, he snatched it off his desk. "This better be important."

"Clarke, it's Noah. I'll make this quick. After we spoke last, I did a little unauthorized digging into her husband. He was in foster care and in that documentation, there was one boy who he had been closest to. I've pulled his name, photo, and latest information on him and sent it to your phone. The interesting part, that man, Richard Parker, was in Mill Creek and Boise. I matched his photo to several traffic camera images around the date of those murders. I'm sure there is more, but I wanted you to know this information."

When Clarke retrieved the last feed on his monitor, his heart stuttered inside his chest. It showed that same man leading Aimee away from his home. Clarke's world went dark. He disconnected the call with Noah and glanced at the photo Noah sent him. Clarke's training kicked in as he snapped to action.

He inserted his ear buds and called Trent. "Aimee is in the car with a man heading toward town," he said, his voice tight with tension.

"I've got them. They just skidded off the road about three hundred feet from your house," Trent reported.

"I'm heading that way now. I'll be on foot," Clarke said. "Keep this line open. I think he's the man behind the murders in Mill Creek and possibly Deputy Jenkins. Noah can put him in the area. He knew her husband from foster care."

Sweeping up his gun from the desk, he palmed the weapon then sprinted up the stairs. He rushed through the kitchen and out the door. Carefully, he eased it open and crept down the steps until he was sure he was alone. The thought of losing Aimee lodged his heart in his throat. He bolted down his driveway and cut through his property toward their location. He knew the exact spot.

Clarke heard everything as he spoke to Trent on the open line racing toward the scene. "Rattle his nerves, tell him what we've uncovered and that we can place him at the scene of two murders. His name is Richard."

"Richard, we know you and Alex Chubb are friends. In fact, we have traffic camera footage of you in both Mill Creek and Boise around the time of some recent murders. I would advise that you surrender your weapon and release Ms. Lang. We need to talk." Trent's voice echoed through Clarke's ear buds. Trent was probably speaking through a bullhorn so he could be heard.

Clarke heard Aimee yelling something but not exactly what she said. "Can you repeat that, Trent? I'm just about twenty yards out."

Trent echoed Aimee's question then said, "I think she may be right. Did you kill those men and Deputy Jenkins?"

Clarke's heart seemed to stop for a moment. Now that he was close enough, he could see and hear the scene unfolding.

"Shut up, bitch," Richard spat.

"Oh, I guess, we were wrong, Aimee, this man isn't smart enough," Trent said.

Richard laughed. "Please, my sheer genius is how I tracked her. I hired the best firm who specializes in security and sensitive investigations to track Sara Chubb's movements while she was in protective custody. They studied the patterns, people, routes, and US Marshals involved with her protection before, during, and after the trial. As you can imagine, this type of surveillance has an extremely high-dollar value attached to it. The outcome was well worth the investment. This firm found Alice Jenkins, who was lonely and grief-stricken. Over time, I earned her trust, and I got my break the day that man torched your home when she called to report that event to Lyndon. I took a drive to that town and found you."

Trent hollered his next question, "So, all of this was to frame Aimee so Alex would be exonerated during his appeal? It's kind of over the top, isn't it?"

Richard tugged Aimee closer. "I may have gotten a little carried away. I didn't realize I'd have so much fun staging crime scenes."

"Richard, let Aimee go, you're under arrest––"

"No," he raged. "You will not save the lady or ruin my plans."

Clarke inched closer, staying in the tree line along the side of the road, making sure to stay in the shadows. "I'm at the edge of the trees, about five yards out," he whispered to Trent.

Trent changed tactics, stating that he'd drop his gun if Richard would lower his so they could talk. This was Clarke's opportunity. Adjusting his footing, he moved forward a few paces until he found the perfect spot that gave him a direct line of sight to his target without placing Trent or Aimee in danger.

Clarke forced a deep breath into his system. Then, he exhaled through his nose in measured release to center his body and mind to take the shot. The opportunity would pass as quickly as it came so he had to be ready.

The moment Richard lowered his weapon to address Trent, Clarke fired his gun. The bullet went straight through the back of Richard's head. He dropped a second later.

Clarke rushed toward Aimee, dying to pull her into his arms, but first, he had to secure the scene with Trent.

"I'm so sorry. I-I brought all this to your door," Aimee said, her tone frantic. "I love you, Clarke. I should've told you that long before now."

"Don't move or touch your face. We need to process the scene. And, sweetheart, I love you too."

Everything had to be done by the book. He donned a pair of gloves and grabbed an evidence bag for his weapon. He disengaged the magazine and emptied the chamber, depositing the bullets into a smaller bag, then placed it inside the larger bag with his weapon. Trent ran the yellow tape and took numerous pictures. While they waited for forensics to arrive, he interviewed Aimee. He had his radio still broadcasting over the wire so the entire scene had been recorded.

She shared everything she'd learned and how Richard had worked to set her up. Now they needed to find that lawyer and bring him in for questioning. When she finished with forensics, they'd taken all her clothing and had given her a white forensics suit to wear with a blanket.

"I'll load the video of him entering my property then escorting her off at gunpoint onto a USB drive," Clarke said.

"You two are cleared to head home. I'll meet you there in a bit," Trent said.

When they reached the house, Aimee headed to the bathroom to shower and change clothes. Her face was as white as a ghost, even with the specks of blood still dotting her skin.

"Take as long as you need. I'll be in the kitchen if you need me," Clarke said in a soft voice. As he walked to the kitchen, he heard Trent knocking on the door, announcing his presence. He let him into his house. "I just got Aimee into the shower. Give me a second to copy that file."

Trent nodded. "No problem. I'll wait here. Hey, does she know about the warrant?"

"Not yet. That's the next bomb I get to drop," Clarke answered.

When he returned to the kitchen, Trent had set up a computer on the table. Clarke flipped the drive to Trent and in a few seconds, the video began to play. It showed Richard coming up the side of the house and scaring Aimee when she took out the trash. It captured their exchange of word and that he forced her to go with him at gunpoint toward Irene's property, where Richard had parked his car.

Clarke pointed at the video. "Did you find the other half of that photo on Richard?"

Trent shook his head. "Give me a second to call Lance. I'll have him inform forensics that we're looking for half a picture either on him or in the car. Do you want to call Lyndon now or after you explain the arrest warrant?"

"What arrest warrant?" a small, feminine voice asked.

Clarke turned to see his Aimee walk into the kitchen. Her cheeks were rosy from a long shower and probably because she'd scrubbed her face one too many times. He slid a chair out for her at the table. She'd change into a pair of yoga pants and an oversized sweatshirt that had a wet spot on the back from her ponytail.

"I'm sorry about that mess, but I had a clear shot, and I wasn't sure I'd get another one," Clarke explained, trailing a finger down her cheek.

She lifted her head to look at him and put on a brave smile. "I wash, so it worked out okay. I'd like this to be my last foray into guns and death."

Trent stood and winked. "You did good tonight. It's over now. I'm going to step outside and let you two talk. Clarke, I'll call Lyndon and update him."

"So, I guess you're going to have to arrest me now?" she whispered.

"Nope, we'll wait to see what DUSM officially says, but from what I saw and more importantly what Richard admitted, I know you're going to be cleared. There will be loose ends to wrap up."

"I can't believe everything Richard did to frame me with hopes of getting Alex released from jail. Everyone who lost their lives because of me..."

At least he didn't have to explain all the new evidence that had allowed Lyndon to obtain the arrest warrant. Richard had already provided that detail plus more. "Hey, you didn't pull the trigger or plan this scheme. The men responsible for all those crimes are Richard, Dean, and Alex. Again, you were a victim and innocent."

An hour later, Lyndon arrived to meet with Trent, Clarke, and Aimee. Lyndon watched the video and listened to Aimee's debrief. Afterward, Lyndon walked around the scene and spoke to various individuals before returning to Clarke's house and escorting Aimee to the family room. Clarke knew it was procedure, but he hated being separated from her.

Trent came back inside and headed toward Clarke. "The medical examiner just found the other half of that picture in Richard's pocket. Where's Aimee?"

"She talking to Lyndon in the other room."

After several long minutes, Lyndon came into the kitchen and asked Clarke and Trent to join him and Aimee. She sat on the sofa so Clarke and Trent sat on either side of her while Lyndon paced.

"I've had Alex Chubb and Richard Parker's lawyer, Dean Walter, arrested and brought to the station for questioning. It'll help to have him corroborate what Richard told Aimee. I'm confident we can help him see that cooperating will be in his best interest. Based on the video and the events that unfolded tonight, the arrest warrant has been voided. She's still part of WITSEC, but my concern is your ex-husband and his lawyer know where to find you. I would recommend that we move you to a new town, but we can talk about that tomorrow. I'll be heading back to Boise to get started."

Clarke got to his feet and tugged Aimee with him. He extended his hand to his coworker. "Thanks, Lyndon. We'll talk tomorrow."

Trent shook hands with the marshal and provided his thanks. He escorted the Lyndon out of Clarke's house and hollered over his shoulder that he'd call him tomorrow.

Finally, his house was empty. He jerked Aimee into his arms and crushed his mouth to hers. He needed a quick taste of the woman he loved. Their tongues dueled in a passionate kiss before he broke it off to tell her. "I love you. Please don't scare me like that again, ever."

"Love you too, but what happens if I have to leave because I've been compromised? Or I could be taken to a safe house for a long period of time until Alex's trial is over. That's not a life for you. It's not fair."

"That's part of your package, which I accept. We'll handle it together. If I have to pack up and move with you, I will. I'm not convinced that'll happen, but we'll learn more in a few days." Clarke pressed a kiss to her forehead.

Damn, that woman had him wrapped around her finger. Now he didn't want to know a world where Aimee wasn't a part of it. He had a plan and soon he'd unveil his surprise.

A FEW DAYS LATER, rays of sunlight filtered through the windows as Aimee lay in bed. She ran her hand over the spot that Clarke's head occupied not long ago. A pink satin bag sat on a sheet of paper on his pillow. She plucked the pouch and note and clutched them to her chest.

A relief she couldn't describe lightened her mood because this nightmare had finally ended. Dean had corroborated Richard's account and had even provided evidence in exchange for leniency. Alex's appeal had been denied due to the new evidence Lyndon had uncovered, and she'd been cleared.

The best part was it didn't appear anyone in Alex's organization outside of Dean and Richard were involved. So, she and Clarke had discussed that it made more sense for her to stay in Mill Creek, surrounded by the people who knew and cared about her. When they'd shared their plan and reasoning with Lyndon, he'd agreed. If something happened, they would address it down the road.

She unfolded the note first and read his message. *Good morning, sweetheart. I have a surprise for you. When you're ready, meet me at Tale Peak. Text me when you leave. - Clarke*

She opened the pretty sack and pulled the beautiful rose-gold heart locket free. When she unfastened the heart locket, the left side held a picture of her family, and the other side was empty. Etched on the back was the inscription *Always dance...*

Tears escaped her eyes at this beautiful and touching gift. He'd given her a way to keep her parents close to her heart. This gift couldn't have been more perfect or thoughtful.

She shot out of bed and jumped into the shower. She couldn't wait to hug and thank him for this precious gift. In short order, she'd finished getting ready, and about forty-minutes later, she sat behind the wheel of her truck.

She fired off a quick text and backed out of the garage. The skies were a gorgeous blue with no clouds. The temperatures had dropped, so she'd grabbed her coat before she'd left. She loved surprises and couldn't wait to see what he had in store.

When she reached Tale Peak, she parked her truck. Clarke opened her door and lifted her out of her seat. His kiss melted her insides. He tasted of mint and coffee, and she wanted more.

When her feet touched the ground, she showed him the necklace. "Thank you for this. I love it. I don't even know what to say—it's perfect."

He lifted her chin with one finger so she could see his eyes. "The other side is for a photo of us."

"Oh, I like that idea, but are you sure? I don't want you to stop doing something you love. And my past is a little checkered."

"You make me happy, and I could give a rat's ass about anyone's opinion except yours. You could feel the same way about me. I've killed my share of people, including a pregnant woman, but you still want me. So, it seems we're a good fit. We have each other, and that's all that matters to me. I've already told you I'm ready for a change with my job. You just helped me to see it."

"Then I say let's do this, because you make me want a future."

"Now you're speaking my language," he replied.

His large hand grabbed hers and entangled their fingers before he tugged her over the ridge and down to a small landing where he had set up a campfire and tent.

She shrieked with excitement. "We're going to camp?"

"We're going to spend the entire day and night here with no one around. Just the two of us and time to do whatever we want," he declared. "Then, we'll have wine, cheese, meats, and crackers for lunch. When you're ready for dinner, I will cook two steaks on an open fire, toast a few s'mores, and we'll enjoy the stars."

She couldn't believe everything he'd done for her. This man had wooed her while fulfilling all her dreams. She wasn't sure why he'd picked her, but she was done worrying about it. He knew her past and hadn't run away from her.

She stopped and looked up at him. "Where's the 'naked, hot, and sweaty' part of this plan?"

His deep laugh filled her heart with warmth. "Oh, sweetheart, I plan to keep you warm and sated for the next five hundred years, starting tonight."

When he dropped to one knee, her heart almost burst out of her chest. He took her hand, rubbing his thumb across her knuckles. Tears leaked down her cheeks for an entirely different reason. The first time this had happened to her, she'd thought she was happy.

The difference today was being with Clarke felt like an electric current surging through her body. He'd mended the hole in her heart, and she knew without a shadow of a doubt he was her soul mate. She couldn't wait to see their story unfold, and just maybe, she might get the family she'd always wanted.

"Aimee, you can be stubborn, but I knew from the first day I laid eyes on you that I wanted you. Then, every day after, you showed me pieces of your heart, which made me fall in love with you."

He removed a box from his pocket and opened the lid. A beautiful, big solitaire diamond winked back at her. He pulled it from the velvet cushion and took her hand so he could slid it on her finger.

"You, Sara Brickley, a.k.a Aimee Lang, are the only woman on this planet who can handle my charm, wit, and bedroom antics. I also happen to love you with all my heart. Please put me out of my misery and agree to marry me?"

Their life together would never be dull, that was for sure. "Mr. Dragoon, I would be happy to be your wife, the mother of your children, the queen of the house...oh, and I almost forgot, the best backgammon player ever."

He stood and tugged her into his arms, lifting her high against his body. She countered by wrapping her legs around his waist and planted a kiss on his lips.

He walked her toward the tent. "I agree, but I think we should practice right now on the proper techniques for creating children."

She laughed and shook her head at this silly, caring, and amazing man she loved.

Dear Reader:

Thank you for reading *Hidden Identities*.

Are you ready for Noah and Jasmine's story? Let the saga continue in *Breaking Point*.

Turn the page for a sneak peek.

XO-Bailey

Enjoy this sneak peek of

BREAKING POINT

Book 3 in the Mill Creek Mystique romantic suspense series

One

J ASMINE WEST FLIPPED THROUGH her interview notes for the umpteenth time at the small desk in her London, England, hotel. The anonymous email she'd received a few weeks ago intrigued her. She'd never seen anything so cryptic. Her source had mentioned that they were a friend of the prominent Dubin family and wanted the truth to come out. That alone made this adventure exciting because she didn't know where it would end up. She'd even titled her article *"Senator Thomas Dubin and Secrets of the Mangled Family Tree."* A burst of giddiness flooded her system due to all the potential story outcomes.

She'd spent the first part of this week in Washington, DC, interviewing some of the senator's past and present colleagues and his late wife's best friend. Her source had suggested she meet the woman, which turned out to be rather informative.

The senator and his wife seemed to have a turbulent marriage, and her trouble with conceiving hadn't helped matters. His wife had been adored by everyone, but no one would talk to Jasmine about the events surrounding her death.

After Washington, Jasmine had hopped a flight from Dulles International Airport to Heathrow to investigate the small town of Holmberry Hill. There were definite concerns of infidelity and a cover-up. This town seemed to be the link.

She finger-combed her hair, now dry enough to sweep up into a messy bun, as she looked out her window at the big red double-decker buses passing. The streets were filled with people dressed for work and play on this early Friday morning.

She tapped her pen against her forehead as she thought. This anonymous source mentioned that Jasmine's photography, her primary source of income, which allowed her the freedom to travel and research, had caught their eye. They'd learned about her journalistic endeavors from her website.

A part of her wanted this exposé to be the story of a lifetime—Pulitzer-Prize worthy. That would irritate her dad because he couldn't downplay that honor. Oh, she knew she'd already succeeded with her photography, but her father would never give her credit for those accomplishments. All Dad saw was that she wasn't married and had strayed from his plan for her life. It was the same for all his daughters—who lived close to him and Mom and raised their grandchildren.

She liked adventure, traveling, and, most importantly, choosing what to work on because it intrigued and excited her. She sipped her coffee, hoping to wipe the fog from her brain. At least she'd gotten a good five hours of sleep, but hopping into another time zone had zapped her energy.

Thirty minutes later, she packed up the last of her belongings and headed toward the car she'd hired to take her to Holmberry Hill. She planned to stay the night at the local bed and breakfast before returning to the States the following day.

When she approached the man waiting at the curb alongside his vehicle, she confirmed his name, then slid across the back seat while he stowed her luggage in the trunk. The steering wheel on the opposite side of the car made her smile. It was those differences that made her adventures memorable.

The overcast day matched her mood. The wipers screeched across the windshield as the car merged into traffic. The driver caught her gaze in the rearview mirror. "Miss West, shall I drive straight to Holmberry, or do you have additional stops along the way?"

"No, please head straight to St. Paul's Church."

She planned to take pictures of the private hospital that closed a little over a year ago, as it was down the road from the church. When that institution closed, various documents, including adoption records, were sent to the church for safekeeping.

Her source had noted that the senator had made several visits to the area. Could the truth be that easy to uncover? Something told her no, but her curiosity had been piqued. The drive into the countryside was beautiful, and the history of the place left her speechless. The brick homes with multiple fireplaces surrounded by lush greenery were truly picturesque. They looked like a Thomas Kinkade painting.

Two hours later, they arrived at Holmberry. The chauffeur drove up the cobblestone drive toward the top of the hill, where the episcopal church stood, peering down over the small town.

Jasmine tapped the driver's shoulder. "Pull over here, please. I want to take some hospital pictures."

She lowered her window and used her phone, deciding to leave her camera in her backpack for now. Once her window closed, the car ambled forward toward the circular drive of the church.

A vehicle was parked in front of the entrance, so her driver opted for the other side to leave the doorway clear. The rental car barcode sticker on the back window of the other car caught her eye. She'd noticed similar ones on cars she'd rented in the past as she bent to grab her backpack from behind the driver's seat.

When she sat up, a large, brawny man exited the church when she sat up. He stopped to survey the area momentarily before descending the steps to head to his vehicle. She had a fleeting thought that he seemed out of place. Nothing gave her a foundation for that revelation other than an instinct shouting at her.

"Please wait here. I won't be long," she said, halting the driver's exit to open her door.

The structure of the old church and its stained-glass windows charmed her. She could only imagine how many events had happened right here over the years. When she glanced to the right, she saw the town nestled below. It created a picturesque view that had a place on postcards, she imagined.

The concrete steps were steep, but when she opened the door to enter the structure, she couldn't help but smile. The exposed wooden beams, ornate carvings, and statues dominated the space, but the decorative windows softened the room with different hues of color. It was breathtaking.

"Welcome to St. Paul; how may I help you?" asked an elderly lady with a duster.

"Hi, I'm Jasmine. I'm looking for Father Duncan."

The woman nodded and guided Jasmine toward a door on the opposite side of the church. Their footsteps echoed as they walked farther into the empty space.

"It must've been hard on the town when the hospital closed," Jasmine said as her gaze took in the church's beauty.

The woman slowed and turned back to address her question. "The residents use the medical facilities in the next town over. The hospital was private and catered to people from around the world who had the means to take care of delicate matters."

That comment swirled around in Jasmine's thoughts, intriguing her with all the situations that the hospital must have handled. Then, one particular question snapped to the forefront. "Do you get many visitors here and for the hospital?"

The woman stopped so she could face her. "No, not really. I wouldn't call this area a big tourist spot. Our busiest days are Wednesday and Sunday." Then she continued her way down the hallway. When they reached the closed door, she cracked it open briefly to converse with someone on the inside before swinging it wide.

Father Duncan stood and extended his hand. "Hello, how many I help you?"

She couldn't help but notice how soft and smooth his hand was. "Hi, I'm here for a birth certificate and an adoption record. I'm hoping you can help me. The father's name is Thomas Dubin."

Father Duncan folded his arms in front of him. "Please, have a seat. I'll go check. I can't remember the last time we had two people on the same day searching for records."

That admission had her sitting up straighter. The image of the man leaving the church flashed again in her head. Never one to ignore her gut, she glanced down at his desk and scanned the surface. There was a basket on the corner of the desk with a file folder and a log of some sort on top. Only a matter of minutes extended between that guy's visit and hers, so that log interested her.

Twisting her head left and then right to ensure she was alone, she removed her phone from an exterior pocket on her bag. Her heart hammered against her chest as she aimed the device at the document. She snapped two pictures, then shoved the phone back into the backpack as she heard the father coming back down the hallway.

"I'm sorry," he said as he reentered the room. "I don't have any records with that name listed. If you have the birth mother's name or the child or adoptive parents' information, I could look again."

"I don't, but could I contact you by telephone?"

"That would be fine," the man said and found a pen. "Here's the number. Can I have your last name for my tracker, Jasmine?

"Yes, it's West. Thank you. I really appreciate your help."

She smiled and exited the office, hurrying toward the car. An insane thought drove her next action, but every fiber of her being told her to do it. This was what made a story. Having the courage to chase the unknown, even if it might be the stupidest idea. That very idea was why she found herself at odds with her parents, especially her father.

He'd prefer she was married and raising her children like her sisters. Instead, she followed the man who'd exited the church right after she arrived. If luck were on her side, and the fact she'd only been inside for a short time, the one-lane country road would slow him so they could catch up to him. It was a long shot but worth the try.

She slid into the back seat. "Remember that car that left right after we arrived?"

The driver turned around to look at her and nodded, his expression guarded.

"Good. I need you to find that car and follow it. I'll pay you double the rate agreed upon, but in cash. And if we do, don't let the man know we're following him."

The driver uttered his confirmation before he returned his focus to the road. He must have understood the urgency because they arrived back to town in half the time. They might not find the vehicle, or this might not lead to anything, but sometimes there was only a fine line between luck, gumption, and hunches.

The driver made a left on the main street that bisected the town and found the car leaving the bed and breakfast where she was going to stay. Her driver followed the car, and it wasn't long until they were back on the roadway that would eventually lead them to London. Her stomach fluttered with both excitement and concern as they tailed the man.

She called the inn to cancel her reservation for the night. Then she sent a text to her big sister to say she was fine and having fun. Her family didn't know the real reason behind her trip, and according to her father, Jasmine had ruined Thanksgiving by booking a trip to the UK rather than celebrating with her family. Once her story was published, she would share all the details about how she'd accomplished it.

The driver cleared his throat. "Miss, it appears he's heading toward Heathrow. Do you want to continue following him?"

She finished sending her text and responded, "Yes, but when he pulls into the rental facility, drop me off outside their office. I need to ride the shuttle, or I'll lose him."

"Forgive me for overstepping, but are you sure you want to do this?"

She gathered her belongings and took out her wallet. "Yes, thank you."

When the car stopped just outside the agency, she handed him the cash they'd agreed upon and exited. The balance would be billed to her credit card. She waited for him to retrieve her bag from the trunk and thanked him for helping her.

As she walked farther onto the property, one of the workers approached her. "Miss, can I help you?"

She'd learned long ago that if you acted like you belonged, most people would let you pass with minimal interference. "I'm heading inside to pick up a bag I accidentally left behind earlier today. I'm so thankful you had it."

"Oh, that's great. Have a good afternoon."

She wheeled her bag through the line of vehicles and toward the crowd of people waiting for the shuttle after completing their returns. She caught a glimpse of the man toward the back of the group, so she turned to the female next to her to start a conversation. This way, she could keep an eye on him while it looked like she was conversing with a friend.

When the shuttle arrived, he boarded toward the rear and stood in front of the door, holding on to the overhead bar. Jasmine opted for a seat in the back of the bus. After all, she was one in a thousand people flying out of an airport to some destination. Why would he think anything different? He didn't seem to be paying her any attention, or he was just good at hiding it.

When he jumped off at the terminal, she followed him and got into the same line. She watched him approach the counter, then was waved forward to the open station next to him. That was when she heard the ticketing agent say Mexico City, so now she knew where he was headed. She bent to retrieve her wallet from her backpack as he passed by heading toward the security.

Jasmine told the ticketing agent. "I need to purchase a ticket on the next flight to Mexico City, please."

The agent asked for her identification, then proceeded to click a ton of keys on her keyboard before coming back with an answer. "First, business, or coach?"

"Coach is fine. I'd prefer an aisle seat, if available."

"It'll be $843.00 dollars, and I'll need your credit card."

She handed over her plastic and stood there while the agent's fingers danced on the keyboard. Finally, she gave Jasmine a receipt and boarding pass.

"The gates are to the left; have a safe flight," the ticket agent said.

Holy crap, what am I doing?

Jasmine's stomach rumbled, reminding her that she had skipped lunch and needed dinner. Once she cleared security and located her gate, she would eat, do a little work on the plane, and then sleep for the rest of the flight.

A pub across from her gate caught her eye. A burger, fries, and cold beer sounded delicious. She had just over an hour to kill before she boarded her flight. When the time came, she paid her bill and moved toward the boarding area, pleased to see that her male companion had boarded with the business-class travelers. At least she knew for certain he was on the flight.

After her group was announced, she forced her eyes toward the rear of the plane and walked right past him. The moment she was clear, she let out a deep breath and found her seat.

The flight was uneventful and quiet, which made her happy. She slept for most of it and had just finished her breakfast when the pilot announced they were preparing to land. Deciding it was best to use the facilities now so she wouldn't risk missing him, she made her way to the rear of the plane. She brought along her small toiletry kit to freshen up and brush her teeth, that way she'd be ready to go when the aircraft door opened.

After the plane arrived at the gate, and she cleared the jetway, she picked up her pace until she had him in her line of sight. She weaved her way through people until she closed the gap, but careful to keep some distance between them. He walked at a decent pace with his long stride, so she had to walk faster than usual to keep up with him.

He exited the airport and climbed right into the back of a waiting Range Rover complete with tinted windows. *Crap!* Her stomach tightened because she was going to lose him. Seeing the taxi line, she dashed over and cut in front of everyone. Since she only knew a small amount of Spanish, she hoped this would work instead of making a big scene.

"*Lo siento, tengo la emergencia con mi familia. Por favor,*" she said to the people in line.

The family in the front of the line relented and motioned for her to take their cab.

"Gracias," she said, then jumped into the waiting vehicle. "*Sigue a ese Range Rover negro. ¡Rápido!*"

The man turned, pointed forward into traffic, and said in perfect English, "That one way up there?"

She saw his line of sight when she leaned forward. "Yes, and please don't make it obvious."

He smiled and steered away from the curb, her back molding to the seat when he stomped on the accelerator. The knot in her stomach increased with every mile they covered. She glanced at her watch and noted they've been driving for close to forty-five minutes.

Her body listed right when the taxi merged lanes and exited the highway. After passing a series of traffic lights and making several turns, the cab came to a stop at an open market. Across the street, the black SUV they'd been trailing stopped behind two identical rovers.

"I'm going to leave you here," the driver announced while he printed the receipt for her ride.

She took the slip of paper and looked it over. "Where are we?"

"Bonita Verde."

The driver accepted the wad of cash she handed him. "This includes your tip, thanks."

After she retrieved her suitcase from the trunk, she moved away from the cab. Glancing over her shoulder, she saw movement across the street. Since her phone was already in her hand she used it to snap a few pictures before removing her camera from her bag and shoving her phone inside.

The weight of the camera felt good in her hands as she moved between the groups assembling in front of the restaurant. She adjusted her lens and snapped a few of the surrounding area and open market.

When she tried to turn back around to focus on the group across the street, a strong hand grabbed her arm and jerked her backward. Shock and fear snaked down her spine. The man snatched her camera from her neck and demanded her phone. Panic flooded her system as a black hood came down over her head. She kicked and screamed, trying to break free or get someone to help her.

The grip on her arm tightened to the point of pain. "This is your only warning," a deep voice said into her ear. "Be quiet and I won't drug you. Do you understand?"

Tears pooled in her eyes and threatened to spill down her cheeks. She nodded. "Are you going to hurt me?"

"I won't, but I can't answer for the others. Why are you taking pictures of my boss? He values his privacy and has found your actions reprehensible."

"I'm sorry, I didn't mean to upset your boss." Her voice wobbled. "I'm visiting the area. If you give me my camera, I'll delete the photos."

There was a loud, grinding sound, and she was shoved into a vehicle. No more words were spoken to her, and forceful hands pushed her to the floor. Her legs were cramped in the small space. At first, the roads were smooth, but the terrain changed and became rough and bumpy like they were on a mountain path. She figured they'd been moving for at least thirty to forty minutes.

Abruptly, the wheels skidded to a stop, and before she could catch her breath, the door behind her opened. Hands slid underneath her armpits, and she was dragged backward and onto her feet. It wasn't long before a tingling sensation slammed her extremities as blood rushed back into them.

The hood she wore was snatched from her head, temporarily blinding her from the bright sun. She caught a glimpse of the man who had taken her camera back at the market before he hopped back into the running rover and disappeared.

A man with a gun in his hand spoke rapid Spanish and motioned for her to walk forward. When she passed him, he prodded her toward a hut and shackled her ankle to a giant cement block inside. The moment he turned back to face her, he holstered his weapon and assessed her from head to toe. Then, his gaze swept over the small space.

Dread filled her, and her stomach churned with anxiety. All she could hear in her head was her father telling her over and over again that she shouldn't travel alone.

"*Quiero tus zapatos*," the man said, pointing at her feet.

A split-second decision had her acting like she didn't understand his words or intent. Having shoes would be better than being barefoot. Seconds felt like hours as he repeated the command and glared at her.

Finally, he squatted in front of her to remove her shoes. His grimace worried her. The moment he stood, something hit the back of her head, and her world went dark.

The clacking of poker chips and male laughter echoed down the hallway toward the kitchen in Noah Parker's new house. He'd officially been a resident of Mill Creek for over three weeks, and he loved it.

The quaint old styling, especially on Main Street, reminded him of an old western mining town. The decorative storefronts, hitching posts, and wooden-planked sidewalks added to the allure. The small-town atmosphere appealed to him. So far, he'd spent his time getting to know many of the residents and eating at all the local restaurants. The area was a foodie's paradise.

Mill Creek was totally different from Washington, DC, and that was a cathartic release. The small town had politics, but those were centric to its residents. Some might say people were nosy, but the residents protected their own. He preferred the different vibe to constantly having to watch his back. Maybe that was harsh, but it was his perspective.

Being closer to his friends and his recent promotion made him happier than he'd ever thought possible. His new role allowed him the freedom to work on special assignments that leveraged his cyber and analytic skills. He loved working for the Federal Bureau of Investigation because he knew his contributions helped to make the world a safer place. There would always be threats, but he could sleep a little easier knowing he did his best to eliminate a few.

Noah turned from the cabinet where he stored paper napkins and plates and asked his friend, Trent Jacobs, a question that had been on his mind. "Do you miss working with our team back at the Bureau?"

Trent opened a package of plastic cutlery. "Yes, but after Dalton's death, everything changed for me. I miss being an agent, but I don't regret becoming the sheriff of Mill Creek. I needed that change for me, even if I had trouble seeing it so clearly at the time."

Noah snorted. "Yeah, that whole hindsight thing's a bitch."

Trent turned to face Noah. "What's gnawing at you? Do you regret moving here?"

"No, not at all, I couldn't be happier. It's just...my father called and pissed me off. He tried to hold the *son card* over my head. He even tried to act like my decision to move here without telling him had hurt him."

Trent's forehead crinkled in confusion. "Why? It's not like you two are close or even communicate regularly."

Noah ran his hand through his hair and sighed. "I know, right? Something about there being a target on his back, and he needs his son to stand by his side. But here's the kicker, he says it's complicated. Blah, blah, blah."

Trent's eyes widened. "What does that mean?"

"Don't know. What I do know is that he only cares about being a senator and getting reelected. Looking back, he was self-absorbed and really lacked the ability to demonstrate empathy. He disappeared from my life altogether after the death of my mom and baby sister," Noah said, shaking his head.

"Sorry, man, his actions were cruel, and there's no excuse. How'd you end the call?" Trent asked in a low voice.

Noah shrugged. "I suggested he use his vast network of resources to save his ass."

Trent's face showed his concern. "You may never get to witness this, but I do believe at some point your father will realize how badly he fucked up."

Noah appreciated his friend's support, but he didn't want to waste any more time or thought on his father this evening. He'd rather focus on what mattered—his chosen family. He grabbed the supplies, then the parmesan cheese from the refrigerator. "Maybe, but right now I have a house full of friends with wallets that need to be emptied. Let's join the others."

"Pizza and beer have arrived," Clarke Dragoon said, his booming voice filtering into the living room from the front door.

"Bring it in here. I have a separate table for food and a cooler," Noah said as he sat and shuffled the playing cards.

Clarke entered the room with two boxes of pizza stacked up in one hand and headed toward the space with all the food displayed. "Hey, what the hell is that green shit?"

Micah, Trent, and Noah all snickered at Clarke, who pressed a case of beer to Kane's chest and pointed at the cooler.

Kane Miller tore into the packaging and buried each bottle in the ice. "Annika wants us to have a healthy choice. It doesn't mean you have to eat it."

Trent clapped his college buddy on his shoulder. "Yeah, go easy on the poor bastard. Annika loves greenery and does push the benefits of eating a salad at every meal. I witnessed it this past summer when they stayed with me."

"Seriously, dude?" Clarke asked and closed the lid on the ice chest after Kane added the last beer. "Well, Aimee made us brownies for dessert. Also, she insisted I bring a plate of leftovers from our Thanksgiving dinner. She's apparently worried you may starve."

Noah started to deal the cards around the table. "It's doubtful that would happen with all the restaurants in this town, but I appreciate her concern because she's a great cook."

Micah Parker raised his hand drawing attention his direction. "Uh, I'd like to point out that I'm the town's veterinarian, and my animals don't know how to cook, so where is my plate of goodies?"

Clarke barked out a laugh. "Good point, I'll let Aimee know she hurt your tender feelings."

Trent folded his pizza slice, ready to take a bite, then stopped. "What about me? Maggie has a lot of talents, but cooking is not one of them. Aimee is aware of that fact because she tried to teach Maggie the basics. Good God, I love my wife, but she could burn water. Both Noah and I suffered on Thursday. I'm pretty sure she overcooked the bird by two hours."

Noah burst out laughing. "It wasn't that bad. I mean, who doesn't love turkey jerky? I keep forgetting that you two are married now. It's weird."

"It's not bad, Noah. You may want to keep an open mind," Trent said.

Noah clapped his friend on the back. "Nah, the whole family thing isn't for me. My childhood zapped that desire. Man, at times, it seems like only yesterday that we were working side by side, chasing Falcon to Mill Creek."

Trent chewed on his food, then swallowed. "Yeah, I know what you mean."

"What are you doing for the FBI now, Noah?" Micah asked.

"I'm working directly with Special Agent in Charge Tim Guzman on a wide range of assignments. The best part is that I have full autonomy while in the field."

Clarke laughed and raised his beer to toast Noah. "That's *special*, but I'm glad you're a permanent resident now. Having Cyber God practically next door is a game changer for sure."

The clanking of beer bottles echoed, and everyone took a drink.

"All right, enough chatter; ante up," Noah said, tossing his chips into the middle of the table.

The next hour flew past as everyone played, ate, and ribbed each other. Noah's pile of chips had grown mostly from Trent and Clarke, along with their incessant whining. "You two want to go another round, or should you drop out so Micah, Kane, and I can get serious?"

Trent leaned back and interlaced his fingers, cradling the back of his head. "Shut up and deal. There's still time to win my money back."

Clarke's beer hissed as he twisted off the cap. "Everyone's entitled to a lucky streak."

"Nah, I think you two just suck." Micah flipped his money onto the table.

Kane removed two twenties from his wallet, then slid one toward Clarke and the other to Trent. "Put your money where your mouth is. You can pay me back later."

Noah added his money into the pot. When his cards were dealt, he arranged them in his hand before increasing his bet. He answered his cellphone on the first ring, not bothering to check his caller ID.

"Hello," he said, holding his money in his hand.

"How's the shoulder healing?"

Noah's eyes widened at that question. He tried to match the voice to a name but came up empty. "Who the hell is this?"

"The one who squeezed the trigger that night in the forest."

Noah's heart thudded against his chest while his mind raced with the implications of that statement. He'd taken a round on the right side of his chest that had collapsed his lung and required surgery to remove the bullet.

The night his team went after Talon, the leader of Falcon––the crime syndicate the FBI had invested numerous time and resources, investigating–– he'd come across mercenary soldiers fleeing the scene when he'd been shot.

"Waltzer?" he asked, his tone cautious yet direct.

"Ah, you'd be correct. I'm sorry about our last encounter. Hazards of the job, right? I have something for you, but you need to hightail it to Mexico City. A female has been kidnapped, and the window to help her will close soon. I'm assuming she's an agent, but I'm not entirely sure. She'll only be at this camp for maybe seventy-two hours before she's moved."

"Excuse me for not jumping at your suggestion. Why are you telling me this and not doing something about it yourself?"

"It's simple. I can't. But I trust you to get the job done like you did for Dalton's sister, Maggie. Your new role will allow you to move quickly while avoiding all the normal red tape the Bureau requires."

"How the hell do you know about my new position? I want some answers that make sense."

"We don't always get what we want," Waltzer snapped. "We're not that different, Noah. We protect those who need it, whether they realize it or not. The only difference is how we engage to get our desired results. All you need to know is that I'm on the right side of the fight. Don't overthink it. Have Guzman inquire about Orion, but watch your six for blowback."

"Who the hell is that?" Noah bit out the question a little harsher than he wanted. "Never mind, I'd rather know what's in this for you."

"You're wasting precious time with needing to be coddled. I only wanted to know why the woman was following me. It's a win-win. You save the girl, and I get my answers. When you arrive, drive to the city of Bonita Verde, and at the resort, the front desk will have an envelope for you that contains the coordinates of her location."

Noah looked up to see Trent glaring at him, but he returned his focus to the call. "How do I reach you?"

"You don't. I'll make contact if it's necessary."

The deafening silence on the line told him Waltzer had terminated the call. Maybe it was the adrenaline coursing through Noah's body now, but his scar burned. He continued rubbing the spot while he processed what he'd just heard. Holy shit, that was one call he'd never expected to get.

"What. The. Hell?" Trent asked in a tight, clipped voice. "Why is Waltzer contacting you?"

Clarke grabbed his seat and turned it around so he could straddle it and rest his arms across the back. Micah and Kane sat watching.

Noah dropped his hand. "The whereabouts of a kidnapped American woman in Mexico."

Clarke's deep voice penetrated the silence. "Do you trust him? How do you know this isn't a setup?"

"My wife will not handle this news well." Trent's irritation was evident by his sharp tone. "Do you think he's looking to tie up loose ends?"

Kane leaned forward. His face was tight. "Waltzer's the guy who shot Noah, right? He worked for the leader of Falcon, who trafficked weapons and drugs?"

Noah nodded while he continued to rub his chest. Waltzer had revealed a key piece of information on the call that Noah needed to research before he shared anything further. After a minute, he responded. "Yes, but I don't sense an ulterior motive. The night he shot me, he had the advantage, but he chose to wound rather than take the kill shot. He's also known about Mill Creek this entire time, so I don't get the sense he's after retribution."

Kane pointed at Noah. "You're actually considering his request to fly to Mexico City?"

"All I've got is animal tranquilizers," Micah added. "They would work on humans with minimal risk."

Noah stood. "Thanks, buddy, but I'll be able to have my gun since I'll be flying on the FBI's jet. There's a woman whose life depends on me finding her. My gut is telling me that this information is solid. So, yes, I need to go, but not until I update Guzman. I'll also do some research during the flight."

Trent stood and gripped Noah's shoulder. "I get why you're going, but be careful. We'll increase our security measures here while you're gone."

"Stay in contact, and let us know what you find," Clarke said.

"Will do." Noah stood and shook every man's hand. "Thanks, guys. I'll talk to you soon."

He headed toward his office to call his boss. He'd see if an FBI agent had been assigned to Waltzer or the region and also try and find out what the hell Orion meant. Afterward, Noah would clean up the mess from tonight before he left.

If the woman in question was not one of theirs, it would take Guzman time to find out if another agency had deployed an asset, assuming they would share that data. If neither was true, could she just be a citizen who happened to be following Waltzer? The clock was ticking if Noah wanted to get to that location to do a little reconnaissance before he attempted rescue.

He planned to take a chopper to the airport in Boise and then fly on a chartered flight. Since his window was tight, he would fly direct and with his equipment. The part he had to figure out while in flight was his exit strategy. His preliminary plan was to get to the coast and take a boat, assuming he could get in, rescue the woman, and get them both out alive.

Breaking Point, Book 3 in the Mill Creek Mystique romantic suspense series is out now.

Have you read the book that started the series?

Enjoy this sneak peek of

TRENT'S REDEMPTION

Book 1 in the Mill Creek Mystique romantic suspense series

One

T HE RAPID KNOCK AT Trent's front door had him hoping that this unexpected interruption would spare him another lonely evening. Hastening his steps, he twisted the knob and sucked in a sharp breath. Nothing would have prepared him for this sight. His partner's sister, and the woman he had dated. Margaret King's haunted green eyes stared back at him. Her blonde hair was thrown into a loose ponytail. Several strands had escaped and fluttered in the evening breeze. Even disheveled, she was still beautiful.

Dread settled in his gut, anchoring a weight to his chest as Dalton's last words filtered through his mind. *Promise me you'll look after her and keep her safe.*

"Maggie, what brings you here?" Trent's mind raced with possibilities, and none settled the growing dread that rotted in his stomach.

Her eyes widened briefly before she found her voice. "Can I come inside?"

"Of course, sorry," he stammered, moving aside and making a sweeping motion with his arm.

She hesitated for a second, then looked over her shoulder toward the driveway. Turning back, she met his gaze and released a deep breath. Remorse slapped him in the face as she entered his home. The last time he'd seen her was about ten months ago at Dalton's funeral. Not once had Trent reached out to see how she had adjusted to life without her brother. Now, the weight of his mistake stood in his entryway. Guilt riddled his body and his gaze shifted toward the floor because he'd let her down.

The subtle scent of oranges and vanilla floated by him as she passed. The moonlight shining through the open window cast a silvery glow across her pinched face. He clicked the deadbolt then flipped on the light before he sat on the sofa, waiting for her to join him. Her feet didn't budge, but her gaze circled the room.

Maggie raised an eyebrow, her eyes blank. "I'm sorry I didn't call first. I thought this discussion would be best in person. I can't believe I had to search the internet for your address."

"I'm glad you're here, and I should have given you my address. There's no excuse for that..."

The tension in the room increased with every second of silence that followed.

"I-I don't know what to think anymore. You might think I'm crazy or worse, have overreacted to drive all the way here." Her voice sounded like sandpaper on wood.

Trent grabbed her hand and swiped his thumb softly across her knuckles. A rush of emotions flooded his system with that simple touch. He hated the strain emanating from her body. "Are you okay, Maggie?"

He released her hand and patted the spot next to him. The cushions dipped as she sat, her gaze lingering on the room and surroundings. "Why do you have scaffolding outside? Did something happen to your home?"

Trent smiled and shook his head. "No, I just finished renovating the interior and have decided to upgrade my roof. What's going on, Maggie?"

She turned to him, flashing a brief smile. "Good. I'm glad nothing bad happened to you. Could I have a glass of water?"

"You can have anything you'd like." He meant those words and vowed to himself to prove it to her. "But you need to tell me what's upset you. What made you drive all this way to find me?"

The single tear traveling down her cheek gutted him. Her resolve and strength may have had her sitting beside him, holding herself together, but her vulnerability undid him. He tugged her body against his, to feel her warmth and the pulse of her heart as he held her tight. To remind her she wasn't alone in dealing with whatever worried her. Even if his actions these last ten months told a different story.

A niggle of hope bloomed in his chest when she hugged him back just as fiercely. This wouldn't erase his absence from her life since the death of her brother, but maybe she'd see it as an olive branch to reconnect them to days long past. To the days when they were friends and all three of them spent time together.

When she sat back against the cushion, dark circles marred the delicate skin beneath her eyes. Trent's mind whirled with a million questions. Had someone hurt her? Had Maggie been with a man who threatened her? Why was she here? All of them remained unspoken because shame swamped his system. Not only was he a shitty person, but he'd broken a promise to his friend.

Dalton would still be here if I'd taken out the shooter in the rafters. Suffocated by the memories of that horrible day, Trent shot up off the sofa, desperately needing air and space. "I'll get you that water. When I return, how about you start from the beginning and explain why you're here? We'll figure this out together."

"Thanks. You're the one person I knew would understand," she said in a mere whisper.

Jesus, what had she been through that would make her run? The woman he'd known was full of mirth and energy. He hated the mixture of defeat and uncertainty radiating from the depths of her green eyes.

"Here you go, Miss Margaret King." Trent handed her a glass of water.

"Ugh, call me Maggie, you know better. My parents called me Margaret, and that was when I was in trouble." She stared into the distance for a moment. "Maggie Moo was the nickname my brother preferred," she added with a slight wobble.

"Sorry, I miss him so much. I just never thought I'd lose him after my parents died. I figured we'd grow old together. It's been difficult knowing I'm all alone in the world."

Trent's heart was clogged with condemnation. "Never apologize for missing him. Dalton loved you. He would've done anything for you. You were his little sister. Hell, I'd known him since training at Quantico, and I knew then, he'd be the biggest pain in my ass and best friend. His death left a hole in our lives." The words he left unspoken were that he'd abandoned her, too.

A soft giggle escaped her lips. "Yes, he could be a pain. He also tried controlling my life down to who I dated."

Trent nodded in agreement. "Yes, he had firm opinions on who should date you and why."

"If I recall, you did, too, since you cited your job as a complication of our relationship. Anyway, blood or not, you've always been a part of my family, which is why I'm here." She forced a slow steady stream of air into her lungs. "You were both logical and rational men who worked from facts to solve life's problems. I've lost count of how often I've endured a lecture about being observant and always aware of my surroundings."

He interjected, "A smart person assessed their situation and acted accordingly. That coincidences rarely, if ever, exist. Yes, I speak that same dialect."

"You are cut from the same cloth as Dalton, which is why I'm in Mill Creek. I've analyzed my situation, and my findings have shocked me." She gulped the cool liquid. Straightening her spine, she continued, "Dalton made me promise—almost to the point of ritualistic chanting—that if I were ever in trouble and couldn't reach him, I should call you. I always thought he'd meant while he was alive…" Tears streamed down her face. "Someone has been following me because I'm Dalton's sister."

Trent's eyes narrowed. She'd piqued his curiosity with that assessment. He then schooled his features so they'd remain neutral. "Why would you think that?"

"I first noticed a white van parked on the street facing my apartment. It appeared after Dalton's death. The days and times were random, but it was the same van. It disappeared for a while, then returned a few weeks ago. I can't explain it, but I got a strange feeling about it."

Maggie fidgeted, cracking her fingers one by one. He sat quietly while she fidgeted with nervous energy. He didn't want to add to her stress, so he gave her the time to process her thoughts.

"How? What made it seem unusual?"

She lifted her gaze to meet his eyes and shrugged. "I only saw the driver and passenger twice, but I'm pretty sure they were the same men from the first time. This sounds bizarre, and I know it does, which is why I didn't report the van to the police. Those men could have lived in the complex or in the area. What happened the other night changed my mind, but instead of calling the police, I headed straight to you. This is personal, Trent, and it scared me."

"I'm glad you came to me." He gently urged her to continue by nodding and keeping his expression neutral. Deep down, his stomach knotted with apprehension over what came next.

A tiny smile crossed her lips. "God, you remind me of him, fierce and protective. I appreciate that you're not judging me—at least until I'm done."

"You're doing just fine, now, keep going."

"Early Saturday morning, I was working at my computer when the fire alarms went off. When I went outside to check, the adjacent unit had smoke billowing from inside. My neighbor appeared outside with her child, panicked, and talking into the phone about a grease fire and firemen coming. I ducked back inside my place to retrieve my messenger bag, which held everything that mattered to me and waited outside with my neighbor. After the firemen arrived and controlled the scene, I was informed that the fire was out, but it would be a couple of hours before I could return. I decided to head to our local coffee shop to hang out while the chaos passed. When I returned..."

The color drained from her cheeks. She lowered her head to stare at the carpet between her feet. "My front door was ajar, again, which I figured was so the firemen could finish their investigation. I caught a glimpse of that white van pulling away. When I entered, everything seemed fine...until I reached my office. Drawers were opened, and papers and folders were scattered across my desk and floor. Then, I noticed a knife stabbed into my desk holding a note that read, 'What did he know?'"

Trent snapped his brows together, his mouth drawn tight. He couldn't quell his reaction to what he'd just heard. The hairs on his neck bristled. He didn't know how, but he'd find a way to slay every one of her demons...or die trying. He owed Dalton that much.

"Why didn't you call the police? Do you know if anything was taken? Were other rooms searched?" Trent squeezed her hand a few times, bringing her gaze upward.

With her other hand, she reached for the glass and gulped the last few sips before she answered, "In my gut, I know this reaches beyond the police. The only 'he' in my life was my brother. My brain went into survival mode. I had to get out of my apartment and get to you. You'd know what to do. I-I didn't look any further. All I kept thinking was, this can't be good to have a knife stabbed into your desk, especially with how he died. I took my bag, hit the bank, and withdrew as much money as allowed. I left my car at the office and called a car rental company. I decided leaving my car behind was best. I stopped at one truck stop to rest, used only cash, then drove until I pulled into your driveway."

She sat still as if she had waited for him to say something. Processing what he had just heard shredded his insides. The last time they had spoken was at the funeral, and that encounter was strained, not ugly or mean, just distant because of him. This was opposite to how he and Maggie usually interacted. Instead, he struggled with his anger and self-condemnation while nursing the injuries he'd sustained that day alongside Dalton. As a result, Trent's job and assignment changed, which deprived him of retribution. He hated the exhaustion etched across her face. Starting now, he would atone for his wrongs.

"Brave and resilient is what you are." A surge of pride and respect flood his system. "You did damn good with disappearing off the grid and adapting in the face of adversity. You're far from an agent but acted cautiously and logically."

Fatigue, stress, and fear radiated from her, but he also saw a brief glimmer of relief. That was something he would build upon.

"Your brother would be proud. Hell, I'm proud of you. I'm also so damn sorry I haven't reached out before now. I own that. My apology doesn't change anything, but I hope my actions will. *If* you give me that chance. I'd say you read the situation right—a clusterfuck for sure."

Her eyes closed for a moment, and her shoulders dipped as tension seemed to fade from her body. Something deep inside Trent's stomach twisted painfully. Had she thought he might deny her his support and protection? Of course, why wouldn't she? It wasn't his intent, but he'd removed her from his life. Another epic screw-up to add to his list that he needed to fix.

He cupped her chin. "I understand why you weren't sure about coming to me for help, so I'll clarify that misconception now. I will always protect you, Maggie. You have my word."

She shifted her head from his grasp and stabbed him in the chest with a finger. "You hurt my feelings, but I'm not blameless either. You have to promise you won't put yourself in jeopardy in any way. I can't stand the thought of losing another person."

The painful truth behind those words constricted his chest. The vibrant woman he had known seemed to have retreated somewhat. Trent snatched her hand, loving how buttery soft her skin was under his fingertips. "Give me your keys. I think it's best to put your rental in the garage for now."

She stood and dug into her front pocket to retrieve the key ring. "Thanks for allowing me into your home, especially with my trouble in tow."

Trent extended his palm and caught the keys. "You always were trouble. I'll give you the grand tour first and point out the highlights from my renovation."

"I thought you liked living out of boxes. You know, afraid of commitment."

"Smart ass," he lamented. "I'm working on unpacking everything."

He couldn't imagine her thoughts when she arrived but was glad she'd come. He started in his kitchen, explaining how his friend Kane had updated everything to stainless steel and gas.

"This is amazing. I love the gas stovetop. That refrigerator must keep you fed for months. It's huge."

"I've heard that bigger is always better," he deadpanned.

She rolled her eyes and protested, "Seriously? You haven't changed one bit."

He flashed her an exaggerated wink and guided her through the rest of the house. When they reached the master bathroom, he showed her his second favorite feature from the renovation: his walk-in shower with multiple adjusting heads that also produced steam. He owed Kane for this gem, too. Her small whimper when she spied the shower didn't go unnoticed. Trent also hadn't missed how closely she followed him the entire time. He'd do anything to diminish the worry radiating from her body. He ended his tour with the room she'd be using and the bathroom.

At the door to the bathroom, he paused and met her eyes. "Why don't you shower in my bathroom while I move the vehicle? You can give me a woman's perspective on my shower."

She leaned her head against the doorway and sighed. "A shower sounds heavenly, but I'll use the guest bath. Will you grab my bag from the front room and put it on the bed?

"Sure, do you have anything in the car you need?"

Her mouth twisted into a frown. "No, I didn't pack any clothing or even think about bringing my bathroom supplies. In my haste, I went with the less-is-more theory. Do you have a toothbrush and paste? And if I could borrow a few things to wear, that would be super. Walking around naked might be awkward."

He groaned internally as his mind conjured several inappropriate scenarios involving her sans clothing. Built like a goddess, with her curves and creamy skin, he'd love nothing more than to see her naked. He caught her staring at his reflection in the bathroom mirror and knew he'd been nailed. His traitorous cock stirred behind the confines of his pants. This woman still caused his mind and body to want more from her. His cue to leave.

"I'll put a T-shirt and a pair of sweatpants on your bed. Leave your clothes outside the door, I'll wash them for you. We'll go shopping tomorrow to fill in whatever you left behind."

She opened her mouth as if to speak, then clamped her lips together as she moved into the bathroom.

"What's on your mind?" he asked.

"Do you have any cereal or yogurt? Something easy to fix."

He put both hands on his waist and cocked one eyebrow. "You can have whatever you want. When did you eat last?"

Her eyes narrowed, and her mouth gaped. "I-ah, a granola at the truck stop."

He shook his head. "You're my priority. That includes food, sleep, protection, and whatever else I've forgotten to mention. Get that through your thick, stubborn, and beautiful head." Trent punctuated his point by wrapping her in a crushing hug. He wasn't sure what else to do, a move so familiar from all the previous times he and Dalton had visited between assignments or while on break.

He sighed as her curves melded perfectly against his frame and in all the right places. A surge of possessiveness roared to life within him, and not only did it startle him, but it also made him back away, breaking their connection.

"Shower, then kitchen," he said in a tone that encouraged no debate.

He headed down the hall and heard the snick of the door as it closed behind him. Needing to put space between them, he'd take care of her car. This woman in his home was Dalton's sister. The same baby sister his partner proclaimed off limits to any man who worked in a risky profession. Dalton was adamant that Maggie should marry a man with a stable job, allowing him to come home every night. A man whose existence wasn't nestled in danger, with the potential to cause her harm because his job encompassed every aspect of his life. Trent had squashed his attraction to her because he hadn't wanted to ruffle Dalton's feathers. Even though he hadn't been exempt from Dalton's censure, he had to agree with the man. She deserved better. She deserved a marriage where her husband would be around every night, a man whose job wouldn't risk her safety or threaten their lives. A fact of his employment he couldn't offer.

RELIEF WASHED OVER MAGGIE's body when Trent agreed with her assessment–she hadn't overreacted. She should never have doubted that he'd support her, but hearing it from his lips alleviated her apprehension. The warmth from his embrace grounded her. If she could press the rewind button, she'd rather go back to when Trent held her in his arms. There was a familiarity to it, and she'd missed the simplicity of knowing someone had her back.

She'd gotten to know him when she went to college in Washington, D.C. and had chosen to live in Dalton's place instead of on campus.

Her brother brought Trent home during break when they were both at Quantico. Not only had they become partners but friends. It wasn't like he was home often with his career, but it gave her an excuse to be close to her brother. She and Trent had dated a few times, but he had ended saying he didn't have time for a relationship due to his career. Her brother would never answer her question, but she would put money down on the fact he interfered.

When Trent smiled and flashed the bluest eyes she'd ever seen, it could melt the panties right off a girl. Never in her life had she experienced such a strong reaction to another person. It also didn't hurt that he was devastatingly gorgeous at six feet tall with his athletic build and all those well-defined muscles. His touch still made her girly parts tingle.

She'd cranked the shower tap to the left. When the bathroom mirror fogged over from the steam, she tugged back the curtain, adjusted the heat, then stepped inside. The hot spray pulsed against her tired muscles and sluiced down her body. She visualized removing Trent's shirt off his body to reveal raised pectorals and a ripped abdomen that flowed into a trim waist with sculpted hips. She bit her bottom lip and moaned. Well, that was what happened when one was sex deprived and surrounded by male hotness.

She adjusted the dial until a cold blast of water jolted her system. That daydream would be her little secret. She needed to stop this line of thinking. He probably had a bevy of beautiful women on speed dial. The type who looked perfect even after a torrential rainstorm. The same type her brother had circling him at all times. A girl could dream, couldn't she?

After stepping from the shower, she dried off and slathered on some lotion she found in the cabinet. She finger-combed her hair and mentally added an actual one to her list of things to buy. There was nothing like a shower to make a person feel human again. Towel wrapped around her body, she padded to the bedroom he assigned. As promised, the clothes and items from her car were sitting on her bed. She removed a stuffed animal from her tote and kissed the cow on its nose before putting it back inside. She'd give anything to hear Dalton call her by her nickname again.

She took in his home as she made her way to the kitchen. It had the perfect blend of cabin and modern.

The center of the room had a wooden dining table with four chairs, and in front of one chair sat a grilled cheese sandwich, her absolute favorite. Especially when she was having a crappy day.

Trent looked over his shoulder, holding a spoon. "You look more relaxed. The tomato soup will be ready in a minute. These are my go-to choices when I need comfort food."

Her insides melted like the cheese in the sandwich.

"Mine too," she said. The part she kept to herself, watching a hot man cook for her, did wicked things to her body. Good grief, she needed to get a grip. He was being nice, not offering her a night of decadent sex. Or a life of love, marriage, and children. The fantasy train needed to stop so she could disembark because that destination did not exist.

The last few months had changed her. She had to find a way to survive before her grief and despair consumed her entirely. Being around Trent has created a few sparks in the recesses of her mind, reminding her of the woman she had been and what they had shared.

"Are you for real? A good-looking man who can cook and isn't afraid to admit that grilled cheese and tomato soup have the power to cure most things in life. I think I've died and gone to heaven," she tossed out and took a seat at the table.

He rolled his eyes and huffed dramatically. "I hate to burst your bubble, but men can do many things these days. I can even load the dishwasher and do laundry, but I draw the line at ironing."

Maggie burst out laughing. "Ah, I needed that. It's been a while."

Trent ladled soup into a bowl. "Feel free to laugh anytime. It suits you very nicely. I also happen to appreciate the eye candy comment."

Did he just flirt with her? She took a bite of her sandwich and moaned. "This is delicious."

"The secret is mayonnaise instead of butter. It's how my mom makes them. Tonight, I want you to promise me you'll rest. I don't like seeing those dark circles under your eyes."

"I'll try, but it's hard to get my brain to stop churning over everything." She blew on a spoonful of soup.

"Well, I promise to keep the boogie men away. Hey, one question, though. Something you said earlier confused me. You said you left your car at the office. Do schoolteachers refer to their classrooms as offices now? Are you still teaching?"

She put down her spoon. "No. I quit teaching."

His eyebrows knit together as he processed what she said, but to her relief, he didn't question her any further. She didn't want to get into it tonight. Her love of teaching had died after she buried Dalton. The burden of life's truths wore her down, and she couldn't handle deceiving those precious faces daily.

Trent filled in the prolonged silence. "We can talk about all of this tomorrow after you rest."

"Okay," she said between a spoonful of soup.

"Oh, one more thing. I'm meeting some friends for breakfast tomorrow. I want you to come. Afterward, we'll head to the store to pick up whatever else you need."

Maggie took a big gulp of water. "I don't want to impose."

"I see your listening skills haven't improved," he muttered sardonically. "We're meeting them tomorrow at eight. I'll have your clothes folded and waiting for you outside your door. You'll love the Knotty Pine Tree. The food is delicious, and I want you to meet my friends, Kane and Annika. They're good people; you can trust them. Besides, your smart actions put distance between what happened in Dallas and here. It'll give us some time to figure it all out."

There was a time when meeting new people and being a social butterfly came naturally, but that part of her died when she put Dalton in the ground. She should label her life accordingly now. BD—before Dalton—and AD—after Dalton.

The scaffolding outside the kitchen window reminded her of a skeleton in the moonlight. She hated the nights the most. All her fears and problems grew into large, creepy monsters that caused her constant worry that whoever left the note would find her.

Trent's Redemption, Book 1 in the Mill Creek Mystique romantic suspense series is out now.

BOOKS BY BAILEY THOMAS

ROMANTIC SUSPENSE

Mill Creek Mystique Series

Watch for the next book in the series
Kane's Reckoning

CONTEMPORARY ROMANCE

Torrent of Hearts us also available in the
Pack Your Bags short story collection

As an only child, Bailey Thomas' active imagination and adventurous nature always kept her busy. Now, she channels those creative powers into storytelling.

Living in the Southwest, Bailey splits her time between crafting heartfelt stories and indulging in her favorite pastimes—whether it's devouring books, marathoning shows, or catching a game.

Life is too short, so Bailey tries to live by her motto of finding adventures that make you smile. She loves to hear from her readers. You can find and connect with her at the links below.

Website/Blog:
baileythomasauthor.com
Instagram
instagram.com/Author_BaileyThomas
BookBub
bookbub.com/authors/bailey-thomas

ACKNOWLEDGEMENTS

I'm so fortunate to have the best readers in the world; none of this would be possible without you. Please leave a review. They are a tremendous help to the author and other readers looking for their next book. Also, don't forget to sign up for my newsletter or follow me on social media to stay updated on book news and events.

Thank you to A Fabulous Productions for creating the stunning print and eBook layouts and outstanding marketing support. You've made everything more manageable and taught me so much.

Lastly, to my Vicki Jean, who has always believed in me, thank you for always wanting me in your life. I love you to the moon and back!